CATCH A COWBOY

Rachelle Paige Campbell

© COPYRIGHT 2024 by Rachelle Campbell Dio

Warning: Not intended for persons under the age of 18. May contain coarse language and mature content that may disturb some readers. Reader discretion advised.

Cover Art Design by: Kelly Moran/Rowan Prose Publishing
Photo Credit: Adobe Images
First Printing
ISBN: 978-1-961967-31-1
Rowan Prose Publishing, LLC
www.RowanProsePublishing.com
Published in the United States of America

FINDERS KEEPERS, Cowboy
Rachelle Paige Campbell

Acknowledgments

Thank you to my friends and family for their support of my career. Having an author in your life presents its own challenges. From staring off into space to holding one-sided conversations, I appreciate that everyone accepts and expects me to jot down notes (and sometimes borrow their names for characters).

The Panera Supper Club, Kelly, Shannyn, Tammy, Kelly, Julie, and, of course, Miss Pamala, remain the best writer friends in the whole world. We encourage each other and sometimes write the demise of someone's enemy into our books. There is no better group for bouncing ideas, commiserating, and celebrating the wins. New writers, the best advice I can give you is to find your people!

Thank you to the wonderful team at Rowan Prose Publishing. Working with you, especially Kelly and Katie, has been the most validating and uplifting experience.

Readers, I am so grateful you have found this book, and I can't wait to take you back to the town of Herd soon. Thank you for the gift of your time.

CHAPTER 1

Stephanie Patricks readjusted her crisscrossed legs on the thick yoga mat, tucking her feet under her thighs, and rested her hands lightly on her knees. In late morning, sunshine brightened the studio. Early September brought golden days with a hint of chill in the air, promising the cold on its way. Her noisy inhalation filled her lungs to capacity as she counted to ten in her head before her loud exhale.

The air in the room whooshed as her class of ten followed along.

She smiled as she met each participant's gaze. She loved yoga, both practicing and teaching. She had no choice but to focus on the current moment. During each session, she forced herself to be present, and not worry about the thousand other tasks on her ever-growing to do list. As a person who took action, she had difficulty with not resolving every situation decisively ASAP. Sometimes, she needed to sit and stew on a problem.

While focused on breath and movement, she found a few moments of peace.

Pressing her palms together, she raised her hands to the center of her chest. "The light within me honors the light within you. Namaste." She bowed, lowering her torso until her forehead touched the floor. She stayed folded in half for another cycle of breath. When she returned to upright, she smiled at the class.

The mixed group of men and women from their early twenties to mid-seventies clapped.

"Thank you. I hope you've enjoyed your vacations and that we'll see you again next summer." She swallowed the small lump in her throat. Three months had passed in an instant. She'd miss her tranquil days here.

With murmured thanks and goodbyes, the class gathered their mats, blocks, and straps and exited the class.

The yoga studio was the corner room of the spa barn at the Kincaid ranch. Ten years earlier, the last remaining legacy ranchers, Hank and his grandson Ryan Kincaid, transformed their business from a traditional cattle operation into a high-end resort. It was a big risk in a small town with no tourism. But Ryan had a vision and revitalized his land and Herd's economy. Within the first year, visitors flocked to the Old West town and the business flourished each following summer.

She was grateful for the opportunity to practice yoga in a brand-new facility with eager students on a gorgeous piece of land. Facing South, the wall of windows flooded the room with natural light, enabling her to turn off the overhead fluorescent bulbs for shavasana. In a building dedicated to massage and facials, quiet and stillness permeated the entire structure.

She liked it here. Teaching was her passion. While instructing adults in the techniques of a Hatha practice was different from her regular job, she enjoyed sparking joy in others. One of the selling points of her vocation was summers off. But she wasn't the sort to sit around. In less than two days, she'd start her fifth year as a kindergarten teacher. She had one full day off.

And was already dreading how bored she'd be. She exhaled a heavy sigh, got to her knees, and rolled the pink and purple mat into a tight cylinder, securing it with her strap.

The door shut slowly.

Typically, the slam that followed the last person's exit echoed in the silent room. Today, the closing was muffled and restrained. She wasn't alone, but she didn't tense. She knew the mystery person's identity. He wasn't betrayed by a sound.

It was a smell that confirmed her suspicions.

Mint and leather. She was reminded simultaneously of a sun warmed car interior on a lazy Sunday afternoon drive and iced tea with the fresh cut herb from a kitchen garden. Unlike the man, both gave her a feeling of contentment.

She lifted her chin, raising her gaze to the newcomer. Her chest squeezed and her throat seized. She frowned. Did that rhyme? Could she work that into a lesson for her kindergarten class? At least then she could turn what would inevitably become another awkward encounter into a positive experience.

Ted Stirling, staff supervisor, pressed a palm flat against the door. With one leg raised and the ankle crossed over the opposite knee, he slipped off a boot. Then he repeated the motion. For a big man, his movements were surprisingly poetic and soft. His balance was impeccable. And his actions? Seeking to respect her space by padding across the floor in socks only solidified what she admired most about him.

He's kind and caring. And he's my boss.

She swallowed a lovelorn sigh. Her body would do at least the minimal motion. Really, she struggled against a full-fledged swoon. He was so dreamy. She knew better. He'd never direct his energy toward her so why let her unrequited crush restrain her? She wasn't exactly tongue-tied in his company. She couldn't remember how to think and speak at the same time.

In bright white socks, he tiptoed across the floor. "Mornin, Stephanie. Figured I'd help you gather your things and get your keys back from you."

The smell of fresh laundry mixed with the other scents, permeating the room. She leaned back on her heels, pressing her knees even harder into the floor. Somehow, he carried every aroma she found most intoxicating in a heady cologne. It was like he embodied a list of her wants. Of course, he didn't know her preferences. How could he when she didn't have the courage to say more than a few words?

Under her knees, the solid surface was unrelenting. Not that it could shake the words out of her throat or stop her palms sweating. She opened her mouth—wanting to deliver a cheeky, flirty comment—and grunted.

He smiled. "Just point to what you need help with, and I'll start loading your car."

Dragging in a shaky breath, she brushed her hair out of her face, her clammy hands extra cold against her burning cheeks. At least her momentary muteness only happened with arguably the nicest person in town. If she couldn't hold her own, she never would have lasted against some of the extra concerned, very involved parents at her school.

She lifted her knees and—balancing on the balls of her feet—slowly stood. The deliberate motions regulated her breathing and her pulse. Grabbing her purse from next to the mirror at her back, she threw the tote-style bag over her shoulder and slung the yoga mat over the other arm, straps creating a crisscross pattern on her back.

As long as she didn't look at him, she was fine. She could pretend she was in charge as the teacher and ignore how his thick lashes highlighted his gray eyes or the deep cleft in his chiseled chin that made him look like a cowboy from an old movie. She crossed the room, averting her gaze, and pointed to a stack of plastic milk crates holding foam blocks and another with woven blankets. "Thank you. I'll get the rest."

She didn't wait to see if he did as she asked. She knew he would. That was the sort of person he was. Within her first few years living in tiny Herd, Montana, she became familiar with every townsperson. Ted always stood out in her mind. Beyond his broad shoulders and good looks, he had a calm, controlled energy she admired.

But she was unable to verbalize at every encounter. Unless she was unquestionably in charge.

The door cracked open, flooding the room with light.

She bent and grabbed the crate holding straps, throwing her purse on top. Turning toward the door, she froze mid-step.

With his back holding the door open, he waited.

She glanced down, he'd slipped back into boots silently. Inelegantly, she jammed her feet into her flip flops, stubbing her big toe. She winced.

He stepped forward.

She shook her head and strolled past him. If he offered her help, he'd wreck her. He couldn't be kind to her. She didn't need to encourage her heart any more to pursue this ridiculous, one-sided, crush.

Down the flagstone path, she continued to the small, employee parking lot behind the building. Hidden from view of the windows behind a row of buffaloberry shrubs, the recently paved rectangle wasn't in keeping with the overall cowboy aesthetic. She was glad for a slight break from the dusty ground.

And, although it hadn't been a problem this year, she was glad to avoid her tires getting stuck in the mud during the typically heavy summer storms. A cool breeze shook the dry leaves of the plants. Snow wasn't too far off.

She shivered and walked to her car.

The little red coupe needed a wash from the dusty, gravel roads leading from town to the ranch. Dirt was the least of the vehicle's woes. The backseat was loaded with plastic containers holding school supplies. In the shotgun spot, she set a banker's box full of files and paperwork from the last civic event—Frontier Days—to the next in a week—the annual charity poker tournament. She'd get around to cleaning and organizing the car over the next week.

She would unload the supplies in her classroom tomorrow. In a few more days, she'd co-host the poker fundraiser. Then she'd put her events files in her bedroom closet to wait until she was called to volunteer again. In a small town, she could be conscripted into service sooner than later. She didn't mind. She set the milk crate on the ground, rifled through her tote for her keys, and popped the trunk. Lifting her gaze, she spotted his gaping mouth.

He coughed.

For a second, reversing the speechless roles was nice. Until she remembered why he gawked. She was the sort of person who constantly made piles. As soon as she cleared away her things, she started a new stack.

Stephanie grabbed her milk crate and strode past, brushing his shoulder as she rounded the bumper. Her arm scalded from the accidental touch. She set the crate in the trunk and removed her mat from her shoulder, slipping the strap over her head. Her cool confidence lasted less than ten seconds.

Ted set the other two crates in the trunk and shut the trunk.

Gripping the tote bag style purse with both hands, she faced him. He looked oddly expectant. If she was supposed to say something, she'd love a script and some lines right now.

"Keys?" he asked.

Duh. She reached into her bag for her studio keys and slipped the yoga studio's door off the clip. She extended the key.

He held a hand out, palm flipped up.

She dropped the key, grateful to avoid any other accidental touches.

"Thanks, Stephanie. Will we see you tomorrow night? It's our last Cowboy Dinner and we like to invite all the employees to enjoy the festivities. Our way of celebrating the season together. I promise, no work."

She nodded. She'd helped at several of the events over the summer but never been invited as a guest. *Not his guest.* He said we. Of course, he meant in his role as the spa staff manager for his bosses Hank and Ryan Kincaid. It was practically a royal we around these parts. The Kincaid Ranch saved the town's economy by transforming from ranching to relaxation.

"Great. I'll see you tomorrow." He reached up like he'd tip the brim of his hat. Instead, he swiped his forehead. "Forgot I left it at home this morning." He chuckled. "Have a good day."

He spun on his heel and strode away.

"You too," she whispered, her words evaporating on the breeze. She walked around her car and hopped behind the wheel. If she ever kept her nerve around him, what would she say?

With each booted step, Ted kicked up more dirt. Striding from the staff parking lot to the barn to lock up and back again to his truck, he walked through a cloud of dust of his own making. He couldn't remember a drier summer. The grass had lost its luster by mid-July. He ripped up roots on the dead lawn with each step.

In a few days, he expected the environmental impact study about the bison's return to the land in his inbox. He and Ryan needed to review the details before sharing information with Joe Staunch. Social studies teacher and part-time tour guide, Joe would ultimately lead all discussions about the herd with the town. With a reputation for respecting others' opinions and understanding the history of the area better than anyone, Joe was the perfect intermediary between the ranch and the town. He was the face of the program.

The reintroduction of the animals was the right decision for countless reasons. But the community would push back. Change was hard. Ted knew he shouldn't try to guess what the study would reveal. He couldn't stop himself. He was brimming with questions and playing out what-if scenarios.

What would happen with the bison next summer? If the prairie grass dried up, what would they eat? Would he have to feed the way he used to for the cattle in the winter, throwing hay off the back of his truck?

Or he could focus on one day at a time and be glad for checking one item off his to do list, getting the studio keys from Stephanie.

He had hoped for more acknowledgment than a nod. He was confident in his managerial skills but worried he put her on edge. Could she give him feedback to improve?

When he had started at the ranch, he accepted a career handling animals. It fit his degree and his personality. He never anticipated he'd be in charge of humans. But he couldn't have predicted any of the twists and turns his life had taken over the last decade plus. If he had? He might have been too scared to take even a step.

Still, he didn't like that Stephanie was so quiet around him. She was known for her capable, take-charge-attitude around town, running a variety of civic events with admirable efficiency. But she never opened her mouth and uttered more than a visceral sound in response to him.

The age gap between them was the prime suspect for her discomfort. He was nearly over a decade and a half older. Their different generations spoke their own languages, he assumed. Beyond that, he carried his emotional burdens in a heavy steamer trunk like he was setting off for a new land and would never return home. He suspected she traveled light. But he couldn't know.

She'd have to speak first.

Shaking his head, he climbed behind the wheel of his pick-up and drove down the gravel road toward the red barn. With one Bluetooth earpiece in, he tapped the steering wheel in time to his favorite music. He learned early on in his time on the ranch, over eleven years ago, that no one in Montana appreciated the Southern California ska punk scene quite the way he did. If he didn't want to listen to the ranchers' complaints about his taste, he couldn't blast the songs he knew by heart on the stereo.

As a transplant from the farming belt in the heart of the Golden state, however, he kept what ties he could to the hometown he had once imagined he'd never leave. He hadn't been back for a year. The longest stretch he'd ever managed without a California sunset or a slice of his favorite pizza. He owed one spot in particular a visit. After he wrapped up the paperwork for the summer employees, he'd make a visit. It'd have to be quick before the chance of snow hung heavy in the air in about a month.

His sister and niece were the only relatives left in their home town. Earlier in the summer, he'd floated the idea about relocating to Herd. She hadn't said anything in response. Oh well. His reasons for visiting wouldn't change if she moved and neither would his hurt lessen. He wanted her nearby. As far as little sisters went, she wasn't too terribly annoying. And her daughter was his favorite person on earth which almost made his sister's bratty years worthwhile.

He pulled the truck to the side of the barn and parked. Jumping to the ground, he pocketed his earpiece and shielded his gaze with one hand. The wooden structure was overdue for a coat of paint but would have to wait a little while longer. He saw no point in doing a job twice. If the owners moved forward with the deck addition, the barn would be plenty beat up during construction. Cutting a giant hole in the back wall and adding French doors guaranteed a touch-up job.

Strolling toward the back of the building, he headed toward the deep low rumble of a heated conversation. Maybe he spoke too soon. Progress couldn't be reached at an impasse.

At the corner, he dropped his arm to his side and approached his bosses. Both equal owners. The eighty-nine-year-old legacy rancher and his thirty-nine-year-old grandson. Scowling at each other in symmetry, like they were mirror twins.

"Ah, good. Sense has arrived. Come over here, Ted. Help explain my side," Hank, the octogenarian, called.

Ryan rolled his eyes heavenward and dug the toe of his boot into the dirt.

Ted wasn't sure he counted as good advice, but he always urged caution. Taking risks was Ryan's forte and how the ranch prospered. Ted needed time to warm to one of the new ideas but ended up in full support. "What's the problem? Didn't we work out the deck's size and position? I have the crew coming to pour footers. I have permits. We are scheduled and ready to start."

"I think we're wasting an opportunity here," Hank said. "This old barn has been fixed up more times than I can count. Why don't we raze the whole thing and build something modern? We keep adapting the structure to fit our needs. Let's take the opportunity to really build what we need."

Ted widened his eyes. Shaking his head, he stared at the ground. If he'd had a guess about today's Kincaid intergenerational debate, he wouldn't have used it on this topic. Demolishing a piece of ranch history? And Hank being the one to lead the destruction?

When Ryan had first broached the idea of selling the cattle and appealing to tourists, he had waged a war with his grandsire, battling to change a single speck of dirt on the land. Ted knew. He'd been part of many of those arguments. Now, Hank wanted to rip out the original barn? Anyone who thought a person couldn't change past a certain age was a fool. "Mr. Kincaid, sir, are you serious?"

"Ha!" Ryan pointed to the cowboy. "See? Told you he'd be on my side."

"I don't want to come between you two," Ted said slowly, drawing the words out to give his brain a chance to catch up. *I know better.*

Grandfather and grandson were equally matched when it came to stubbornness. Only the girl next-door, Ryan's girlfriend Meg Hawke, could cure either of their pig-headed ways. The Kincaid men shared a blind spot for her. She could almost do no wrong. What would she think about the new idea?

"Mr. Kincaid, you're right," Ted said, stroking his jaw. "It would be great to have a clean slate. We'll be scrambling to retrofit the interior to meet the needs of the event guests and staff."

Hank lifted his chin and grinned broadly at Ryan.

"But I agree with Ryan."

Ryan clapped Ted's shoulder. "Good man."

Hank glowered.

"I'm not in favor of keeping the old barn forever." Ted held up his hands in surrender or defense, whichever proved the more effective stance against either or both of the Kincaids. "You have a good point about the needs for an event. We squeeze into a tiny storage closet when we need something. We'll no doubt be storing at least double or more. Abby Whit has spoiled us about catering because she's on wheels. Her kitchen is parked outside, and she hauls everything in as needed," Ted said.

"Hey, you're supposed to be talking up my plan." Ryan frowned.

Ted held up his hands. He didn't want to choose a side and sometimes the stubborn pair insisted on all or nothing. "The biggest argument to keep the barn is simple. We can't risk losing time during the start of the summer season if the build goes long. And builds always go long."

"My thoughts exactly," Ryan said. "We'll get a new barn. Eventually. We have to know the events are going to pull in a profit first."

"Oh, they will. With Meg in charge, I don't doubt it." Hank extended a hand to his grandson.

Ryan shook it with a smile.

Hank was a gracious enough loser to admit defeat. Of course, he was also wily enough to include praise for Ryan's girlfriend. Sharp and nimble, Hank was a formidable ally or foe. Ted always kept his caution around Hank. "I was heading inside to double check provisions for tomorrow night. I invited Stephanie, after she handed in her key," Ted said.

"Good, good. Did Stephanie get out ok? Was she pleased with working for us this season?" Ryan asked.

Ted stroked his jaw. "I think so, not like she'd tell me."

Ryan chuckled. "Yeah, why do you have to be so scary all the time? You don't have to inspire fear to earn your employee's respect."

Ted scowled. He couldn't take the joke for fear of the truth hidden in the jest. Was he intimidating? The ranch was his first experience as a boss. He didn't want anyone frightened of him.

"Oh, give the man a break." Hank interjected. "Not his fault the woman clams up around him. It is peculiar though."

Ted agreed. She was a puzzle. He admired her spunk and bubbly personality. He'd glimpsed her beaming smiles directed at others. Whenever he neared, however, he heard nothing. He supposed it shouldn't matter. But it did.

He could fight his own battles but was always grateful for a reprieve. Especially about Stephanie. All he wanted out of life was to keep the status quo until he reached the end. He was most definitely not looking for romance and kept his guard up around his matchmaking, elder boss. With so many years between himself and Stephanie, they'd have nothing in common and no reason to interact besides work. If he was going to pursue a friendship with someone, however, he might choose her.

As the silence stretched, Ted became aware of the collective stares of his bosses. He cleared his throat. "She did a nice job. Hopefully, she'll be back."

Ryan nodded. "Wait a second." Scrunching his face, he turned to his grandfather. "Why is he a man, and I'm a boy?"

Hank shrugged. "I never had to wipe his butt."

Ted smiled at Ryan's red cheeks. Not a lot could embarrass him, but Hank knew every touch point. While the pair weren't Ted's family by blood, he was glad they'd embraced him anyway. Tragedy spurred him to uproot his life and change everything he'd ever known. Where he landed was just about perfect. With the opportunity to work with animals again next spring, he couldn't ask for more.

He wanted everything to stay perfectly the same forever.

At the main road, Stephanie signaled and turned toward town. She had agreed to an end-of-summer lunch to savor every last second, even though she'd end up talking about work. Her destination was The Golden Crown saloon. She was meeting with her fellow kindergarten teachers—and arguably her best friends. In another town, the location might be a scandalous destination for three teachers before noon. Only about a third of their school population resided in Herd. The rest of the kids came from neighboring towns in the greater surrounding region. The likelihood of running into students and their families was small.

Named for the failed prospecting discovery that established the town, when a would-be miner fished someone's golden tooth out of the creek on the current Kincaid ranch, the saloon was less rowdy bar and more family-friendly bistro. It was also the only full-service restaurant in town. During the summer and on warm weekends, Abby Whit operated a food truck from the disputed land near the church at the end of the street. Her food was exceptional but her location was al fresco. Stephanie had doubted her fellow teachers wanted to spend their last few hours of summer exposed to any passer-by.

She drove down Main Street, past the blacksmith shop and the antique store, past the costumed Old West portrait studio and General Store, parking in front of The Golden Crown. Turning off the car, she glanced at the banker's box full of her plans for next week's event.

James, the saloon owner, was kind enough to host the annual, historical dress encouraged, fundraiser. After three years, he understood what was needed and expected. Still, she liked to be fully prepared and work through the entire checklist several times over.

A knock on the window had her snapping up her head.

"You coming inside?" A very pregnant brunette asked, leaning an arm on the roof of the car.

Stephanie scrambled out of the vehicle, grabbing her purse off the center console. "Lauren, you should be inside and off of your feet."

The other woman waved off her concern, resting both hands under her swollen belly and leaning her back against the old hitching post in front of the building. "I'll have plenty of time to lay around later."

Stephanie eyed her dubiously. She'd never heard of any parent of multiples finding time for rest after their sweet, twin bundles of joy arrived. But she also knew better than to disagree with Lauren and especially not now. Calling her bluff only provoked a challenge. "Let's get a table. I'm hungry." She rubbed together her palms and continued to the door, holding it open for her friend.

Stepping inside, her eyes adjusted to the dimly lit interior. The Golden Crown saloon was a large space and had hosted an occasional hundred person plus reception when needed. Most days, however, the place felt cozy with smaller vignettes created by huge posts throughout the room.

A polished, walnut bar took up the length of the building, hugging one wall. Behind it an antique mirror reflected the patrons' faces as they savored their drinks. The sweet smell of sawdust hung in the air, a throwback to the early days when The Golden Crown used it to mop up spilled beer and spit tobacco.

At a table near the back, under a kerosene style hanging light, an older woman stood and waved.

Stephanie and Lauren strode toward their comrade.

Kelly Strong was nothing like her namesake. From her soft and flowy garments to her hushed voice, she was the matronly type Hollywood would cast to portray an early childhood teacher on screen.

To her good friends, Kelly was known for her deep laugh, strong drinks, and love of family. Her kids were in college, only a little younger than Stephanie and a decade younger than Lauren. Kelly never treated the women as a mother hen but rather worked hard to guide them as a trusted and respected mentor.

Kelly pulled out a chair for Lauren.

Lauren sank into the wooden seat like a bag of horseshoes.

Kelly grabbed another chair, tugging it out from the table. "For your feet."

"I'm fine," Lauren protested weakly.

Kelly shot her a teacher face and returned to her spot.

With a sigh, Lauren rested her feet in the chair and propped one arm on the table, sitting in profile. "This is probably better anyways. I can't scoot my belly under the table."

Stephanie sat in the free seat. "Are you sure you want to start the school year? You can still change your mind. Bill understands."

Their principal was well regarded. Raising twins of his own, he appreciated Lauren's situation better than most. Definitely better than Stephanie. She only vaguely grasped the impending changes to her friend's life. With a husband, Lauren's world was already a step removed from Stephanie's. Kids would only heighten the differences between them.

"I'm fine. I can't take any more babying. Steve is monitoring my every move. Wouldn't surprise me if he pops in." Lauren rolled her eyes.

"He's excited. Good for you and him." Kelly pushed a water glass forward.

Lauren grabbed it and drank.

Stephanie was glad for the break from Lauren's gripes about her sweet, nurturing husband. If opposites attracted, the pair were a perfect match. Not to discount Lauren's good qualities. She and her husband shared kindness. But their difference was in the delivery. "Soon enough, your kids are grown and gone. Your job is done like that." Kelly snapped her fingers. "If you need anything, you call me. Any time. No questions asked."

Lauren nodded.

"I'm looking forward to a good year," Kelly continued and turned to include Stephanie in the conversation.

With so much happening in their personal lives, Stephanie didn't like to admit she felt like an outsider at times. She had too much to do for wallowing or self-pity. *You get one life, what are you going to do with it?* Her mom's mantra pushed her forward every day.

"Me, too," Stephanie chimed in. "I might stop by and drop off another round of supplies at my classroom." She smiled, feeling it down to her toes. Creating a safe space for every kid in her class was just as important as providing them with the tools to excel and love learning. She had a new plan for the school year to further erase any differences. She wanted everyone on an equal standing within her four classroom walls.

Focusing on her kids was better than thinking about her one-sided, unrequited crush.

"I need a good, smooth, quiet year," Lauren said, her gaze sliding to Kelly's.

Kelly shook her head.

The motion was so slight, Stephanie might have thought she imagined it. But with five years of working together as a duo before Stephanie was hired, the pair sometimes exchanged looks and non-verbal communication with significant implications. "What is it? What's wrong?"

Kelly frowned.

Lauren leaned forward. "Nothing's wrong, per se. But be careful. The PTO president's youngest kid is in your class this year."

"Oh, okay." Stephanie tipped her head to the side. She'd only had positive interactions with the woman, Candace Vane. When Stephanie first had her idea to do a fundraiser to cover the costs of food service for the entire building, thus eliminating any difference between kids receiving free and reduced lunches and those paying full price, the woman had supported her and had called on a corporate connection that met the donation, thus doubling the gift and adding breakfast to the offerings. "Do you suppose she requested me?"

"Maybe?" Lauren grimaced and shook her head. "I taught the eldest Vane child my first year."

"What was the problem?" Stephanie asked. "My interactions with Candace have all been good. She has a real heart for the school and doing her part."

Kelly darted her gaze side to side and leaned forward. "She likes to play saints and martyrs. Either she portrays herself as utterly magnanimous and you adore her because she's so selfless. Or you are her persecutor and how dare you when she's only trying for the greater good. She never does anything without seeking public support."

Stephanie puzzled over that, folding her arms over her chest, and nibbling her bottom lip. Was that her angle? Trying to be esteemed by the public at large? Did people really spend so much time caring what others thought about them?

"Just be careful is all we're saying," Lauren said.

"I will. But don't worry about me. You'll be on leave soon," Stephanie said. "Focus on staying healthy for your babies."

"I want you there when I get back," Lauren murmured.

Stephanie lifted her menu, cutting off the unhelpful conversation. Talking wasn't her style. She much preferred taking action over pretty words. When her plan was in full effect and the kids were excelling, then she'd be vindicated.

She didn't want to be on edge at school. After a summer tiptoeing around Ted Stirling, she wanted to fall back into her role as self-confident, career woman. She appreciated her friends' words but knew she'd have to live the experience to understand for herself the caution they urged.

Thankfully, a server approached the table and took their orders, clearing the way for a total conversational shift. She would do what she did best. She only had to survive one more awkward encounter with Ted, and then she vowed to put her feelings for him away for good. What was the point in liking someone if she was too scared to say hello?

CHAPTER 2

Stephanie was nothing if not maddeningly self-aware. As predicted, her day off was torturously long. When the clock finally struck five, she grabbed her tote style purse and headed out her apartment door. An early riser her entire life, she forced herself to stay in bed in her one-bedroom apartment in the complex between the regional school she taught at and Herd's historic downtown, roughly ten miles of empty prairie separating her from each. She'd had to drive another fifteen past town to reach the ranch, putting more miles on her car over the past three months than in the past three years.

Meal prep and laundry kept her busy most of the day. She liked the days she didn't need to drive at all. The newer apartment building sat in a redeveloped strip mall complex. If she'd wanted, she could walk to the little coffee shop on the corner, past a convenience store, gift shop, dry cleaners, and two-screen movie theater. But she didn't need anything else keeping her awake today.

She could have stopped by school to drop off the supplies taking up her backseat. But she hated to drive even a single mile extra. Besides, she'd wake up early enough tomorrow morning with plenty of time to unpack her car long before another teacher arrived and asked if she wanted help.

As a do-er, she resisted any hesitation in a plan. Working with another person—even for something as simple as unloading a vehicle—meant she'd have to slow down and explain herself. She preferred to be in charge without any hint of micromanaging. When her younger brother had married, she'd officially handed over making his appointments to his wife. Her sister-in-law had been shocked an adult didn't know the number for the dentist or when the next physical was due. With two, full-time working parents, Stephanie had taken care of Tyler, earning praise in the process.

Late in the day, leaving for the cowboy dinner, she exhaled a heavy sigh. She was eager to get on with her life and excited to see Ted, despite the churn of her tummy. The scenery passed in a blur. If she had spared a glance, however, she wouldn't have enjoyed the view.

The prairie grasses and wildflowers died early in the season. A lack of summer rain dried the ground until deep cracks broke the earth. For the first time ever, she'd welcome the snow and—with it—the hope of quenching the parched earth.

At long last, she pulled her car in front of the ranch house. Parking at the end of the circle drive, she grabbed her purse off the shotgun seat and exited the car. She swung the tote over her shoulder, tucking her hands into her jean jacket. The late summer evening held a chill in the air. She probably should have worn something more substantial than her favorite cotton sundress and ankle boots.

She wanted to look nice. Just in case. Crunching the gravel under her heel, she crossed in front of her car and continued around the side of the main house. She had only talked to Ted—successfully—once. During her audition to teach, she led him and Ryan through a class. When she leaned into her skills, she was confident. As long as she held still in tree pose, she conducted a conversation with ease.

This evening presented a challenge. Her prospects for success were very slim. Balancing poses were hard enough without adding a plate full of baked beans.

A screen door slammed shut.

She jumped.

"Stephanie?" A feminine voice called.

Stephanie stopped and raised her gaze to the covered, wraparound porch. Squinting, she spotted the face of her newest friend and waved. "Hi, Meg. How are you?"

"I'm doing very well, thank you. But I think you're the person who should be answering the question." Meg walked down the front steps and stopped at her side.

Why? Stephanie sucked in a breath. Had Ted said something? About what? She hardly replied with one-word responses to his questions. Her skin burned. Of course, he could be joking around behind her back.

"Ready for school in the morning?" Meg asked, crinkling the corners of her brown eyes as she smiled. The pretty brunette wore a floral dress that floated around her. She moved with an ease Stephanie envied. *Because she was the girl next door and knew this ranch by heart? Because she was lucky in love?*

Releasing a shaky breath, Stephanie smoothed her hair behind her ears and nodded. "I'm all set."

Meg looped her arm through Stephanie's.

With almost five inches height difference, Stephanie focused on the ground as the pair started walking. After a few steps, she found the rhythm. Meg was considered average height. To Stephanie, however, she was tall.

"I'm glad to see you. This has to be your busiest week of the year, huh?"

"Well . . ." Stephanie considered that. The start of the school year was quickly followed by the holiday season. Between work and civic life, she operated in a loop of busyness. Once winter came, her town commitments diminished as her career ramped up with parent-teacher conferences, curriculum meetings, further education, and after-school activities. Then came the spring and summer and the return of tourists. Did she ever have a slow time of year?

Meg chuckled. "Never mind. I think you're always busy."

"I like to be productive."

At the back of the house, they crunched brittle, brown grass under their feet, careful of the deep cracks in the dry earth. Stephanie missed the sweet smell of fresh-cut grass but watering the lawn would cost an exorbitant amount. She lifted her gaze toward their destination.

The doors were fully opened. Light spilled out and the buzz of conversation floated past, welcoming company for a fun evening.

Cars parked on the grass next to the barn. During the summer, resort guests were the primary customers at the cowboy dinners, thus not needing a large parking lot. Had Stephanie been presumptuous to park in front of the house? She nibbled the inside of her cheek.

"Do you need an extra hand at the poker tournament?" Meg asked. "The auction was pushed back so we aren't leaving for another week."

"Oh, that would be great." Meg sighed. "Can I stop by the store on Thursday?"

"I'll be there. I might be working on my packing list. I haven't visited San Francisco in years."

"I've never been." Stephanie couldn't hide her wistful tone. Images of cable cars and brightly colored Victorian homes flashed in her mind.

"Really?" Meg pulled back, studying her. "I had family nearby years ago. I'm not excited to see how much has changed. But I am looking forward to visiting my favorite spots in the city."

At the entrance, Meg unhooked her arm and leaned close. "I confess my volunteer involvement at the fundraiser won't be entirely selfless."

Stephanie tipped her head to the side. "It won't?"

Meg shook her head. "I would love to pick your brain about event planning. The ranch's next venture was my idea. But the more reading and research I undertake, the more I'm overwhelmed."

Stephanie nodded. "I understand. Believe me. When I first took over Frontier Days, the task seemed Herculean. You have to start small and be willing to learn. I have a few checklists I can copy for you as a starting off point. Weddings are a different beast."

"Maybe I can convince you to help me part-time?" Meg asked. "We both have full-time careers demanding the bulk of our attention. If the business takes off, an on-staff coordinator will be hired. It'll be a bare bones operation at the start."

Stephanie nibbled the inside of her cheek. She preferred to work on one event at a time rather than a vague promise to help out indefinitely. She liked having clear deadlines and set budgets. If Meg asked for wedding help for her nuptials, Stephanie would agree straight away. "I'm not sure I can give you an answer without more specifics. I'll help where I can. I'll bring copies of my calendars, too. Everything I have, I'll share."

"I'd appreciate it, thanks," Meg said. "I better see what trouble Hank is getting into," she murmured.

"Don't let me keep you. Thanks for the escort." Stephanie smiled.

Meg strolled forward without a glance backward, like she owned the place. She almost did. Her family had owned the next-door ranch, and were one of the town's founders. She grew up spending summers on her land and this property. Dating Ryan Kincaid, the owner's grandson, she'd no doubt be a part of the legacy of this land very soon.

Stephanie was happy for her and knew the now very serious and seemingly inevitable pairing had been a lifetime in the making. Would it take her that long to work up the courage to talk to Ted?

A shove from behind pushed her forward.

She gasped and turned, eyes wide.

"Sorry, Stephanie," Joe said, peering around the large box in his outstretched arms. "I didn't see you."

"Totally my fault for lurking. Can I help?"

"Actually, yeah. Grab one end, please."

Stephanie nodded, not that he could see, and did as directed. While she'd heard whispers of a job opening on the ranch at the start of the summer, she owed her position to her friend, Joe. She'd help him however he needed.

In the K-8 school, she had the opportunity to get to know her fellow teachers as they shepherded their kids from one grade to the next. Joe taught middle school social studies. In a year, he'd be working with her first class of students. She marveled at how fast time sped past for the kids while she barely changed.

"Just behind the catering table," Joe said. "I'll walk backward." He sidestepped until he stood in the position.

"What's in the box?" she asked.

"Huh?" he called.

"What are we carrying?"

"The box?"

She blew out a sigh. Curiosity wasn't enough of a conversation starter tonight. She didn't really care. But she'd made an effort twice, might as well go for the third time. "What is in the box that we are carrying?" she raised her voice, hovering just under a yell.

He stopped walking and started to lower the box to a table.

With her attention focused on the cardboard, she set it down, straightened, and her skin flushed.

Ted stood next to Joe, quirking an eyebrow at her.

In amusement? Oh, please let her be anything but a source of ridicule.

"Thanks," Ted said. "The box has favors for everyone, to celebrate another great year. We have a photographer set up near the band, and we'll pass out commemorative frames. The photos will be mailed."

"Oh," she murmured. Again, the words caught in her throat. She might have only thought the response.

Ted focused on the box, slipping a hand under the flaps at the end.

"Are you trying to open it? Use a knife," Joe said.

"No, I got this." Ted waved him away.

She scrunched her nose. What was it with men not accepting help when offered? If Joe said nothing, would Ted have pulled out his own pocket knife?

"First, you have to grip it. Then you rip it," Joe said.

Ted chuckled. "Okay, Bogey Lowenstein." He rolled his eyes and ripped the box open.

"Wait? What?" she asked.

His comment snapped her out of her stasis real fast. Was that all it took? Adding in a hearty dash of utter bewilderment to loosen her tongue? Too often, in Ted's company, the useless muscle lolled in her mouth.

Two male faces stared at her with mixed expressions of amusement and outrage.

She wasn't in the wrong here. If they wanted to make bizarre comments, they'd have to explain themselves. And for once she found her voice.

She spoke? In front of a witness? To him? At a public event?

Ted widened his gaze. Her confusion was enough to make him ignore the very painful paper-cut he'd given himself from the surprisingly well sealed box. He should have used a pocket knife. Once Joe opened his mouth, however, it went against Ted's code to give his friend the satisfaction. That was their friendship in a nutshell. Fine and dandy until one opened their mouth gave the other advice. No matter how prescient.

"Who's Bogey Lowenstein?" she asked.

"Ah! She speaks." Ted grinned and widened his stance on the old pine boards, folding his arms over his chest. He couldn't believe his luck any more than he understood her lack of knowledge of one of the seminal movies of his generation. "And I'm offended. It's not who, the question is, what's a Bogey Lowen-stein?"

She darted her gaze from one to the other. "I'm supposed to know what that means?"

"It's a classic line from a great movie," Joe said, exasperated.

Her eyes widened.

This was the first time she'd engaged in a conversation with him. Ted hated to waste it by being offended. But he was equally as flabbergasted as Joe. "It's from 1999?"

"I was five." She shrugged.

Joe groaned.

I was in college with Liv. And just like that, the moment shattered. Not that it mattered. Ted was never moving on from losing the love of his life and definitely wasn't looking for a connection with someone so young and unhurt by the world.

Stephanie was sweetness and light. She didn't know pain the way he did. He hoped she never would. They'd never have anything in common besides their zip code.

Ted scrubbed a hand over his face. "Regardless, the film has one of the best soundtracks of all time."

"Truth." Joe raised his hand and fist-bumped Ted.

"I thought the music from that time was all horn lines and . . ." She frowned. "What was it called? Ska?"

Joe threw up his hands. "This is too much."

Ted agreed. Maybe he liked her better not speaking if she was going to challenge the pop culture pillars of his life. But he was equally amused at finally having a conversation with her. He couldn't let it go. "What's better than ska? It has a point of view and a message."

"And that is?" She asked, staring at him with a quizzical gleam in her sapphire eyes.

Ted enjoyed seeing any expression other than confusion and bewilderment on her pretty face. He'd probably regret giving her an answer. Her tone hovered between teasing and serious consideration.

"Because every song I've heard had the same, vague, parents don't understand vibe," she continued.

"Ah. Okay. I get it." Ted regained his footing. "You prefer country slash pop?"

She nodded.

"Aren't some of the most popular songs too hyper focused on the artist's personal life? Why dunk on someone else's ex?" Ted asked.

Her cheeks turned pink. "Heartbreak is universal. The specificity makes it more relatable."

Did she have a bad break-up in her past? Opening his mouth, Ted wasn't sure he wanted to know. The idea of Stephanie dating someone made him feel as hot and weary as he did after a long day of mending fences under the summer sun. But he liked talking with her. What he would have said remained a mystery.

Joe paled, whiter than the clouds, and stepped forward, hunching his back.

"Stephanie, please cover for me," Joe hissed. "Hank's coming towards us with Abby, and I really don't want to be bamboozled tonight."

"No, you're an adult. Just tell him to back off," Stephanie said, rolling her eyes. "You're starting to be rude. Be honest with Mr. Kincaid. Although, I don't understand why you don't like her. She's the only person even remotely interested in your town history project."

Joe glared. "Once I finish the interviews and publish the book, I can promise you everyone will be interested."

Ted studied the pair. He had the sense they'd had this conversation several times before. He hated feeling like the third wheel, especially with them. But he couldn't insert himself into a chat he only guessed at.

Hank Kincaid had spent the summer heavy-handedly manufacturing meet-ups between Abby Whit, food truck owner, and Joe. Ted should be grateful he wasn't on the old man's radar. Love wasn't part of his future. He clung to the memories of romance like a comfortable pair of faded jeans. Someone new wouldn't know his moods or understand his love of silence.

He'd come to Montana seeking peace on his own terms. While he'd become part of a community, slowly over time, that hadn't been his goal. Friends he cared for like family was an unexpected gift. He wouldn't ever seek more. He wouldn't challenge fate again.

"She's hiding some kind of secret," Joe said.

Stephanie rolled her eyes.

"Or she's laughing at me," Joe rushed to add. "Either way it's awkward. Please, come on. I'll owe you big time."

"I flat out refuse." Stephanie shook her head. "The last thing either of us needs is a rumor that we're together spreading through town."

"Fine," Joe bit out the word.

"Besides. I like Abby. I don't understand your issue. If she's catering," Stephanie licked her lips, "I'm eating every plate I can. The food truck is only operating for a few more weeks. I won't get a chance to stop by again once school is in session."

Heavy, bootsteps clicked against the wooden plank floor.

Joe scrubbed a hand over his face, wiping away the grimace.

Smart. Hank deserved no less than everyone's respect. He'd been a town mainstay, supporting any neighbor who needed help and never asking questions. While he might have a bit of a reputation as a gossip, he didn't push. People shared.

About six months into Ted's tenure, he confided in Hank. The pain could never fully be eased but sharing helped shift the boulder off his heart. Hank didn't demand an explanation or play by play. When he had lost his beloved Susie, he had sought Ted for a chat. The pair had reached an even deeper bond.

Hank clapped a hand on Joe's shoulder. "Good evening, everyone. Nice to see you, Stephanie."

"Hi, Mr. Kincaid. I'd better get a seat while I can." Stephanie smiled and waved, backing away.

Joe might have uttered *coward*. Or maybe Ted's imagination filled in the dots. But he had enjoyed the evening's unexpected encounter, learning more about both his friend and his former employee.

He'd been corrected. She was only fourteen years his junior. In the grand scheme, the difference from twenty to fourteen was marginal. But at least it explained why perhaps she never really attempted to talk to him. She probably had no idea what to say.

If she didn't, she wouldn't be the only one.

The problem with falling in love at fifteen and getting married at twenty-two was he'd only really interacted with one girl outside of his family circle. And when he vowed forever, he meant it. He'd shake off his concerns about his run-ins with a random acquaintance. *Except she wasn't random, and she was than an acquaintance.*

"Ted?" Hank snapped his fingers.

With a shake, Ted focused on the new group. "Sorry, thinking about what to do next."

"Good man," Hank said, nodding. "I'm going to steal Joe, if you don't mind. Since Abby's here, figured it's a good time to talk logistics."

Joe frowned. "We don't really want to interrupt her in the middle of service."

Hank waved off the comment. "Oh, it'll only take a second."

"I'm all set here. Thanks for your help, Joe," Ted said, sort of enjoying his friend's frustration.

"Right this way." Hank gestured down the table.

Joe smiled and turned, flashing a finger behind his back.

Ted chuckled. After Hank successfully paired off his grandson and their beautiful next-door neighbor earlier in the summer, he focused his newly found matchmaking energy on Joe. In this case, Ted didn't mind being forgotten.

In Ted's back pocket, his phone vibrated. He pulled out the device, staring at the screen.

Jen Cade: We're here.

His palms went clammy. Why now? Was something wrong?

He'd called his little sister a few days ago, and she'd given him no clue about a visit. His heart slammed into the front of his chest. The text was plural. He could rest easy that had to include at least two. If it was three?

Swallowing the lump in his throat, he dried his hands on his jeans. He could be cordial—if distant—to his niece's father. Jen would expect no less. Probably why she'd given him no warning about her impending arrival. If he snuck out now, he could be back in fifteen minutes.

The crowd settled at tables. The photographer roamed the room, snapping candid pictures. The staff helped Abby carry covered trays from her food truck outside, through the side door, and set them onto chafing dishes. Meal service would start soon.

Everything was set-up and running smoothly. But he couldn't disappear, abandoning his post without a word.

Crossing the room, he pulled Ryan from a conversation with Meg near the bandstand.

"I need to go to my cabin. I should be back in half an hour. Forty-five minutes, tops," Ted said.

"Why?"

The question wasn't unexpected. Ted shifted his weight uneasily. He wasn't sure he knew the reason and didn't want to lie.

"Should I be worried?" Ryan tipped his head to the side. "Do you need someone to go with you?"

"No need. Nothing I can't handle." *Liar liar.* Ted cleared his throat. "I'll be back soon."

"Okay." Ryan nodded.

Without further explanation, Ted spun on his booted heel and stalked out of the building. In a few long strides, he crossed the lawn and made his way through the maze of vehicles. He wrenched open the door of his truck, turned over the engine, and peeled out of the parking spot. He reached his snug, wooden, two-bedroom cabin on the other side of the pond, opposite the tourist cabins. Parking his car next to an SUV pulling a trailer, he hopped to the ground.

"Unc!" A little voice called and barreled into his legs, nearly knocking him over.

Chuckling, he reached down and grabbed his niece, embracing her in his arms for a big bear hug. The little girl always looked askew. Her curly mop of thick hair fought against any attempts at taming it. So did the child. He kissed the side of her cheek and, for the first time in twenty minutes, he felt calm, his pulse slowing and his breath evening. "Maddy. So good to see you. I didn't know you were coming." He set her back on the ground and raised his gaze.

His sister sat on the front stoop.

Alone. Thankfully. He refrained from releasing a heavy sigh. With limited time and a complicated custody arrangement, his sister's ex-husband had joined them on visits to Montana in the past. Ted preferred advance notice in such situations. Relief that his former brother-in-law hadn't joined the pair wasn't a particularly charming response to the impromptu family reunion.

"Hi, Teddy." Jen pushed off the top step, dusting her hands on her sherpa jacket and jeans.

Only a few inches shorter, she shared the same gray eyes and brown hair. He often thought she looked like him in a wig. Not that he'd ever say so. She had a wicked right hook.

He pulled her in for a hug.

She returned the embrace and released a shaky exhale. "I got a job at the local hospital. Like you recommended."

She could have called and told him. She knew he hated surprises. Little sisters never stopped being frustrating. He dropped his arms and studied her face. "And everyone is okay with that?"

She nodded. "He's taking a job overseas. We both decided I should be near family. He'll visit us here."

Ted pressed together his lips, holding himself back from what he wanted to say. He wouldn't speak ill of a man in front of his innocent child. When he'd floated the idea about the job opportunity, he'd received no response from his sister.

He figured she wasn't able to pursue the option or wasn't interested in a move. He couldn't blame her. With a child and an ex, her life was complicated without uprooting everything for her brother. Besides, he'd been the one to leave their childhood hometown. If he wanted family close, he should have stayed.

"Are you 'cited, Unc?" Madison asked.

He smiled down at the little girl. "More than you can know. Come on, let's get you settled inside."

When he lifted his gaze to Jen, he noted the dark smudges under her eyes. Exhaustion clung to her like chains. She was here. He'd keep them both safe. If he had to watch his tongue around Maddy, so be it. But he'd never let down the people who loved him. Not after failing one person so completely that he'd never be fully healed.

CHAPTER 3

Stephanie chose her career because she loved children. Summers off was one of the selling points, too. Until she started working and realized the break wasn't relaxing for a person who thrived on external validation.

In that aspect, she supposed she'd never shake her childhood lessons. Her parents instilled in her that a person could have it all as long as they weren't afraid of hard work. The phrase was motivation and cover. Happy to shine the spotlight on others, she shrank in the overhead glare of a direct beam and kept to the background as part of her head down approach to any job.

Since she'd started working, she focused on any chance to make someone else's day a little brighter. She could worry about her own happiness at some distant point in the future. Or if she ever worked up the courage to speak to Ted again.

Behind her desk, she yawned and glanced at the clock on the opposite wall. She had ten minutes to show time. Last night, after the dinner, she had stayed up too late watching the movie he mentioned. She still didn't quite get the appeal. Was that his high school experience?

The amount of in-person interaction was what shocked her the most. Of course, without social media or even widespread cell phone usage, she supposed that was what they had to do. Speak to each other. She cringed. She'd rather send a text than have to look at her crush in the face and worry what her expression said.

A knock sounded on the door.

"Come in," she called and stood, brushing her hands on her skirt. For work, she dressed in bright colors with often cartoonish, cutesy themes. Today, her shirt dress was covered with crayon appliques.

"Good morning, just checking you're all set?" Bill, the principal, asked, entering the room. Dressed in his usual suit, he also used his wardrobe to set him apart in his role. Without the collared shirt and dress shoes clicking against the twelve-by-twelve tile floor, the kind, soft-spoken man wouldn't be nearly intimidating enough for the older kids.

With a smile, she strode toward the neat stack of school supplies she'd unloaded from her car. She pointed to the boxes of crayons and pencils. "I'm ready. Although, first day of kindergarten usually involves more tissues than markers."

The middle-aged man nodded enthusiastically. "I'm sure you're right. The incoming class is our largest ever. I'm stopping in to double check if you, Kelly, and Lauren have any last-minute requests."

"No, I'm good." She grabbed the stack of fliers off the top of her desk, holding the text to her chest. Was he truly here to offer bland first day greetings? Or had Kelly and Lauren met with him?

"You're aware you have Candace Vane's daughter, Amelia, in class this year?" he asked.

"I am." Stephanie dragged out the response.

"Candace asked for you specifically."

"Oh, that's nice." Stephanie released a shaky breath.

He tugged at his necktie, loosening the Windsor knot.

"Or . . . it isn't?" she asked.

"If you need any support, please come to the office. If you anticipate any problems, you don't even have to knock on the door. Just enter and tell me. Keep me in the loop."

Two warnings in less than twenty-four hours had to count for something. She wasn't the type to follow other people's advice without question. But she always listened when someone shared a personal anecdote. Still at the start of her career, she remained mostly untested. "I appreciate it. I have worked with Mrs. Vane for the past several years."

"You have, and the free meals for all program has been wonderful. She can be formidable as either an ally or an enemy. Be careful."

The bell rang over the door, metallic clanging reverberating through her.

She jumped, the papers in her arms fluttering. "First day. That always gets me."

He chuckled. "Have a wonderful day, if you need anything, you know where to find me." He turned and strode out the open door.

When her boss was out of sight, she released a heavy breath. She wasn't a brand-new educator. She could handle her class and was eager to lean into her strengths.

High-pitched chatter mixed with the squeak of sneakers against the freshly washed floor. The doors whooshed and crashed from constant opening and shutting. The organized chaos of the school year began.

In a few minutes, she'd have to go pick up her kids from the multi-purpose room, shepherding her students down the hall after the older kids were settled upstairs. She held her papers out, scanning through the text again. She never second-guessed a decision and especially not when her motives were so clear and logical. But all the talk lately left her slightly off-balance.

On the fliers going home today, she spelled out her expectations of the year. She wanted her kids to learn in a safe, fair environment. To that end, she was limiting volunteer opportunities in class. She hated seeing the tears of children whose parents both worked and could not be the mystery reader while other children's moms and dads stopped by on multiple occasions per week.

She'd been that kid without any parental involvement. She'd taken it upon herself to be her brother's mystery reader to save him the pain of everyone else feeling special and him feeling singled out. Neither had she wanted her wonderful parents—with two equally high-powered careers—to feel guilty they couldn't take off time.

At the wall of cubbies, she slid a brightly colored sheet in each slot. While parents might initially balk at the change, they would come around. Earlier in the summer, she'd informed the families of her incoming class about the shared school supply format. The crayons, markers, and glue sticks would not be kept at each child's desk. Instead, she would have supplies available for everyone from a communal table. A few had raised complaints insisting their student should have their own supplies, but after discussion about teaching the importance of sharing, parents had agreed. She wouldn't have to worry about this.

The bell rang again.

With the last paper in the final cubby, she pulled back her shoulders, plastered on her teacher smile, and strode into the now quiet hallway. Everyone was safe and equal at school. She wouldn't flinch from her purpose.

She breathed deep, inhaling the smell of freshly sharpened pencils and industrial cleaner as she walked from her classroom to the multi-purpose room at the end of the corridor. With each step, the buzz of furtively whispered conversations filled the air. She would miss this.

While nothing had been officially announced, the large incoming class signaled a change in the town and the school's future. The economic rebound—spurred in large part by the success of the Kincaid ranch—meant more families moving into the district and others staying put. She was glad everyone could earn a solid livelihood.

The expansive school boundaries weren't being redrawn with the population boom. But the building couldn't house too many more grades of seventy plus kids. She'd been pleased to teach roughly fifteen to eighteen children each year. At twenty-four, this would be the most students she'd taught on her own ever. She'd student taught a large class and found the situation overwhelming.

An idea had been floated to separate the kindergarteners into their own building. She'd miss the other teachers. The elementary grades were a family within the larger community. They worked together, sharing ideas and practices for the benefit of the entire school society.

The multi-purpose room's door stood ajar.

She entered and stayed close to the wall. She waved at the first and second grade teachers, and stood next to Lauren and Kelly.

"You're late?" Kelly whispered, leaning close.

Stephanie gripped her elbows behind her back. "First day pep talk from Bill. Nothing to worry about."

Lauren stepped forward out of the line of teachers. "Good morning boys and girls."

"Good morning, Mrs. Simmons." The chorus of voices of the first and second graders filled the room.

Lauren smiled at the room, meeting the gazes of the confused kindergarteners on the ground in front. "When I call your class, I'd like you to please stand up and form a single file line. Your teacher will lead you down the hall to your new classroom. If you aren't sure who your teacher is, please wait until I ask for the remaining students to step forward. Miss Patricks' class."

Stephanie stepped forward and grinned.

A gaggle of children stood, gathering their backpacks and lunchboxes. They formed a somewhat single file line. A few pairs clung to each other.

With her finger as a guide, Stephanie counted to twenty-four and flashed Lauren a thumbs-up. "Please follow me."

A little girl dressed in head-to-toe pink, with a huge, satin bow expertly tied around her ponytail and velvet ballet flats, stepped forward as the line leader.

Stephanie fought her frown. The child assumed the first-place spot and the others let her. Not a good omen. Stephanie kept smiling. If she had to guess, she'd wager the child was Amelia. She carried herself with the same confidence as her mother. Stephanie had good interactions with the parent and wouldn't read too much into the child. But she also counted herself a good judge of character, and worried about the mean girl vibe she got from the too-sweet-to-be-genuine expression.

"Please follow me," Stephanie repeated, this time with a little more confidence, and turned. As she exited the room, the little girl put her hand in Stephanie's.

She glanced down and smiled, again fighting the urge to recoil. She wasn't a fan of the teacher's pet. Favoritism wasn't her style but could be a struggle against a person's natural inclination to gravitate towards one over another. Under the guise of turning to glance over her shoulder, she dropped the little girl's hand and counted again to twenty-four. She checked the numbers two more times as they walked the twenty yards to her classroom. At the door to the room, she stopped. "Good morning class. I would like to shake everyone's hand as you walk inside. Please find your name on a cubby and place your backpack inside. Then, if you'll take a seat on the brightly-colored carpet in the story corner, we'll start today with a book."

Kneeling, she held out her hand to the little girl. "Good morning, I'm Miss Patricks."

"Amelia Vane," she said and bounced into the room.

Stephanie turned to the next child, a little boy with tear-filled eyes. Pulling a tissue from her pocket, she extended it.

The boy blew his nose, loudly, and held it out to her.

She had a long day ahead, but she'd focus on one step at a time. This would be the best year ever, she'd except no less. And avoiding the snotty sides of the tissues whenever possible was key.

Ted paced outside the closed door, clicking his boots with each step. He hadn't stepped foot inside a school in over two decades and never this particular building. But some things a mind and body couldn't forget. The whiff of pencils tickled his nostrils and brought back the long-forgotten anxiety of coloring in bubbles on a standardized test. He did well in school, but tests overwhelmed him every time.

As his ribs tightened, his vision blurred. He stilled, leaning against the painted, concrete wall.

"Unc, you okay?" Maddy asked, shaking their clasped hands.

He glanced down at his niece, swallowing the bile rising in his throat. He wasn't the one who should be nervous. He wouldn't be starting a new school a day late. He cleared his throat. "Yep. Sorry, squirrel."

The bell rang.

The loud clang preceded the classroom door opening and cacophony of high-pitched voices filtered into the hall.

Maddy ducked behind him.

"Alright, single file behind me please," Stephanie said. Her voice was kind but firm.

Until yesterday, he hadn't really heard it. Was that only yesterday? Might as well have been a year ago. After he had settled his sister and niece into the extra bedroom at his cabin, he had returned to the Cowboy Dinner. Jen and Maddy were invited but skipped it, following the long drive they were wiped. By the time he had finished and returned home, he knocked on their bedroom door and opened it to see the pair curled up together and snoring in sync. They'd been so peaceful. He hadn't had the heart to wake his sister and get more specifics about her move or her next steps. He'd regretted that choice all day.

Stephanie walked backwards into the hall and turned, glancing over her shoulder. Frowning, she froze for a moment.

Wearing a crayon-patterned dress, she embodied her role as a kindergarten teacher. He'd grown used to seeing her in yoga pants and ponytails. He'd never noticed that her hair only grazed her shoulder or how the light made the blonde shimmer.

She wore minimal makeup, but she looked more pulled together than he was used to.

A child pushed another forward.

"Please, let's be careful of everyone's space," she said, facing her students again. She walked backwards, facing a line of boys and girls.

When she glanced his way again, she dropped her gaze to the child. Nodding, she flashed him a thumbs up. "We'll go to the multi-purpose room again for dismissal and then I'll come back to the classroom. You'll be called by your bus or your last name if you are being driven home."

Was that directed at him? Should he duck inside the room?

She tilted her head toward a classroom door and shot him a look.

Yep, he definitely stood out. In dirty jeans and an old flannel peeking under the hem of his brown coat, he came straight from the ranch without changing. He had washed his hands but that was the full extent of his cleaning up before his arrival. As the last child in the line filed past, he tugged gently on Maddy's hand and strolled into the classroom.

Bright colors greeted him from every corner. Posters with cheerful greetings, inspirational messages, and class rules were interspersed on the two long walls. Opposite the door, a wall of windows overlooked the playground and in front a play kitchen sat behind a large alphabet motif rug. To the left of the door, cubbies hugged the corner. Circular tables with little chairs filled the center of the room.

He breathed easier. The space was warm and inviting. "Let's sit. Miss Patricks will be here in a minute." *Hopefully.*

He didn't like the way Maddy's lower lip quivered or her sheepish posture, her chin practically glued to her chest as she stared at her feet. She'd been fine until she saw the other kids.

Had he missed something? In the car on the drive over, she hadn't stopped chattering about going to school. He'd been glad for her enthusiasm.

At the table closest to the adult-sized desk, he pulled out two chairs. He sat, his bones creaking.

Maddy giggled.

With his bent knees almost at his shoulder height, he felt like a bear riding a tricycle at a circus. The image was ridiculous, and the position was painful. He didn't care. Earning her smile was worth the physical cost.

Like usual, he had arisen before the sun to take care of the horses. Animal husbandry was his favorite part of the job, and he left his cell in his truck's cupholder for a spot of peace as he started his day. But when he had returned to the vehicle, he'd missed about a hundred calls from Jen and frantic texts.

He had no choice but to head home. At his front door, his sister had explained what she had failed to mention the night before. She needed to return to California, to finish her final shifts and finalize both the sale of her house and her custody arrangement. The new job hired her sooner than she intended but she couldn't pass up the chance. She'd be gone for the next ten days, coming back for a weekend visit before finishing her last week at her current job.

She would have stayed in California and moved with Maddy in a few weeks. But Maddy needed to start school. Jen had filled out some forms online but didn't get a chance to stop by and drop the paperwork. If he showed up, he could probably manage the rest of registration.

Overwhelmed, he hadn't done more than listen as the information was tossed at him. No sooner than he found his voice, he had watched his sister maneuver the SUV and trailer and head down the road the way she came. He'd turned to a still sleepy Maddy.

He had never stepped in as a parental figure. His role had always been the fun uncle. Right now, she needed security. He had no idea what to do with a child. But he couldn't show fear. There had to be some similarities between skittish animals and small kids.

So, he had fed her and loaded her into the truck. They had spent the rest of the morning doing his usual work. She wasn't as much of a hindrance as he feared. But neither could he modify his schedule every day to be child friendly. While he had toyed with the idea of keeping her with him until her mother returned, he understood he'd be doing them both a disservice. After lunch, he couldn't delay the inevitable any longer. He needed to get her into school. Luckily, he knew just who to ask for help.

The door shut with a gentle thud.

He turned toward the sound.

"Hello," Stephanie said softly, approaching with eyes only on Maddy. "I'm Miss Patricks. I'm a teacher."

For a split second, he was jealous. She addressed the little girl with such care and attention. He wanted some of that, too.

Stephanie walked to their table, pulling out a seat opposite and sinking down. "What's your name?"

"Madison Cade," the little girl whispered.

Stephanie beamed. "It's a pleasure to make your acquaintance, Madison. Do you have a nickname you like?"

The little girl nodded.

"Can you tell me what it is?" Stephanie asked.

Maddy froze, turning toward him with a deer in the headlights expression of terror.

Jen did a good job raising her daughter to be afraid of giving any information to a stranger. But—with any luck—Stephanie wouldn't be unknown for long. Mentally, he shook himself. She wouldn't become closer via him. Stephanie would be Maddy's teacher. He put a hand on his niece's shoulder. "This is my niece, Maddy. She arrived in town last night, and I guess I messed up her first day of school. Her very first day."

"Oh, that's where you went?" Stephanie said the words in a rush.

She knew I was gone? He widened his eyes.

She coughed. "Sorry, at one point Hank needed you and . . ." She waved a hand. "Doesn't matter. Did you go to the office? Fill out registration? I didn't have an extra name on my attendance list this morning." She wrinkled her brow.

He liked her cute look of confusion. But his screw-up wasn't her fault. "My sister had forms I was supposed to bring but then I lost track of time today." He glanced down at his niece. Her hand felt tiny and vulnerable in his grip.

"Did you just walk in?" Stephanie shifted her weight from one foot to the other.

"No, I stopped at the office. I gave them my I.D., but I told them I was here to see you." He hated the off-balance feeling of not knowing exactly how to right a wrong and worse, letting down his niece in the process. "I really need some guidance here. Can you help?"

A curious look passed over her face. An almost triumphant gleam to her eyes. She smoothed her hair behind her ears and focused her attention on Maddy. "So, Madison, are you starting kindergarten?"

Maddy nodded.

"Well, that's perfect. I teach kindergarten," Stephanie said. "Would you like to be in my class?"

Yes, please. Relief washed over him. If Maddy ended up in Stephanie's class, she'd be safe and looked after. He wouldn't worry.

Maddy faced him, her mouth gaping.

"It's okay, squirrel." He rubbed a hand over her back and glanced at Stephanie.

Stephanie mouthed the word *squirrel?*

He shrugged. When his sister showed him the ultrasound, he couldn't make sense of it. The blob in the center had looked more like a tree rat than a baby. "You can talk to her. She's nice."

Stephanie smiled. The expression came from deeper than the lift of her lips. Her eyes sparkled and her whole body seemed to radiate with happiness. From a single, obvious, statement? Was his opinion important to her?

He couldn't let it be. For both their sakes. He was glad she warmed up enough to talk to him. If she returned for another summer on the ranch, she wouldn't be so on edge again. She was a sweet person and so light and full of life. Her bubbly persona was a genuine gift.

Maybe being on her turf, she felt confident enough to take the lead. While he wanted a change in their interactions, from silence to friendship, he complicated that by needing her help. This time, the power balance shifted toward her.

"Yes, please call me, Maddy. I would like to be in your class." Maddy exhaled a heavy sigh. "Did I miss a lot today? Will I be behind? Did everyone make best friends? Is anyone else new?"

Stephanie grinned. "You did not miss anything, and I don't think you'll find it difficult to make a best friend. We have a nice class. It's big. With you, we'll have twenty-five kids."

"Is that too many?" He shifted forward on the hard, molded plastic seat. "Can you teach that many kids?" He hated to impose on her. He couldn't imagine watching two five-year-olds let alone twenty-five. Would Maddy be shifted into another class? She warmed up quickly and had a knack for making friends. If something went wrong, though, he wanted to know. Stephanie would keep him informed.

"I'll be fine. Why don't you head to the office and start the paperwork?" she asked.

He reached inside his coat pocket, pulling a folded stack of papers. "My sister, Maddy's mom, already started filling out the forms. I need to drop them off. But I think I have more to do? Something about proving residency? Do you know if everything is online or if I'll have more to fill out or . . ." He was rambling.

Stephanie smiled. "Wendy, in the front office, can help with every question."

Stephanie was such a calm presence. He found her comforting. Maybe he hadn't messed up too much. Letting down Maddy was far worse than the lecture he'd get from Jen when she learned what happened. "Thank you. I'll do that."

Stephanie nodded. "Maddy, do you have any questions I can answer?"

"Yes." Maddy slipped her hand out of his and crossed her arms over her chest. "Trick or treating. How does it work here? In California, we have sidewalks and live close to each other and go door to door. Unc lives in the middle of nowhere here. I didn't see any sidewalks when we drove to school from the ranch. It's all country." She sighed.

He covered his mouth with a fist. Her put-upon-tone always tickled his funny bone. Maddy was serious from birth, an old soul trapped in a child's body.

Stephanie nodded. "At school, we hold a costume parade for parents and uncles to attend. Then we have a party in the afternoon. Instead of trick or treating from one house to another, the town holds a big trunk or treat. It's a lot of fun. Cars and trucks get decorated and park up and down Main Street. You go from car to car. Don't worry, you'll get plenty of candy." Stephanie winked.

He hadn't ever attended the Halloween event. By October, the weather was cold and night fell early. He usually completed his evening routine with the horses and, with the exception of poker night, was back in his home reading over his supper by six.

Now he was looking forward to attending the special holiday celebration. He'd loved Halloween as a kid. Children were a gift, forcing the grown-ups in their lives to snap out of their doldrums and look at the world with wonder. Did Stephanie experience that on a daily basis thanks to her job? Or was she just sort of magic on her own?

With hands pressed flat against his thighs, he forced himself out of the too small chair with a groan. His knees cracked. He was relieved he hadn't been trapped in the seat. Although, he wouldn't mind a few more minutes in Stephanie's classroom. The space was comforting and cozy, as warm as the teacher.

She shot him an expectant look.

He cleared his throat.

Stephanie flashed him a thumbs up. "Can I show you around my classroom, Maddy?"

"Yes, please. Does everyone get a cubby?" Maddy asked, her voice chipper.

He strolled to the door and glanced over his shoulder.

Stephanie and Maddy spoke with animation, totally focused on their conversation and not him.

He preferred the status quo. If any change was going to happen, though, this one was welcome. Having his family near would be worth the momentary upheaval. But that was it. Pretty young teachers who'd never known heartache—and good for them, he'd begrudge no one a lovely life without hindrance—were best left to their own devices.

CHAPTER 4

Stephanie held open the door to the multi-purpose room with her back. The second day of school passed in a blur. She liked to leave her students with a sunny smile and a positive affirmation. She wanted everyone to feel good about their school day.

Teaching kindergarten, she learned staying calm was paramount to success. Getting overly worked up about anything aggravated both good and bad situations. With a gentle reminder tomorrow held no mistakes, she could encourage those students who had a difficult time in class.

As usual, Amelia and her oversized, satin bow led the line.

Stephanie bit the inside of her cheek. The child was well-behaved. She spoke and acted with a sugar sweetness that set Stephanie's teeth on edge. No one could be so cute all the time. How did the little girl act when Stephanie wasn't watching?

Tomorrow, she'd institute classroom jobs and give everyone a fair turn at leading the group. She waved and winked at each student as they passed her into the room for end of day pick-up. At the back of the line, Madison strolled forward with confident swagger.

Stephanie was glad. The other students welcomed her instantly. The room was tear free for most of the day. The school year was off to a banner start.

"Bye, Miss Patricks. I can't wait to see you tomorrow." Maddy squeaked.

"Same, Maddy. Have a good night." Stephanie stayed in place until her classroom reached their marked spaces on the wooden floor and sat. Then she stepped away from the door and strode back down the hall. Inside her classroom, she shut the door and exhaled a heavy sigh.

The first week was always an adjustment. She forgot how much energy she had to summon and utilize for each day. Being present required a lot of focus.

Rolling her neck and shoulders, she started her work of preparing for the next day. She cleared the dry erase board, wrote out the next day's in-class announcements, and picked up stray items for their lost and found. Back at her desk, she organized the thick stack of photocopied worksheets she'd requested which would carry her class through the end of the month, and checked her to-do list.

She opened her laptop and pulled up her inbox to check on any messages she had missed. During quiet time after lunch, she usually caught up on her emails from parents. A few trickled in later in the day. Sure enough, she had a message from Candace Vane.

Curious, she clicked on it and scanned the text, sucking in a sharp breath. Candace had issue with the reduced volunteer opportunity, and her daughter didn't like sharing classroom supplies. Stephanie reread the missive but wasn't exactly sure the point of the email. A warning? A threat? General observations?

No request was made. Stephanie wasn't sure a response would be the best course of action. Both complaints were part of Stephanie's strategy to create a safe space for all. Candace was financially blessed, or so she gave that impression to everyone in town. Stephanie balked at the idea of flaunting status in general but especially in front of five-year-olds.

With her fingers hovering over the keyboard, she tried to think of the best way to handle the situation.

A knock shook the door.

"Come in," she called.

The school secretary, Wendy, opened the door and entered. "Good afternoon, Miss Patricks. Sorry to disturb you. I'm here with one of your students."

A hiccupping cry bounced off the walls.

Stephanie stood, rushing out from behind the desk and pulling the pack of tissues out of her skirt pocket. "Of course, of course."

The child was hidden behind Wendy's legs. The pair stopped near the first table.

Stephanie knelt on the ground and glanced at Wendy.

New girl. Wendy mouthed.

Stephanie widened her eyes. "Maddy? Sweetie? Can you tell me what's wrong?"

The little girl peeked around Wendy's knees. Her face was swollen and red. "Unc isn't here."

Stephanie shot her gaze to the clock on the wall. Almost an hour had passed since the end of school. In a silent room, she often lost track of time. She hadn't realized how late the day had gotten.

"I can't get ahold of him," Wendy said.

"No problem." Stephanie stood, dusting her hands on her skirt. "Maddy, I can call him, and we can read and color while we wait for him, okay?"

Maddy let go of Wendy and lunged for Stephanie's outstretched hand, the backpack dangling off her back and threatening her balance.

Stephanie hadn't asked any questions yesterday. She should have. Where were the little girl's parents? Why was she suddenly living with Ted? Stephanie stroked the child's back. Maddy had such a great first day. Bile rose in Stephanie's throat, and she struggled to swallow it. She hated this ending.

Wendy offered a grateful, sad smile and strode out the door.

Stephanie led Maddy to the carpet and pulled a bin from the shelf under the window, full of coloring pages and crayons. "Let me call him," she said softly and handed a tissue.

The child blew her nose and extended the used tissue.

With years of training, Stephanie didn't flinch as the snotty square was dropped into her open palm. The little girl stopped crying. That was the most important thing at the moment.

Maddy raised her gaze, nodded, and sat on the carpet, rifling through the bin with determination.

Stephanie crossed the room, dropping the tissue into the waste basket, washing her hands in the room's sink, and returned to her desk. In the bottom drawer, she retrieved her purse and found her cell phone. She dialed Ted's number. He'd given it to her over the summer in case she needed anything while working on the ranch.

The phone rang and rang, never clicking over to a voicemail box. Then the line died. She dialed it again.

She'd never called. What was the point if she couldn't speak? When the situation involved one of her kids, she trusted she'd find her voice. She would always have her students' best interests at heart.

The line rang and rang. Then nothing.

Dialing again, she couldn't imagine where he was or why he didn't set up a way to receive voice messages. *Pick up pick up pick up.* From the corner of her gaze, she studied the little girl coloring with gusto. Stephanie was glad Maddy didn't react.

As she held the phone to her ear for the fourth redial, she flushed with frustration. Wherever he was, and whatever held him up, he had a responsibility to his niece that took precedence. She had a clear—if atypical—solution. He'd asked if he could list her as an emergency contact. She'd agreed, not imagining she'd ever be required to step up and drive her student anywhere.

"Maddy, I have a booster in my car. I can drive you to Unc's house and talk to him about pick-up. Is that okay?"

Maddy got to her feet with a huge smile. "Yes, please."

Stephanie smiled. Was this a gray area? Would Bill frown at her for taking charge in this way? She'd take care of the child first. Grabbing her purse, she waited as the child put the bin away a bit haphazardly.

Stepping out into the hallway, she darted her gaze from one end to the other. Most of the other teachers had left for the night. The off-pitch tones of fourth grade band filled the space. She held her hand out to Maddy and led the child out the doors to the teacher parking lot.

She settled the child into the backseat of the car, hopped behind the wheel, and turned over the engine. Her pop music playlist launched as she steered out of the lot and onto the main road. When the song approached a questionable lyric, Stephanie turned off the stereo and glanced in the rearview mirror.

Maddy faced the window, her swollen cheeks still puffy but her eyes less red.

Stephanie focused on the road. She had a lot of driving to do tonight, and if it was all in silence, she'd never last. Exhaustion overtook her in the quiet moments. "Do you have favorite songs to listen to in the car?"

"Mommy and I like musicals."

"Really?" Stephanie glanced in the mirror again, catching the child's emphatic nod. She would have figured Maddy would say the soundtrack to an animated movie or the kid-friendly versions of current songs. She kept both on her school-approved playlist. "Any musical in particular?"

"My favorite is the Christmas one because . . ."

Stephanie smiled. "Because it's Christmas? No explanation needed. I don't think I know which one you're talking about."

"The one with the sisters. Mommy and Unc sing that song."

"They do?"

"Unc always has to tell Mommy which way to turn."

In the rearview mirror, Stephanie met the little girl's gaze. "What do you mean *turn*?"

"Mommy and Unc have a routine. Just like the movie. He's a great dancer."

He dances?! Oh, she had to see that. Stephanie's icy ire thawed as her imagination took control. But something else came into clearer focus.

Maybe her ability to speak to him was the clearest indication she was over her ill-fated crush. She felt a connection with him but maybe her lonely heart planted a false idea. When she did meet the right guy, she wanted to be a priority. For the first time in her life, she would be someone's number one.

Shaking the can of white spray paint, Ted bent and marked an x on the ground. With a hand to his aching lower back, he groaned. His day had skidded downhill like a truck left in neutral. The last guests had checked out yesterday. The seasonal staff had departed by midday. And he was caught somewhere in the middle.

Today, he had started the work of figuring out how much he had to do while the weather cooperated. Surveying every building for needed repairs, he'd been called to the barn to oversee the start of the deck. But the crew had never arrived. And at some point, the markings of the deck had been washed away, so he had rolled up his sleeves and taken care of business.

Most days, he didn't feel like he was forty-three and middle aged. After a day spent on repetitive physical tasks, ending his chores by bending over and marking the ground for the proposed deck behind the red barn with several cans of spray paint, he reconsidered. His muscles ached and tweaked. When he talked to Stephanie, he didn't feel any younger.

She'd been so delightfully deadpan when she had called his favorite movie out of touch. He smiled despite himself. Rolling back his shoulders, he straightened, shrugging off annoyance. At least he finished this task.

He was never afraid of getting his hands dirty. Physical labor had kept him sane when he lost his wife. No one expected to be a widower. Let alone at the age of thirty. Their organic farm had only started turning a profit when Liv was killed in a car accident.

Grounded with a job that demanded the use of his muscles more than his brain, he worked each day methodically as he checked items off his to-do list one at a time. Life on the ranch was easy—if not especially meaningful. That was okay. He wasn't the boss worrying about employees. He did his tasks and didn't get caught up in anything that could add deep commentary on his life choices. For that, he had his family.

The start of the morning was surprisingly smooth. Maddy was an old soul. She made thoughtful—often hilarious—observations and connections on the world around her. Dressing herself with care, she had helped him pack up her bag for her first day of school. When he had dropped her off, he had lingered in case she needed another hug. But she had never turned around. She had strolled into the school like she owned it. He couldn't wait to hear how her day went.

Icy dread gripped him tight. His palms went clammy, his forehead beaded with a cold sweat, and he frowned at the low tilt of the sun. *What time was it? Oh no, I forgot Maddy.*

Spinning on his heel, he ran to his truck, parked in front of the barn.

Tires crunched gravel.

He lifted his gaze.

Stephanie's little red coupe neared.

What was she doing here? He had to go get his niece. He opened the door to his truck and found his cell in the cupholder. The screen was full of missed calls from her.

"Hey, I've got her," Stephanie shouted, her voice carrying out an open window.

Ted slammed the truck door shut and approached the slowing car. With a hand shielding his gaze, he spotted Maddy on a booster seat in the back. *How could I have forgotten to pick her up? How could I have let her down?*

The red car stopped.

He reached for the rear door handle, waited for the click of the lock, and then opened it.

"Hi, Unc," Maddy said, her face looking a little red and her cheeks chapped, but otherwise okay.

He could have cried. His knees buckled, and he locked them to hold his position. "Hi, squirrel. I'm so sor—"

"BZZT," Stephanie said.

Huh? He met her gaze in the rearview mirror.

She shook her head and mouthed *no.*

He wasn't supposed to apologize? He'd let down his niece. What was expected of him if he wasn't allowed to grovel? He turned back and unbuckled the seatbelt.

Moving out of the way, he stood next to the car and waited for either female to direct him on what came next.

"Can you hold my backpack?" Maddy flung it at him. "I'm gonna run up and tell Mr. Hank about my day. He asked me to." She yelled over her shoulder, racing across the lawn toward the back of the ranch house.

She didn't want to yell or cry? She didn't want a hug? He held the pink and purple bag and watched her climbed the porch and let herself in the back door.

He exhaled a huge shuddering breath, rolling his shoulders forward and hunching. "Thank you for bringing her home. I can't believe I forgot."

He wanted to shrink to the size of an ant so someone could squish him under their boot. Abandoning Maddy on her very first day of school ever? Jen expected more. Maddy deserved better. What if he didn't have a friend who cared enough to bring the little girl home? He met Stephanie's gaze. "I owe you."

"It happens."

Her voice was oddly flat.

He slipped the backpack onto a shoulder and turned, facing her. Had he disappointed her, too? Was he less than in her eyes now? He didn't want that. "I am truly, truly sorry."

"I know you are." She softened her face, just a little, glancing at the ground. "Sorry I cut you off mid-apology. I didn't want you to get her worked up again. She was in tears at school. I calmed her down on the car ride."

He appreciated she was the expert here, and he'd have to follow her lead. But he didn't like her darting gaze or crossed arms. She was standoffish. While she'd only recently begun to speak to him, she was a sunny, open-book. Not today.

"I promised my sister. I really hope I didn't scar Maddy."

"We've all been left by a parent or caregiver." Stephanie lifted a shoulder. "It's almost a rite of passage."

Was it a painful experience for you? Her hesitation hinted at something he couldn't decipher. He was intrigued.

"Where are her parents?" Stephanie asked, frowning. "I'm sorry to put you on the spot. But what is going on?"

"My sister and her husband divorced when Maddy was a baby. They've been good co-parents since the beginning. She doesn't know any different." *Thankfully.* Jen and her ex fought from day one. A mismatch from the start, Ted wanted to warn her that if the easy time was complicated the relationship was doomed.

But he hadn't offered an opinion. Knowing his stubborn sister, she would have ignored him. Or, worse, she pushed him away. She needed him and vice versa. So, he kept his mouth shut. "Maddy's dad is moving overseas for a job. My sister is starting at the hospital soon but needed to finish up her job and sell her house. She came on Labor Day so Maddy could start school."

"A little abrupt. She didn't give Maddy a chance to settle in."

He held up his hands. "Maddy is so good at being flexible with plans. My sister takes that for granted. I know I do."

Stephanie nodded.

He waited for her to ask more. She had every right. He'd put her in a tough spot.

"How long is your sister gone?"

"She'll be back for a visit in ten days. She'll be up here for good the week after." He held his breath.

Stephanie wrinkled her brow in the cute way he understood meant she was working through an issue. He hoped it didn't involve calling the authorities about his negligence.

She tipped her head to the side. "Do you want help with the afternoon pick up? I can drop her off after-school if that makes life easier."

Oh, it does. He dropped his shoulders and exhaled a heavy sigh. "That would be wonderful. I'm great at getting up early. Once I'm on the ranch, I lose track of time."

She nodded. "I did, too."

"I truly am so sorry this happened today. You can't choose the memories children make." He scrubbed the corners of his eyes, wishing he was stuck in a bad dream. "I love that little girl so much, and I don't want her holding onto the time Unc let her down. I never want her sad."

"I appreciate that sentiment, but you can't beat yourself up over every mistake. Isn't it better she sees you accept responsibility, apologize, and move on? Give tomorrow your best shot. You can't and shouldn't give a child some perfect, no problems worldview. That's just not real life."

"What is?"

She lifted the corner of her mouth in a half smile. "Trying."

Could it be that easy? With parents in another state, Maddy depended on him. Intellectually, he'd grasped the concept. Until he was left in charge as the sole adult, he hadn't tested the weight of the role. Now he carried every ounce.

"You should take her home, explain what happened, and let her move on. Read a book. Make a good memory. She had a great first day at school."

"Thanks, I'll do that."

With a nod, Stephanie strode back to her car. As she moved, a hint of citrus wafted past his nose. The smell was sweet like candied orange slices.

"Wait," he called.

She paused, glancing over her shoulder.

"Can you stay for dinner?" He shouted, his voice cracking. He hadn't intended to ask. But now he wanted her to stay and prove that he was a capable guardian. "You've driven over here. It's getting late. I owe you."

"I don't know." She tapped a finger against her chin.

"Did you already eat?" he asked.

She frowned.

His foolish question hung in the air. "It's just... I thought I smelled candy. Like oranges?"

"Oh, that's my shampoo." Her stomach growled. "Now that you mention food, I am hungry." She covered her stomach with her arms, muffling further sounds. "Should I trust you with cooking? It involves some time management skills that might be out of your wheelhouse?"

He chuckled. He liked her teasing. "I'm great at dinner because I start in the morning. It's my go-to slow cooker alfredo. Maddy's favorite, and she has quite the discerning palate."

"Okay, sounds good." She tucked a loose strand of blonde hair into her ponytail. Her cheeks pinked.

Great, with a few exceptions, they were back to normal. She spoke now, which simplified and challenged their interactions.

But he could handle the change. He was interested in friendship and Maddy's well-being. If the twin goals could be combined, he'd come out on top.

Chapter 5

Sitting on the opposite bank of the pond, the snug log cabin stood apart from the guest cabins. With a stone chimney on one side and a low-pitched roof over the porch, mirroring the entrance of the larger ranch house, the charming, one-story building blended perfectly with its surroundings. The setting couldn't be more picturesque if it had been created by an artist.

Stephanie slowed her car as she neared the front of the house. Maddy rode with her uncle, giving Stephanie a break from Maddie's chatter. Her mind took full advantage of the quiet to daydream.

She pictured sitting outside in a rocking chair at night in the summer, catching fireflies. On a crisp autumn morning, she'd cuddle under a blanket, sipping a hot cup of coffee. In winter, she'd bet the smoke curled from the chimney in wisps while the home nestled in a snowbank, demanding its occupants slow down and enjoy the indoors for a spell.

Every scenario included Ted. It was too easy to imagine. She'd always been glad for her boundless depths of creativity, but now she hated it. Her one-sided crush was doomed to remain unrequited. First, he'd been her boss. Now, she was his niece's teacher. Each association raised ethical concerns.

But if they were a couple? Her skin flushed thinking about the warmth of his smile. Her toes curled, remembering the tenderness and vulnerability when he realized he forgot his niece.

Parking next to his truck, she pocketed her keys and grabbed her purse off the shotgun seat. Out of the car, she strode up a flagstone path toward the front door. Could she regain her righteous indignation and find her confidence—and voice—again?

He'd been so earnest and so genuinely upset when confronted about his mistake. She'd lost her balance. But she hadn't wanted to slip into the old patterns. She wanted to move forward. The night of the cowboy dinner sparked a change. Teasing him about his pop culture taste had been natural.

If Maddy hadn't shown up, would the encounter have been a one-off? Stephanie would have returned to teaching full-time with no excuse to stop by the ranch. Would she have spoken again if they bumped into each other in town? Or would the moment simply have been a shared memory that floated past with no significance?

Lifting her fist, she knocked on the door.

The knob spun.

She took a step back.

Pulling the door open with a smile, Ted waved her to cross the threshold. "Please, come inside."

Cautiously, like a sudden movement would snap her out of the moment and back to reality, she entered the home, stepping into a small entryway onto a handwoven rug. The rectangle was—at first glance—red. With closer inspection, however, she noticed the variety of shades of rust, burnt orange, and salmon, coming together. It was the sort of piece someone might pick up at an artist's fair. Did he buy it? Was it a gift?

She lifted her gaze, studying his profile as he shut the door. She really didn't know him. For as much as she knew that his gray green eyes never crinkled when he smiled, she had no clue about his personal life. He kept himself removed.

Maddy, at least, wouldn't let him remain aloof. When she returned, his sister would humanize him, too. Nothing like family to suddenly force a person to stop faking and start being real. Would Stephanie be close enough as a friend to witness the change?

"I hope you don't mind waiting for a few minutes." He gestured to a room on the left. "Maddy wants to set the table."

"Of course, not." She turned toward the open doorway leading to a sitting room.

A large window overlooked the front yard. The stone fireplace took up most of one wall, the mantle extending over low, built-in bookcases on either side. A pair of leather armchairs with ottomans sat before the fire. A worn quilt was thrown over the back of one. Again, a surprising touch of softness and care. Was that why he smelled like leather? Did he fall asleep in the chair?

Heat crept up her neck, and her ears burned.

Opposite the window wall, a smaller doorway opened to the eat-in kitchen. No TV? How did he watch his beloved teen movies? She faced him, readying her question.

"I'll go and check on her. She loves to decorate and could take the whole night if not otherwise managed." He wiggled his eyebrows. "What would you like to drink with dinner?"

"Water, please."

He nodded and walked into the kitchen, through the other doorway.

Interlacing her fingers, she strolled toward the bookshelves, curiosity lifting her onto her toes. Above the bookshelf nearest the window, she spotted a certificate mixed in with candid photos. A college degree? She was both surprised and unshocked. Any time her role as a teacher came up, he spoke with a deference about education. What did a cowboy study in undergrad?

She narrowed her gaze and studied the words Animal Sciences.

Sparing the degree only another momentary glance, she turned toward the other frames. She recognized Maddy and assumed the pretty woman, who looked like Ted in a wig, was his sister. Leaning closer, she didn't spot any other mystery woman in any of the pictures. Childhood photos were mixed with a few recent shots, most including Maddy. If she had to guess, she'd wager the sister provided all the images.

She exhaled a heavy sigh. She was glad she hadn't spotted any romantic shots of him and another woman. Just because Stephanie's love life was non-existent didn't mean anyone else's was. He had fourteen years on her. He had ample time for a meaningful romantic entanglement. She couldn't get jealous about his past, and she should know better than to snoop.

She studied the top shelf. Near the window, she bent and read the spines of the books in the dim ambient light from a wall sconce. With each title, she widened her eyes a little more. *Young Adult fantasy novels?*

"She's almost ready."

Stephanie straightened, stiffening, and tweaking her lower back. She sucked in a sharp breath.

"Sorry, didn't mean to startle you."

"I'm fine." She forced a smile and gestured toward the shelf. "I'm a little surprised by your book collection. Did you get these for Maddy? They are advanced for her reading level."

He folded his arms over his chest. "No, those books are for me. I love them."

"You do?"

"Is that wrong?" He lifted a brow.

His expression was quizzical. She hoped her tone wasn't judgmental. She loved to read and hated when she was condemned for enjoying romance novels. Still, she was surprised by his choice. She cleared her throat. "I've never met a cowboy who loves dragons."

"Maybe I'm not really a cowboy."

She widened her gaze. He wasn't? Who was he? She nibbled her bottom lip. Or was he flirting with his cheeky comments? Her cheeks heated.

"I wanted to let you know. I apologized to her and told her the new plan." He took a few steps closer and stopped a foot away. He dropped his hands to his sides. "Thank you. You're really helping me out here. How much do I owe you for gas?"

"Oh, that's not necessary." She waved a hand. Standing near, she had the perfect opportunity for an up-close perusal. She didn't need to look to know concern would be etched in a deep furrow across his brow. She shook her head. Once she made it through the first month of school, after the poker tournament, she'd start a profile on an online dating app and get over her crush.

"Will you get in trouble for driving a student home?"

"It's a temporary solution. It'll be fine." She hoped it would be, but she wasn't exactly sure. She wasn't breaking any hard and fast rule. She'd have to remember to tell Bill to stay ahead of any gossip. "I'm glad you two talked. She's a great kid."

"That's all her mom."

"Not her dad, too?"

A shadow passed over his face. Earlier, he had spoken so highly of how his sister and her ex co-parented. What wasn't he saying? Something lingered there, but it wasn't her place to push her way into family dynamics.

"Dinner is served," Maddy's high-pitched voice called. With an apron wrapped around her waist and a paper towel draped over her arm, she appeared in the doorway.

He leaned close. "She's playing restaurant. She's the maître d', and server, and chef."

Did that mean they were on a pretend date? *Might be the closest I ever get to the real thing.* Her cheeks burned, and, with her luck, he'd spot her heightened color.

Taking in a deep breath to calm her nerves, she breathed in his mint and leather smell. Instead of peace, her pulse jumped. She'd always thought the smell was from handling saddles and reins. Now that she knew how he lived, she'd picture him here, in his chair near the fire, reading aloud with his deep voice.

Why not torture herself a little bit more with a pretend date now? She swallowed. "We'd better go. I've heard this place doesn't take reservations."

"Yes, it's exclusive." He winked.

Standing behind Stephanie, Ted pressed together his lips, holding in his chuckle. He was glad to use the woman as a shield.

Maddy expected to be taken seriously, always. Even when she was being exceptionally cute like right now, pretending to run a restaurant. He knew better than to laugh, however sorely tempted he was to start chortling.

"Table for two?" Maddy asked, stopping by the only table in the whole house.

He loved booth seating. When the opportunity presented itself, and he only had himself to please, he purchased a pair of high-backed, oak banquettes and slid a table in the center. He always felt cozy and warm, and could imagine he smelled garlic and oregano like he was at a pizzeria.

Stephanie turned him, widening her eyes as she glanced over her shoulder.

"Three," he said. He wasn't quite sure how to interpret the teacher's look. Surprise? In a good or bad way? The whole week had been one unexpected moment after another. He wouldn't take offense at something else going off script.

"Of course." Maddy nodded and pointed to one side of the table. "Please be seated."

Stephanie slid into the appointed spot.

Maddy turned toward him. "Excuse you."

Again, he swallowed the laugh. Eight times out of ten, she mastered the cliched sayings she heard from adults and TV. Those two instances she got it wrong, however, tickled his funny bone every time.

Maddy slid into the booth, pressing against the wall.

He joined her, taking the outside seat. His knee brushed Stephanie's.

She blushed and tucked a strand of hair behind her ear.

He sat straighter. "Please, dig in."

Maddy wasted no time. She spun her fork in the pasta and slurped.

He smiled at Stephanie, but she focused on her meal, neatly twirling the noodles onto her fork. The sauce covered pasta fell off the tines.

She glanced up. "Do you have a spoon?"

He nodded, slid out from the booth, and crossed the kitchen. He pulled open the utensil drawer, and at the loud sound of Maddy's chewing, grabbed the extra napkins off the top of the counter. He handed the spoon to Stephanie and a napkin to Maddy.

The little girl blotted her face. "Thanks, Unc." Her words were muffled with a full mouth.

He frowned and sat, scooting next to his niece. He'd have to work on her manners if they had more company. Did he want that? From under his lashes, he studied Stephanie across the table. Using the bowl of the spoon, she created a perfect pasta swirl on her fork and raised the bite to her mouth.

He held his breath. He hoped she'd like it. When he threw together dinner in the slow cooker that morning, he hadn't thought he'd have to please anyone besides himself and his niece. But it was nice to share a meal with someone else. He'd grown used to keeping his own company and ate mostly by himself. The Kincaids invited him to supper at the ranch house about once a week. He enjoyed the often-teasing chatter but didn't mind returning home to eat in silence the next day.

Would she get in trouble for staying? She assured him she wouldn't, and he had to take her at her word. It was nice to have support. With his niece, he was so out of his depth for full-time care. He'd babysat but never longer than a few hours. He didn't anticipate Maddy's needs. He had a lot to learn and was glad for the teacher across the table. Serving her a meal was a simple way to show his thanks for her help today and what he was beginning to realize would be almost every day while his sister was gone.

Stephanie reached for her napkin, dabbing her mouth. "This is really good. Can you send me the recipe?"

"Sure, of course. It's really easy. I'm not much of a cook. But I have a couple recipes I like."

"Isn't that better? My grandmother always said *jack of all trades, master of none.*" She took another bite.

He considered her words as he started eating. She had a shyness to her but the more they talked, the more he felt he knew her. And the more he knew he couldn't overstep. Stephanie was so positive, resilient, and caring. He couldn't remember ever being bright and shiny with no predestination.

Marrying his high school sweetheart after college graduation meant he'd been checking off one to-do after another. He loved Liv. She'd been his past, present, and future. For fifteen years, he didn't have to explain himself. He lucked into meeting the person who knew him best before he could even drive a car. And then, all he had to do, was go along with her plans.

Losing her was devastating. Thirteen years later and he still wasn't sure he'd ever find who he was again. His interactions with Stephanie were nice and a pleasant diversion. But their situation was temporary. He could be appreciative and fully aware of the limits of the arrangement.

"I can't wait to bring Shakes home," Maddy said.

With a start, he frowned. He'd been in his own zone, mindlessly eating and unaware the other two were conducting a conversation. He looked down at his empty plate. If something named Shakes was coming into his sanctuary, he needed to get involved. He reached for his water and cleared his last bite. "What is Shakes?"

"Not what. Who," Stephanie said behind a napkin.

"Our class pet," Maddy said. "Everyone gets a turn to take care of him for a weekend. And then you add to his scrapbook. And I can't wait to show him the ranch."

Class pet? He shuddered. Oh, those poor creatures. Shouldn't one of the animal rescue organizations have put a bill forward banning class pets from schools across the country? He remembered a series of terrified, anxious hamsters sitting in glass aquariums near the teacher's desk and a window. A few had been lost during their weekend stays with his classmates.

"Shakes is a stuffed animal," Stephanie said. "He's a Golden Retriever, to be more precise."

He dropped his shoulders.

She arched an eyebrow. "You don't like animals?"

He shook his head. "I love animals. That's the problem. Didn't you see my degree?"

She nodded. "I did. What is Animal Sciences?" She propped her elbows on the table, resting her chin in one palm. "Is it Veterinary Medicine?"

"It can be a pre-vet course. It can also focus on the science and technology of enhancing animal products with well-being. My focus was on more general agriculture."

"Why did you pursue it?"

My wife. "I grew up in farming country. As a kid, everyone focused on adapting to the newest technology and efficiency. I was more interested in old techniques. Organic was starting to become a buzz word when I was in high school. In college, I started to pursue the idea of everything in relation to one another. I studied animals to understand the interconnectivity of life and the land."

"Wow." She leaned forward. "You were a farmer?"

"For a time."

"How did you end up ranching in Montana?"

My wife died. Again, he left the biggest reason unsaid. He missed Liv every day. He didn't hurt when he thought about her or talked about her. But having to drudge up all the emotion again to explain himself was draining. Although, he had the oddest sensation that if he ever wanted to talk to anyone and be understood not pitied, Stephanie would be the person. "Farming was tough on my own. I sold the farm and started wandering. I wanted to focus on animals and my little portion of the job instead of constantly being responsible for a big picture. I was in Montana, passing through and met Hank. He offered me a job."

She crossed her arms over her chest, her mouth gaping.

"Is that not what you expected?" He didn't want to care, but he did. Her opinion mattered.

"I suppose it's as good a job interview story as any other. Weren't you scared to start a career with no experience?"

He shrugged. At that moment, when he had met Hank, he hadn't been scared of anything. In the aftermath of the worst days of his life, he had operated without fear. "I'm an avid reader and hard worker. Learning to cowboy was good for me and gave me direction." And, being so focused on studying for his job in the early days, he hadn't had time to think about anything else.

"Are you excited about the bison?"

He nodded. "I am. It's a chance to learn. I'm always grateful to take on something new." And he was. He'd been wandering around the country, considering an RV, when he'd decided to visit Montana for a while. He liked to be grounded and hadn't needed much convincing to transplant his uprooted self on the ranch.

Ryan and Hank were content with his resume and references, and Ted had proved himself adept in the role. Stephanie was the first person to prod. But her questions didn't feel intrusive, and he found himself answering.

She set her napkin on her plate. "Thank you for a delicious dinner."

Do you want seconds? He wanted to stall her. He wasn't eager for her to leave. But he didn't want to apply any sort of pressure to convince her to stay longer. "Of course, my pleasure."

Stephanie slid out of the booth seat and turned toward her plate.

He reached a hand to still hers.

She jumped at the touch.

He drew back his hand. "It's quite alright. We'll clean up. Let me walk you to the door." He stood and motioned for her to walk ahead. Following behind, he kept several feet distance between them. At the door, he strode in front of her, to hold it open. "Thank you again for your help."

She nodded. "It's no problem. Have a good night."

With her gaze downcast, she didn't look up at him. He watched her get into her car and waved as she turned over the engine and reversed out of the spot onto the gravel road. Shutting the door, he crossed back into the kitchen. "Okay, squirrel. You go take a shower while I clean up the kitchen. Maybe we can read after you talk to Mommy."

"Three chapters?" Maddy looked expectant.

"Hmm." He stroked his chin. "Maybe two. If you hurry."

The little girl raced out of the booth and down the hall.

He chuckled. He wasn't quite sure what to make of the day, but he knew he had hours left before he settled into bed. And for once, he was excited.

CHAPTER 6

On Thursday night, Stephanie was still puzzling over Wednesday's unexpected dinner date. Not date. Her cheeks flushed. Lifting her gaze, she scanned the saloon. She'd arrived too early for the dinner rush and was—blessedly—alone. With one day until the poker tournament, she'd stopped by to review plans.

She reached for her glass of ice water, her hands slipping against the condensing sides. Sipping the cool drink, she relaxed. Last night hadn't meant anything. And, in case anyone got the wrong idea, she had knocked on the principal's door first thing that morning and explained exactly what happened and what would be continuing. He'd raised no concerns. As she expected. Her crush on Ted remained unrequited and inconvenient. But she would push through.

Following another successful school day, she had dropped off Maddy at the cabin but remained in her car. When he had spoken to her over a pasta dinner, he had held himself in check. He answered more personal questions than she had ever thought to ask before the quiet moments in his home. A niggling doubt, that she wasn't hearing the full story of his past, bothered her. Instead of confronting him, she backed off. She didn't want to push too far and make him shut down.

James Rabbitt, saloon proprietor, approached her table. He'd grown a full beard, and was almost unrecognizable. Only the historical garters he insisted on wearing over his shirt sleeves, like the original owner of The Golden Crown, gave away his identity. "Thanks for the updated timetable for tomorrow night."

"My pleasure, truly."

He chuckled.

After several years working together, he knew to take her at her word. She loved a schedule and an organized event. Until Candace Vane stepped up, Stephanie had run the evening with James for support in the food and beverage logistics. Even with the other woman's involvement, much of the planning still fell to Stephanie. She wasn't upset about being left to tackle most of the work alone. She was never one for group projects.

"Can I get you anything besides water?"

"I'm meeting Meg. She'll be here soon. I'm sure she'll be hungry." Stephanie leaned forward studying James' red blond beard. He looked more like a Viking. Typically, he took great care at accuracy for the grooming habits of a nineteenth century man for the special, costumed evening. "Interesting choice."

"Oh, this isn't the final look." He stroked his beard, smoothing the whiskers. "I'm shaving tomorrow right before opening the doors to the ticketed event. I'll be sporting an Imperial."

She appreciated that he thought she was educated enough to know the term. But she wasn't Joe the social studies teacher and town-historian. She participated in one historic event a year.

"Mutton chops connected with a mustache." He gestured with his hands.

"Oh." She couldn't visualize the description. She liked a clean-shaven man. Like Ted. She ignored the heat in her cheeks. When she had the chance, she'd have to search for the facial hair style on the internet. "I'm sure Joe will approve."

"It's hard to beat the waxed mustache from last year. A crowd favorite. But I like to try something new." James smiled. "I'll grab a couple menus." He walked away from the table.

The door swung open, light filling the entrance. A cool breeze snaked into the room.

Stephanie dragged her attention toward the front. Meg strode in, swinging her brown hair over her shoulder and waving at James and the other occupants she recognized.

As the last of her founding family in town, Meg Hawke was the closest Herd came to royalty. Her relationship with Ryan Kincaid, member of the other prominent family, solidified her status as town darling. Until recently, however, she'd felt like she didn't belong. Meg had confided to Stephanie her struggles with her place in the community. Stephanie remained aghast that the confident, beautiful woman ever questioned herself.

"Sorry I'm late." Meg stopped at the table, her floral skirt catching on the breeze. "Hey, did I see you at the ranch today?" She sat opposite and scooted the chair closer to the table.

Stephanie fought a groan. So much for avoiding the topic of Ted. Better to address the situation head-on with the only person who guessed about the crush—or the only one to say so to Stephanie's face. "You did." She nodded. "I'm helping Ted and his niece."

"Oh, I heard about his niece. I haven't met her yet although Colby has." Meg smiled every time she mentioned her rescue dog, Colby. The one-time stray was a pampered pup now and could most often be found asleep on a well-padded surface. "Hank says she loves the little girl."

"I think it's hard not to like her," Stephanie said. "She's in my kindergarten class. I haven't met her mom though. Have you?"

Meg shrugged. "No. Ted is close to his family, but usually he goes to visit them. Although, according to Ted, his sister looks like him in a wig."

Stephanie chuckled. "I concur."

Meg arched an eyebrow. "I thought you hadn't met her?"

"No, I've seen her photo in Ted's cabin."

Meg lifted both brows clear into her hairline.

Stephanie covered her mouth with a hand. If she'd done that earlier, she wouldn't have blurted such a suggestive statement. She hadn't behaved inappropriately and wouldn't incriminate herself. Straightening, she dropped her hands flat to the table. "Nothing happened. I'm dropping Maddy off for Ted at his cabin. He is having trouble navigating the afternoon pick-up. Yesterday was sort of a surprise that it happened, and Ted was nice enough to invite me in for dinner as a thank you. It's strictly business." She turned and reached into her tote, grabbing her clipboard, and ignoring Meg.

Meg couldn't possibly read Stephanie's mind. Stephanie wouldn't allow it despite her friend's reputation for being a shrewd judge of character. Their friendship was in its early days. What began as a mutually beneficial exchange of skills and time at Frontier Days in June continued naturally over the summer.

By the time the poker tournament approached, Stephanie couldn't fathom asking for help from anyone else. Stephanie pulled the sheets off the clipboard, handing a stapled stack to Meg.

Meg accepted the stack of sheets without comment.

No matter what may or may not be happening in her personal life, Stephanie wouldn't lose sight of her focus. The poker tournament raised funds and eliminated the stigma for the families that relied on the help. She'd heard stories of some kids not eating lunch so they wouldn't be spotted getting their meal at a free or reduced price. If she didn't fight for the kids, advocating everyone should be treated equally, she worried no one would. She couldn't let anyone down.

"Corporate sponsorship?" Meg asked after checking the sheets.

Stephanie nodded. "Yes, Candace got the backing. Last year, her corporation supported the event with a very generous in-kind donation. She didn't want to ruffle anyone's feathers so she approached a friend."

"Must be nice to have high-powered friends."

"Better than enemies." Stephanie hoped her under the breath comment hadn't been intelligible. She hadn't received any further communication with Candace since the annoyed missive earlier in the week. If she was upset, she'd let Stephanie know. Still, something nagged.

"What's wrong?" Meg asked. "If it's about you know who, you don't have to worry. I won't tease you. Just consider me a sounding board."

"Thanks. No, this is about my class." Stephanie sighed. "I think I've annoyed a parent. But I know everything will be fine."

"Dare I ask what happened?"

"The long and short of it is the parent does not agree with my management style. The parent thinks they deserve more of a say in how I run my classroom."

"And does the parent have a valid argument?"

The question was asked without any inflection. Stephanie flinched all the same. She wouldn't write off one parent's frustrations as invalid or unimportant. Everyone had a say when it came to their child. She respected that each parent was trying their very best for their kids. She'd been blessed to only have loving, involved moms and dads in her classes so far. What would happen with the reverse? She shuddered. "Yes, but my side is valid, too." She had another note already sitting in the cubbies for the kids to put in their backpacks tomorrow afternoon. "I'm probably making something out of nothing and being defensive. The parent sent an email with a comment. If they want to discuss the situation, I know I'll get a phone call or a meeting request."

"You know you'll always have my support. And not just because I need your help, too."

"Thanks." Stephanie bent and grabbed an accordion file off the ground. The heavy file landed with a thud on the table. "Speaking of my help."

Meg widened her eyes and gulped. "Your event checklists?"

Stephanie nodded. "And a little bit more. I included some contracts, budgets, planning calendars, etc. I wanted you to get an overview of what goes into an event. Although I'm not sure all the information is transferrable to the ranch. Most of this came from my brother's event a few years ago. Weddings will have their own set of issues. I gather you'd have a list of preferred vendors for your guests to choose. You might be able to glean a bit of how far in advance you'd ideally need to book." She paused.

Meg reached for her water and sipped, drinking steadily until she emptied the glass. "This is a lot of information. I knew asking you was the best first step. You're an expert. I can only imagine what a good teacher you are for the kids. They're lucky to have you. If the parents can't appreciate your work, you should come to the ranch. We'd value you. Handsomely."

"Thanks." Stephanie smiled through her gritted teeth. Chasing a big payday wasn't her style. She hadn't needed it to be. With her college education fully funded by her family, she started her career debt-free and continued to live that way, saving whatever she could. "I just wish I could be a little bit more like your boyfriend. Ryan has strong beliefs and a unique vision. He's celebrated."

Meg frowned. "Well, I'm not sure your situations can be compared. I don't fully understand what you're dealing with but the scenarios are different."

"Because I'm not rich?"

"No, because you don't have the ultimate authority for your decisions. You answer to the parents. Whether everyone agrees on the methods or not, you and the parents are bound by a duty to the children. Ultimately, the parents carry the final choice. They are responsible."

Stephanie couldn't argue with that. Maybe she'd been focused on the wrong aspect of her battle. She'd remember every side of the argument going forward.

"I'm sure Ted won't raise any complaints." Meg shot her a knowing look. "If you're worried about getting on your crush's bad side..."

Stephanie's cheeks flushed again. "Am I that obvious?"

"Not anymore. Now that you sort of talk around him, you don't make it so clear how you feel."

Stephanie pressed cool fingers to her hot skin. In a small town, every action was observed and studied. Doing so wasn't necessarily a conscious choice on the part of the observer. Patterns became expectations. Any behavior out of the ordinary would be observed as a curiosity, not necessarily to stoke gossip. Her little conversation at the dinner continued to draw notice and get comments.

"I'm proud you've found your voice," Meg said.

"Well, maybe it's because I know nothing will happen." Because if Ted was going to make a move, he would have done so by now. Stephanie partially took her summer job to spend more time around him. But the plan backfired. Instead of forced proximity, she'd ended up complicating their roles by becoming his subordinate. And now she was his niece's teacher. Could the situation ever be simplified?

"Don't say that around Hank, he might take is as a challenge and set you two up."

Stephanie snorted. "If I thought that would work, I would have told Hank how I felt years ago. Matchmaking might be old fashioned, but it is effective."

"I don't think a set-up is a guarantee."

It worked with you. At the start of the summer, Hank pulled out all the stops to throw Meg and Ryan together. Within a month, the long-time frenemies were officially the town's favorite couple. Stephanie wouldn't mind a little of Hank's meddling magic.

"Are you sure you're not interested in Joe?" Meg asked.

"And mess with the set-up between him and Abby?" Stephanie lifted an eyebrow.

Meg chuckled. "Hank won't push with Ted. He might be the only person to get a pass."

Stephanie frowned and leaned forward. "Why?"

Meg lifted a shoulder. "He's a widower."

Stephanie hadn't known. The explanation answered so many questions. She understood why he was alone when he had such kind soul and warm heart. Losing someone must be the hardest tragedy to overcome. Pressing a hand to her chest, she rubbed her aching heart. The biggest question remained. Would he ever be ready to try again?

Inside the old red barn, Ted held a measuring tape to a wooden board and pulled it taut to the end. He lifted the end, letting the tape recoil slowly back into its case and grabbed the clipboard he'd left on the ground. With a pencil, he checked off the last of the boards.

It had been a good, too busy to think, sort of day, exactly the kind he'd come to the ranch for. Running from one task to the next didn't leave a person with any time to themselves. For good reason.

At the same time the lumber had been delivered for the deck build, another crew had poured the footings outside. The concrete mixer had needed extra care, navigating around the old building. Ted couldn't stand in one place and direct the guys where to stack the boards. Too bad the back wall hadn't been pushed out yet, or Ted could have directed everyone from one spot. Instead, he was in and out the entire day.

With men and machinery everywhere, he'd been in the center of the storm, directing the chaos. The mechanical whir of the saw, appropriately slicing each board and post to order on site, had mingled with the hum of the mixer to create a white noise symphony. Ted had signed the lumber receipt with the caveat he'd be checking each board. After setting the posts in the concrete, the crew had called it quits and left.

In silence, Ted filled his lungs and immediately his mind drifted, wondering what Stephanie was up to. He could barely take care of himself let alone watch out for his niece. He couldn't take on more people. He was better off alone.

But he hadn't been lonely until he realized what he'd been missing. That was the sting. A person could know something with the certainty of absolute zero and still find themselves struggling to reconcile the head and the heart.

Maddy had arrived on the ranch an hour earlier, in the midst of the day's work, and been happily ensconced in the ranch house with Hank and Colby. He probably needed to head up to fetch her and start thinking about dinner. Before Maddy came, he survived plenty of days on a piece of fruit and a cup of coffee until he headed into town for dinner. That wouldn't fly with taking care of a child, and he didn't need his sister thinking she couldn't count on him when it mattered.

He wanted Maddy and Jen nearby, just not as the sole responsible adult overseeing everything. At least he'd managed to look pulled together once, for Stephanie, when it mattered. Maybe she wouldn't totally think him an old fool.

The big barn doors slid open, the wheels squealing on the track. He'd add *oil hinges* to his list.

"Hello," a deep, gravelly voice called. "You still back there?"

Ted smiled, striding to the entrance. "Yes, sir, Mr. Kincaid."

Hank Kincaid, sunlight glinting off his white hair from the open doorway, surveyed the interior. "Huh. With all the tables stacked up and the chairs in storage, I'm having a hard time picturing what it'll look like. Do we need more tables? Less?"

"I think we'll be fine." Ted scanned the space, trying and failing to gaze with fresh eyes. He had no problem imagining the space.

During the tourist season, the barn came alive with evenings of dinner and dancing. Some of the local teachers formed a bluegrass band and were happy with the opportunity to perform regular gigs. Stephanie had sung with them a few times. Her voice was as sunny and bright as her personality. She had lit up on stage.

"Hey, you were supposed to get me," a deeper voice, slightly out of breath, added. Ryan Kincaid entered, his chest heaving as he pressed a hand to his side.

"Boy, I can't wait around all day," Hank said.

Ryan lifted his gaze to the ceiling.

Ted pressed his lips together. The eyes to the sky was all the eye rolling Ryan allowed himself in the presence of his grandfather. The eighty-nine-year-old man was spry, both mentally and physically. He did what he wanted, when he wanted, and what he didn't want was answering to the child he'd raised. Even if said child now stood over six feet, was closer to forty than four, and had single-handedly saved the family legacy with the idea to sell off the cattle and transform the ranch into a resort.

No, Hank still had his opinions. Ted cleared his throat and tucked the clipboard under his arm. "I was checking the boards again. Everything is correct. I'll be ready to start with the flashing and ledger board tomorrow, if Ryan has time to help."

"I'll see you tomorrow morning after the school drop-off, come get me," Ryan said.

"Great. Should we head outside and see the footings?" Ted asked.

"Lead the way," Ryan said.

Ted strode through the open door and around the building. He'd spent most of the summer planning the deck build. The project demanded precision in its execution both for the scope and timing, to not disturb the guests. As he rounded the last corner and the site came into view, he gasped.

No amount of x's on the ground or hastily drawn sketches could prepare him for the scale of the actual construction marked with concrete footers. The deck was to be built in such a way that, if needed, they could eventually extend the boards to wrap around the sides of the building. He'd fought against starting with that vision. It would ruin a visitor's first look at the historic barn. He wasn't a history buff like his buddy, Joe, but he did have an opinion on the ranch. He'd soaked the ground with his sweat and hoped he'd memorialize himself on this land. Somehow.

Hard to live forever if you don't have kids to remember you after you're gone.

He turned around to gauge his bosses' reactions.

Ryan stroked his jaw.

Hank nodded. "It's good. I trusted Meg. She has vision. But I'll admit I was worried. Seeing this now?" He rubbed together his palms. "Gives me ideas."

"Ideas?" Ted frowned.

"He's circling back to his matchmaking. He'll twist any comment into an infinity loop for his favorite topic," Ryan said.

Ted's heart hit the front of his chest. Hank couldn't be thinking about him, right? Ted wasn't looking. *And if I was, I found my own match.*

"Boy, now you've scared him." Hank shook his head. "Don't worry, Ted. I have big plans for my birthday celebration. I'm not plotting anything for you."

Ryan sniggered. "Your birthday celebration is the whole ruse. You've got to back off. Joe and Abby don't need this much time to plan. And, even if they did, they could tackle a lot on their own."

"That's not the point." Hank spit onto the ground.

Ted could find his voice for his friend. Joe didn't dislike Abby as much as he had expressed his frustrations and concerns about her. *She's hiding something, and I think it's big.* Joe had told

Ted at the last poker game. "Mr. Kincaid, sir. I have to caution you. Joe doesn't care for Abby. I don't think they could even be considered friends."

"There's a very shaky boundary between love and hate. Those two have something," Hank said.

Ryan shook his head.

"Maybe you should set him up with someone else?" Ted asked.

"I thought about Stephanie." Hank stroked his chin.

Ted caught his breath, the air burning his lungs. If Hank set up Joe and Stephanie, the pair would be happy. As a couple, they'd make a lot of sense with so much in common. Hank was one for one on his matchmaking skills. He'd probably score another win with those two.

"No spark there," Hank said. "And she's too young."

Slowly exhaling, Ted didn't find much relief. If Stephanie was deemed too young for Joe, what about Ted? He was two years older than his buddy. He shook his head. The conjecture didn't matter. While he never intended to be alone forever, that was his lot in life, and he wasn't going to change course now. How could anyone else claim his heart? Even a good person with a sweet, soft smile could break him.

Focusing on status quo was his path to a contented life. He loved and cared about his family and was happy to have them unexpectedly close. Despite his love of a friendly game of poker, he wasn't a gambler. When he had married his high school sweetheart, he had lucked into a once in a lifetime love. No guarantee he could find that again. Marriage didn't come with a warranty. If he had a kid, he still didn't have any assurances. He could end up divorced like his sister. Was that fair to a kid?

"Ted?" Ryan asked.

Ted lifted his gaze. He hadn't realized the conversation continued without him. But he was glad for it. "Sorry, thinking about the next steps on this project. Did you need to discuss your birthday?"

Hank grinned. "That's why you're the best cowboy we've ever had. You're always looking ahead and spotting problems. I don't think we'd be able to reintroduce animals to the land without you here."

"It's quitting time," Ryan said. "Your little lady is getting hungry. We came down to fetch you for supper. Will you join us tonight?"

Ted nodded. These men stepped up for him at a time he'd been so lost. And again, their kindness and caring extended to him like he was their kin, too. They invited Maddy into their lives without a second thought. "That sounds wonderful." He meant it. Status quo might not be overly ambitious but it was peace. He wouldn't lose that for anything.

After dinner at the ranch house, he drove home and started the new nighttime routine at the cabin. While Maddy showered and brushed her teeth, Ted swept up the kitchen floor and ran the dishwasher. Having a house guest forced him onto a schedule.

If not for the little girl, he'd probably have missed dinner and started the deck. Working around the clock was his norm. He could push himself past pain and through hunger, if he engaged his muscles and his mind in manual labor.

"Unc? Can we read?"

He lifted his gaze to the pink pajama clad child. "Of course. First, I promised Mommy we'd video chat."

"Yes, please." Maddy grabbed the cell phone off the table and handed it over.

Sliding onto the bench after her, he unlocked the screen and dialed his sister. He handed the phone to his niece and sat next to her, angling close.

"Mommy!" Maddy squealed.

"Oh, sweet girl. Hi! I've missed you!" Jen sounded exhausted and wistful. Like she could start crying in a second.

He wouldn't be surprised if she did. She was doing her best in a tense situation. His sister shouldered a lot of worry and guilt. Maddy was the proof of his sister's wonderful parenting skills. Remembering Stephanie's advice, Ted had to insert himself in the call and aim for levity. "Don't worry about me."

Maddy giggled. "Unc is here, too. Mommy, I can't wait to show you everything. Mr. Hank and Miss Meg and Colby and the barn and school and Miss Patricks."

Jen chuckled. "Sure sounds like you've settled in. Good job, sweetie. I'm glad I'll have a local to take me around town."

Maddy beamed at the praise.

Ted almost sighed. Jen regulated her voice to normal. Crisis—and bad night's sleep—averted. "How is everything? No hiccups?"

"None whatsoever," Jen said without hesitation.

Ted swallowed the sigh of relief, glad to know they'd be nearby for good. Ted wasn't sure he could go back to living totally on his own. The girls wouldn't always share his house. Taking care of Maddy grounded him, and he couldn't give it up. In a few years, he could look forward to off-tune school concerts and maybe attending a few sports events. He couldn't wait.

"I'm heading to work soon," Jen said. "I'm off tomorrow, and then I'll work six days straight. I'm driving up with some of our things next weekend."

"Not everything?" Ted asked.

"I'll have one more week of work before I close on the house. Slight hiccup. The movers will follow me in two weekends."

He didn't mind, but he couldn't quite comprehend what his sister was going through. The separation from her child had to be excruciating. He couldn't let the call linger or everyone would be sad, realizing what they were missing. "We'll be happy to see you."

"Mommy, do you want to see my backpack and my papers?" Maddy stood on the bench and jumped over him. Holding the phone, she raced to her bedroom.

Ted chuckled. His motion sickness prone sister was in for a doozy. But he wasn't going to micromanage the call. He'd give the pair space.

Maddy could dazzle her mom with tales of school, and he could be grateful for the twist of fate that brought his family to his chosen hometown even if he avoided adding to his list of nearest and dearest. He refused to read into the motivations for Stephanie's help. She'd be kind to any child. Maddy was special to her family.

He was grateful. Because he couldn't be anything else.

CHAPTER 7

In her high-necked prairie gown, Stephanie stood perfectly straight. She had no choice. Sitting was uncomfortable. Running was impossible. Talking too loudly was most definitely not an option. The worst part about her ensemble? She didn't even have pockets. Her historically accurate dress seemed to shrink the longer she wore it. She took in the deepest breath she could and calmed down. Not long to go now.

While the poker tournament was nearing its end after several loud, raucous hours in The Golden Crown saloon on Friday night, she remained in constant motion with no opportunity to slow down or sit. Helping wherever she could, she had run to the back to grab her cell phone, almost forgetting to snap a few pictures of the event to share on the school website, loan to the town's tourism page, and keep as a personal memento of another successful night.

The outfit restricted her ability to perform even the most basic of her tasks. At least her wardrobe was temporary, and she'd been born over a century later, long past the fashion for up-to-the-chin collars and floor length hemlines. She was glad she didn't have to teach her students in the school-teacher garb she wore. Although, she wondered if some might enjoy not having a teacher focused on them but too attuned to her own aches and pains.

Pushing through the swinging door from the employees only area to the main room, she plastered on a smile and pulled up her camera app. Angling her device this way and that, she snapped hundreds of photos in a handful of minutes as she circled the perimeter. At the start of the evening, the circular tables were occupied with card sharks. As the play dwindled down, only one table remained with an active game. Couples, families, neighbors, and friends now gathered around the buffet tables, enjoying the meal their entrance fee purchased. With her device, she captured smiling faces and heads thrown back in laughter. It was a fun evening for a good cause. Everyone got the memo.

For the most part, the crowd was attired in nineteenth century costumes. The annual event had become a town spectacle. Locals stashed period clothing for the tournament. Kim at the Old West photography studio began an enterprising side-hustle, renting out her costumes to interested tourists. The room was filled to capacity with bowler hats, vests, corsets, and ruffles.

She would be jealous of the women dressed in saloon girl outfits, if the corsets didn't look more restrictive than the tight collar on her gown. She had a role to play at the end of the evening to officially close the night and needed to look the part. Still, she was sweating through the dress and couldn't wait for a cool shower and soft pajamas at home.

Striding past the bar, she snapped a couple shots of James in action. His beard was definitely the stand-out facial hair of the year. Most of the other men stuck to either a moustache or beard. A handful sported a few days of scruff, also in keeping with the time period. No one had taken the same level of care as the saloon owner. She angled her phone and snapped a picture, flashing him a thumbs up before crossing toward the last table still in play.

Hank Kincaid operated as the house. The local blacksmith and a man she recognized but didn't know sat in front of him. Joe and Ted were there as well.

She held her breath, transfixed watching Ted. With his cards face down on the table, he stared straight ahead. He could have been carved from a glacier. Nothing showed in his expression. He barely breathed, holding still and steady. Even playing a game, he exuded safety and certainty. She'd been drawn to those qualities. *I'll always be able to count on Ted.*

The longer she studied him, the chillier she grew. She crossed her arms, tucking her phone into the crook of her elbow. She couldn't snap pictures and risk the flash disturbing the men.

Hank dealt two cards to each player.

Ted focused on the game, providing a rare opportunity to study him. Gray hair threaded through his temples. Not a ton, but enough—along with the fine lines around his mouth and eyes—to highlight their age difference. She didn't find the years between them insurmountable. She liked his cautious approach to the world. She found herself barreling ahead and flailing around, but she liked that he was more thoughtful.

The players placed their bets.

His gray eyes flashed like melted silver. For a split second, he warmed up like he'd been plunged in a crucible.

The change was slight, but she noticed. And his moment of victory was contagious. She smiled for him, feeling the heat from her head to her toes.

Hank gestured for the players to show their cards.

"Pair of Kings," Ted said. The others sniggered and took sips of their drinks. Hank pushed the pot to Ted.

She took a step forward, eager to congratulate him. A cold hand seized her elbow and squeezed. Wincing, she turned and frowned at the back of a saloon girl.

She let the woman drag her from the crowd, across the room to the corner near the kitchen. She wouldn't cause a scene and interrupt the last table at play. Her mind reasoned the kidnapper must be an acquaintance, and she was in a very public place. She wasn't about to be snatched, no matter how many of her true-life crime shows told her otherwise.

Free of the crowd, the woman turned.

Stephanie sucked in a sharp breath. Her eyes almost bugged out of her head.

In arguably the skimpiest saloon girl costume of the evening, Candace Vane glowered.

"Oh, hi." Stephanie pressed a hand to her collarbone and forced a laugh. "Good evening, Candace. I didn't recognize you. No wonder I hadn't seen you yet. I'm glad you found me."

"I thought you were deliberately snubbing me."

The haughty tone befit royalty. The corresponding sniff and lift of her chin complimented the expression. Only the costume ruined the effect. "I apologize if I gave you that impression. I think this might be the best event yet." Stephanie smiled, the corners of her mouth lifting in a shaky grin.

"I know it is. The corporate donations alone have secured the program for the next year."

"We couldn't do any of this without you."

"Hmm. Interesting. I appreciate your praise. I thought I must have offended you somehow." Candace studied her bracelets.

Stephanie darted her gaze, looking for escape, a witness, or solid ground. Anything to hold onto. The subtle cut of each word sliced deep with repetition. "Of course you haven't offended me." Stephanie forced a laugh.

"We aren't quite the partners I had imagined." Candace lifted her gaze and held Stephanie's with an unblinking stare. "You didn't respond to my email on Wednesday."

I completely forgot. The stifling costume threatened Stephanie with heat stroke, trapping her flushed skin under a high collar and long sleeves. She hated being scolded and did her best to avoid reprimands. "My sincerest apologies. I didn't realize you required a response. Your email didn't pose any questions or ask for any action."

Candace lifted her hands to her tiny, corseted waist. "At least this went well. Let's return to more formal terms, Miss Patricks. From what I gather from Amelia, you have been showing a lot of particular attention to specific children at the expense of the others."

Stephanie's throat went dry. "I don't follow."

"Oh, I'm sure you do. Your closeness to one child and her guardian hasn't gone unnoticed. Since I seem to be on the outside looking in, maybe this is the natural end of my help with your fundraiser."

Stephanie was speechless. Threatening the kids and calling her out, Candace cut her down to size. Hot emotion bubbled up inside Stephanie. She wasn't sure if she should laugh or cry.

Candace strode past Stephanie, brushing against her shoulder.

The shove was too powerful to be an accident. Lauren and Kelly had warned Stephanie about Candace, but she wanted to believe she'd taken the measure of the woman during their years working on this event together.

With a glance over her shoulder to make sure no one noticed, and she wouldn't be missed, Stephanie strolled toward the antique half door. At least she had the valid excuse of putting away her phone to steal a moment to calm down. She pushed her way inside and continued to the line of hooks near the back door. She shoved her phone deep into the bottom of her purse.

Filling her lungs, she caught a hint of mint and leather. And she almost collapsed and started to cry. She pulled back her shoulders. Ted must have noticed her disappearance. She wanted him to care about her so much more than he ever could. But it wouldn't be fair to him if she leaned into his solid chest and hugged him, though she desperately longed for his strong arms to wrap around her and reassure her everything was okay.

Her world was changing. Whether she wanted it to or not. She wouldn't compound her sins by dragging him down with her. No matter how tempting.

She turned, brushed her hair out of her face, and smiled as she strolled towards the one person she feared really saw her. She wished he'd be her friend and nothing else right now. "Hi, Ted. Good round out there. We should get back."

"Wait," he murmured.

She felt the softly spoken words down to her bones and the light tone frightened her worse than Candace Vane's bluster and fury. Stephanie twisted her fingers to stop from doing something over the top, like reaching for him. She was a fool to imagine anything more than the momentary friendship based on her helping him out. She couldn't seem to make her heart understand.

We could be happy if you let us.

For the past several hours, Ted was unnervingly aware of Stephanie's every move. Without turning his head, he knew exactly where she was in the room. It was torturously hard to keep his focus on his game-playing. But he managed. Somehow.

He had debated skipping the event. After a long day of work on the deck, he ached. Every muscle in his body was strained from unusual twisting and stretching. As had become their habit, Stephanie had pulled her car in front of the ranch house and walked around the wraparound porch to flash him a thumbs up. Then, Maddy had let herself into Hank and Ryan's house and Stephanie had left.

He'd wanted to talk to her and thank her. The rest of Maddy's week had been much smoother since the grown-ups in her life had started working together. As a result, his world had been restored to its axis. Was this what prompted his sister to put aside her differences with her ex? For Maddy's sake? He hadn't understood the importance until he'd lived it.

He had been holding a piece of metal flashing when he had spotted Stephanie on the porch, and couldn't do more than nod his head in acknowledgement without ruining his work. She deserved better. Exhausted from his labors, he wanted to kick back at the cabin with Maddy. He'd never been so grateful for a weekend. What would next week, the first five days of school, bring?

He looked forward to quiet and a weekend spent recharging. But Ryan volunteered to babysit since he was dog sitting for Meg. The pair, Colby and Maddy, were evenly matched in energy levels, making the job easier as the child and dog entertained each other. Ted thanked Ryan, grateful. Ted had to show up and support Stephanie's event. Friendship required kindness from both parties. He couldn't offer her more of a relationship, but she deserved every ounce of his respect.

He was good at playing poker. Participating in a tournament was hardly a stretch for him. Careful to never play with the seasonal ranch hands, he had a standing weekly group and, as he expected, those five were the last men standing in the tournament.

When Meg had approached the table during the last hand, she brought with her a strange sense of calm. He relaxed at her nearness, maybe because he didn't have to subconsciously track her around the room. She stood close enough for him to catch a whiff of her citrus-y smell. And then he'd been dealt a winning hand.

He accepted his winnings, turned his head toward her, and frowned. She disappeared. Reaching a hand to his chest, he rubbed the dull ache in his ribs. One person in a crowd shouldn't hold the power to make or break an event. For him, she did.

"Hey, Hank, will you watch my chips?" Ted asked the dealer.

Hank arched a brow. "Okay, but we're only taking a quick break before the last hand."

Ted nodded, pushing back from the table. He accepted the congratulations and positive comments from friends and neighbors as he wove through the crowd. Everyone knew the evening's winner didn't take home the pot. The money was donated back to the school as part of the fundraiser. But the winner earned a positive reputation in town. In a small community like Herd, a person's integrity was prized above all else.

He spotted the door to the kitchen still swinging. With a frown, he noted the angry saloon-girl nearby, nostrils flaring like a bull.

His pulse raced. Was Stephanie in the back? Was she okay? Slipping through the door while it swung open, he carefully strode into the kitchen.

His boot slid on the tile. He froze but slid forward a half an inch. He stared at the floor. He hadn't realized how slippery tile could be with his all-purpose boots. With his gaze on the floor, he didn't see her approach he felt the change in the air as she tiptoed toward him.

"Hi, Ted," she said. "Good round out there. We should get back."

He heard the hitch in her words. Had she been crying? Her face was a little red and puffy. What happened?

He was terrible at dealing with tears and his flight control took over command of his body at the first sign. Right now, however, he wanted to stay here and comfort her. *We are friends. Friends don't abandon each other.*

She brushed past his shoulder.

"Wait," he murmured. When he turned his head to speak, he stood only a few inches away.

She froze.

Up close, he couldn't even see her breathing.

Dressed in a high-neck gown with long sleeves and a busy print, she was one of the women portraying the Ladies' Society for the Health and Moral Well-Being of the Youth of Montana. The group had worked to abolish gambling in Herd during the early days of the town. They'd been unsuccessful.

She shouldn't be the most beautiful woman in the room, but she was. Her unusually tight posture was all wrong. She was lightness and positivity. She should never have a second of sadness. He had enough for the both of them. He'd take on even more pain if he could spare her a second of sadness. She should always be bright and happy.

Dragging in a shuddering breath, she stepped back and met his gaze. She offered a tight smile. "I'm okay. Don't worry about me."

It's hard not to.

"I'm just preparing for my big entrance." She reached up and pinched her cheeks. "You had a great round out there." She repeated her earlier praise.

"I got lucky." Could his winning streak continue? It hadn't. For much of his life, he had one perfect thing, one good moment, or one glorious victory. And then everything crashed down around him. *What if my luck changes?* "What happened? Why are you upset?"

She sighed and shook her head.

"You can tell me. We're friends . . . right?" He desperately wished that were true. Because that was all he could ever have with this special, wonderful human. And he needed her goodness and spirit in his life. He'd lose that when Jen returned. She would assume control of the pick-up and drop off. She would meet with Stephanie for parent teacher conferences. Jen would step up in all the ways involving Maddy. And he'd have no reason to speak to Stephanie again. Until the summer? June was an impossibly far off date in the vast and distant future.

"You're right, we are." She took in a deep breath. "To be honest, it was a little bit of a power play. Someone trying to put me in my place. Under their heel."

He'd dealt with that before and—if he ever left the ranch—he would probably have to face it again. "Do you need me to do anything? Can I help and speak to someone?"

"No, but you're sweet for trying." With a shaky breath, she stepped forward.

He opened his arms wide and wrapped her tight in a warm hug. Until he made the gesture, he hadn't known what he'd intended. Holding her felt right. He needed the embrace, too. She'd been slumped and defeated. He wanted to lift her up figuratively and literally.

After a few seconds, her breathing evened, returning to normal. She kissed his cheek. "I'm needed for my grand entrance." She strolled toward the swinging door, pulling back her shoulders and lifting her head high.

He liked this version of her almost as much as the soft peck she'd planted on his cheek. He let the light touch soak into his skin.

She turned. "Come on, you better go win it all so we can finish this night properly."

He had to take her word that she was fine. He had hoped hugging her would reassure him that she was okay, he wasn't sure it had. He knew she was the same sort of prideful as he was. Like recognized like. And more than anything, he was certain sometimes a person had to tell others what they wanted to believe about themselves. But the reflection of himself didn't change what he wanted. Her dampened spirit had only a tiny flicker of its usual spark. He cleared his throat. "Okay. See you soon."

Striding past her, he headed straight toward the table. At his sides, his hands shook. Not from nerves but the sudden desire to reach out and touch her again. He sat at the table as Ryan announced the last hand.

The final round was quick and—shockingly—Ted won. He didn't lose it all at the last minute. He was applauded and clapped on the back.

The front door of The Golden Crown crashed against the wall.

The room fell unnaturally quiet. The crowd parted.

Standing into the center of the saloon, holding a sign reading *For the Children*, Stephanie strode in with her band of other modestly-garbed women. She played her role to perfection. Joe had researched the event but allowed Stephanie to take liberties with the script. She demanded the cowboys cease and desist at once.

At the table, she lifted her chin and held his gaze. He adored the flicker of amusement and cheek as she continued to rail against him. Finally, she finished. He pushed the winnings forward. The crowd erupted into cheers. After a few minutes, James announced the record-setting donation amount, everyone clapped, and the evening concluded.

Ted tried—unsuccessfully—to catch her eye but Stephanie had stepped away to finish up her duties for the evening.

Playacting for one night was okay. But he preferred the real person under the costume. From the corner of his eye, he caught what looked like a heated argument in the opposite direction. He turned his head and observed Joe and Abby at war again.

Ted shook his head. Hank was usually a shrewd judge of character. There was no way he would find success matching up Joe and Abby. Ted had a surefire way to take the heat of Hank's matchmaking off his friend. If Ted made a move on Stephanie, he'd be sure to grab the old cowboy's attention.

Ted glanced at Stephanie, smiling so pretty near the bar. Holding her hadn't been about anything more than providing comfort. What he found, however, had shocked him. She belonged in his arms, as natural as pulling on a hat on a sunny day. The longer he'd held her, the more he realized he needed the warmth of another person's embrace too.

He didn't want to need her but couldn't deny the way she enhanced his life. Was that emotion tougher than fighting against lust? While it might be more tempting, he'd hold strong against her allure.

He had his family in town now, and she had her own life. She deserved so much more than a broken-down old cowboy like him. But a tiny part of him, deep down, wanted her in his life. As more than friends.

CHAPTER 8

Stephanie parked in the driveway of the cheery yellow house, and turned off the car. Reaching for her travel mug, she took one last long sip of the cooled coffee. She hated room temperature coffee. Today, however, she savored every last ounce of caffeine and peace. Saturdays should be for sleeping in. The day after the poker tournament, however, was anything but restful.

Last night, she'd gone home exhausted and spent the night tossing and replaying the past few hours. She'd been shocked by the confrontation with Candace. The PTA president's threat to stop her participation—and thus the majority of the fundraising—left Stephanie speechless. Could the other woman be so vindictive she'd impact children's welfare over a personal frustration?

Before Candace's involvement, the event raised only modest sums to help pay the lunch balance owed by a few students at the end of the school year. Since the woman took over the project, however, the increased corporate sponsorships had helped raise their goal to almost unimaginable heights, covering the fees for every child.

Stephanie was upset, frustrated, and disappointed. Inwardly, she raged against Candace for threatening a program that did so much good out of spite. Mrs. Vane, she corrected herself. Formal terms only with an eyeroll. In the moment, Stephanie hadn't stood up for the kids. She'd acted like a coward.

If she was honest, she was more annoyed with herself both that she'd let the event depend so heavily on one person's involvement and that she hadn't practiced her due diligence in reaching out to a parent. She had put herself in a questionable spot.

Compounding the issue was driving Maddy every day after school. If she didn't know Ted, would she have helped him? She couldn't argue that it was on her way home. She had to drive miles out of her way and circle back. She'd informed Bill, keeping administration abreast of the unusual situation. But deep down, she knew she used it as an excuse to see Ted. Otherwise, she wouldn't have any reason to fan the flickering flames of their new friendship.

A knock on her window snapped Stephanie to attention.

Lauren stood next to the car. "Are you planning on coming inside? Or are you busy plotting an escape?"

Stephanie pocketed her keys and swallowed the cheeky response. She was here because after three early morning texts, she'd agreed to help Lauren today. Otherwise, she'd still be in bed resting.

Slowly, Stephanie opened the car door, grabbing her purse off the center console as she slipped from the driver's seat. "Sorry." She shut the car door. "Lost in thought."

"Remember, you said any time I needed help?" Lauren's voice shook, heavy with emotion.

Stephanie reached for her friend's hand and squeezed. "I did, and I meant it." She forced a smile.

Lauren sniffed and pulled her hand free, swiping her eyes.

Stephanie knew better than to ask what was wrong. Lauren never responded to that question. She bristled like a cactus growing spikes on time-lapse when pestered about private matters. As her fluctuating hormone levels impacted her emotional state, she would not appreciate any prodding.

"Did you get home late?" Lauren asked. "Are you tired?"

Stephanie shook her head. "I'm ready to get started. What's today's project?"

"Nursery furniture. Packages have been accumulating in the room. I didn't want to open anything until I could organize. I finally got the furniture yesterday. But it's all in flat pack boxes and needs to be put together. And I have to get the room straightened and sorted. Steve doesn't understand the urgency."

"I'm sure that's not true." Stephanie struggled to keep her voice even. Lauren was sensitive to tone without the added upheaval of her changing body.

"It is. The packages arrived late last night. After seven. I wanted to get started. But Steve had to go into the office this morning for monthly inventory. He made me promise I wouldn't start on my own. The room is packed, and I can't do anything."

Stephanie nodded solemnly. Obviously, Steve hadn't read enough of the baby books to grasp the importance of nesting. And he assumed he could reason with his agitated wife. Stephanie would have to talk to him. "I'm here. I'll get to work, and you can tell me where everything goes. Okay?"

Lauren inhaled and exhaled, loudly. Her nostrils flared. Her eyes went a little wild.

Stephanie remembered the same breathing techniques from her sister-in-law's pregnancy. She copied the pattern for two rounds. "Better?"

Lauren smiled. "Yes, much. Come on in, and I'll get you another cup of coffee before we gets started. You probably need it after last night."

Stephanie pressed her lips together. Her honest reply would only worry her very distressed pregnant friend. Stephanie followed her friend into the house, slipping off her shoes inside the front door and climbing the stairs to the second level. "I'm okay. A little hard work is all I need."

The Cape Cod style home boasted three bedrooms and two bathrooms on the upper floor. Stephanie tried not to notice her friend's labored breathing as she climbed the steps. She remained silent as she approached the open doorway.

"I'm relieved to hear you say that. Because here we are." Lauren's voice caught.

Frowning, Stephanie peered inside and dropped her jaw. Boxes filled every inch of the room like some complicated stacking game gone awry. Steve was right not to let Lauren start assembling on her own. Or at all. She was liable to hurt herself even stepping foot inside.

Telling Lauren her husband's judgement was sounder than hers wasn't a good start. None of Stephanie's thoughts were helpful or encouraging.

So, instead, she faced her friend with a smile. "Why don't you rest on your bed? I will start moving the boxes out so I have room to work on the furniture. That might take me a while. Once I start building, I'll let you know so you can tell me where to put the pieces."

"I know it's lot. I can't remember what is inside every package anymore. I really need to set up the room."

"It's no trouble. I'll help today, and then you can take your time with the little things, and you'll feel so much better." Stephanie utilized her most placating tone. "Are you going on a babymoon soon?"

"Maybe." Lauren sniffed. "I don't really want to go anywhere. I feel miserable. What's going to change if I go to a hotel? Will my heartburn suddenly stop? Will the babies stop kicking my bladder at three am?"

"A night away might be a nice mental break," Stephanie said, interjecting her voice with as much whimsical optimism as she could muster. "You could let someone else cook and clean. Take a few days off."

"I'm not sure. I have so much to do."

"Don't worry about this." Stephanie waved a hand at the room, not able to assess the space again without pulling a face. "I'll get everything straightened and sorted."

"Thanks, Stephanie. Truly." Lauren wiped at her eyes. "You're such a good friend. It's why I don't want anything to happen while I'm gone."

"Gone?" Stephanie cocked her head to the side. "Where would I go? I don't take vacation during the school year." She hadn't taken a real trip in years. She'd love to but always used her time off to help her friends or visit her brother.

"No, I don't mean a trip to the beach. I'm talking *gone.*" Lauren widened her eyes.

Stephanie frowned at her friend. "Gone like fired?"

Lauren nodded.

A chill swept down Stephanie's spine. Lauren wasn't the sort to gossip or invent a story. Had Lauren heard about the argument last night? Had someone been listening? Or was Candace spreading the story?

Stephanie gritted her teeth. Candace Vane's threats rattled, but Ted buoyed Stephanie's flagging spirits. Lauren hadn't been at the event. How would she know? "What do you mean?"

"I had a dream a couple nights ago. It was so real, but I didn't want to call you and tell you over the phone. I've been waiting to talk to you in person."

"Ohhhkkkaaay," Stephanie dragged the word.

"You were called into Bill's office and cleaned out your room." Lauren reached for Stephanie's hands and squeezed. "Please be careful."

Stephanie swallowed her sigh. Dreams weren't reality. Her heartbeat returned to normal. "I will." She pulled her hands free. "You were missed last night. No one rings the school bell to publicly shame the gamblers with quite as much gusto as you."

"Did Kelly take over for me as the dowdy school marm?"

Stephanie nodded. Her relief at not being gossiped about was fleeting now that she realized a frustrating truth. No one had taken notice of her distress and disappearance last night. Neither had anyone spotted that she had returned disheveled and overwrought.

While she was glad to avoid more gossip, she couldn't help but wonder why she flew under the radar. Was everyone too wrapped up in their own problems? She still wanted to matter to someone. Her childhood insecurities resurfaced in an instant. She drew in a deep breath.

Ted saw.

He might never look at her the way she wanted. He might never offer her more than a polite friendship at arms' length. But he still cared. She'd accept the crumbs of his affection like a starving woman.

"I think I will lie down." Lauren yawned. "Only for a little bit."

Stephanie waited until her friend disappeared down the hall before entering the nursery and shutting the door. She sank to the free spot on the carpet, resting her back against the door. Hot emotion tickled her throat and eyes. Frustration? Anger? Both?

As far as the town was concerned, the fundraiser had been another success. Ted's comfort had felt real. Unfortunately, both highlights were tainted by her mistakes that led to the argument with Candace, and the potential loss of fundraising going forward.

Sharing her concerns with Lauren would only reveal her sense of guilt. She hadn't done anything worthy of condemnation. Focusing on someone else, she remained out of the spotlight and in control. But she couldn't shake the unease that had taken hold. Her only way out of her problem was to get through it. She'd find a solution both to the funding and to fighting Candace's veiled threats. She stood, dusting her palms on her jeans, and got to work.

Despite being exhausted from a nearly sleepless night, Ted sat at the kitchen table in the ranch house, eager to get on with his day. The night before had left him with a sense of unresolved issues and nagging worries. He'd hated witnessing Stephanie's breakdown.

A kind, caring person should be treated with respect. She shouldn't be crying in the back at a successful event she had spearheaded. Anyone would feel angry and defensive on her behalf. But he didn't want the surge of protectiveness.

He hadn't experienced the rush of anger for another person in years. Until only a few months ago, he had avoided any sort of emotional sway in either direction. He chalked his feelings up to friendship. He'd be as protective if something happened to Meg as Stephanie. The only difference was Meg had Ryan to defend her.

He didn't want more. Scratch that. He couldn't handle more. Under the bench, he crossed his ankles and leaned forward, resting his forearms on the table.

Last night, he had picked up Maddy from the ranch house and tucked her into bed, he spent the rest of the night staring at the ceiling. He had no clue how to best move forward with his feelings. The word elicited a shudder. Hadn't he left behind inner turmoil years ago? He didn't want to go back. Unable to sleep, he had arisen and escaped with what he did best, work.

With his niece in tow, he'd come to the ranch to discuss the results of the study that popped into his inbox late yesterday. He had dashed off a text to Joe for good measure. Maddy had scampered off with Hank, Meg, and Colby, on a walk around the property.

Ted had let himself in, following the grumbles as his friend, Ryan, slapped buttons on the coffee maker. Ryan paid him no attention as the coffee brewed.

Fine by Ted. He let his mind wander to another problem. How to entertain Maddy for the next two days. He'd already used every trick he had and then some, looking up Internet articles about how to keep kids happy and engaged. He was glad he only had one weekend solo. His sister returned next weekend for a quick visit.

He wouldn't let either his sister or niece down. Now that he had Maddy here, he wasn't sure he'd be able to return to the way things were before. He'd be happy to relinquish his role as the sole decision maker for the little girl's health and well-being. But he loved hearing her funny thoughts, and reading out loud together after years of silence in his cabin.

He suspected he wouldn't find contentment by himself anymore. To his surprise, he needed people. His comfortable hermit lifestyle had been destroyed. He'd knew he'd be lonely once his niece left and moved into an apartment with her mom.

And Stephanie wouldn't have any other reason to drop by and interact with him. He'd miss that, too. The admission made him shift and squirm. He wouldn't run from the discomfort. Friendship was the full extent he would offer either of them. She had to understand.

The coffee maker beeped.

Ryan poured himself a cup and turned, facing Ted as he sipped.

Eye contact and a nod were Ryan's typical greeting before the first cup of coffee. Despite being a legacy rancher, Ryan wasn't a morning person. The morning after a late night, the minimal responses were hardly surprising.

Ted needed action not circumspection. He did not want a discussion about the event or what happened. He'd steer the conversation. "Did you get a chance to look over the report?"

"Sort of." Ryan covered his mouth with a hand, ineffectually shielding a yawn.

Ted turned away. Nothing good came from pointing out his friend's exhaustion. He was tempted to ask why Ryan was so tired. Ted had stayed late to help clean-up The Golden Crown following the poker tournament and woke up early with Maddy. The little girl rose with the dawn every day no matter how late she'd been awake the previous night. She had requested chocolate chip pancakes for breakfast. Ted had been up for hours already.

Ted looked at his friend and boss again, studying the other man. Ryan had accepted babysitting duties alone. Had Maddy run him ragged? Had the dog? Before Ted had adjusted to the energy and noise levels from his niece, he must have been in a similar state of exhaustion to those around him. Why would he do that? And then it clicked. Ryan was ready for fatherhood, or at least wanted to prove his caregiving capabilities to Meg.

"Did I miss anything interesting?" Joe asked from the doorway.

Ted watched Joe stroll in with a notebook and pen. His smiling countenance and loose gait giving him a jaunty air.

Ryan might have groaned or growled or both. Sipping from a mug, it was hard to decipher if he'd made any noise at all.

"A rehashing of last night?" Joe asked, arching a brow, and shooting pointed stares at both men.

Ted wasn't about to bite. He might be curious about Ryan's sudden caretaking side but not enough to put his own behavior under the glare of his friend's shared stares. Ted didn't want Joe asking where he'd gone before the last hand. "Thanks for stopping by so early on a Saturday," Ted said. "I'm sure you'd rather be sleeping in on your first weekend of the school year."

Joe slid onto the bench across the table. Opening his notebook, he uncapped a pen. "Of course. I'm anxious to get my part of the project underway. Bison education."

Ryan dragged his feet, his slippers scuffing against the slate tiles as he approached the table. He glanced at the armchair at the head.

Ted caught his breath. Did Ryan dare assume Hank's throne?

Ryan slid next to Joe on the bench. "Me, too. I scheduled a meeting with the zookeepers to get a little more insight into the care and handling. Ted, I'm sure I'll have to make another trip and I'd like you to join me next time."

"Thank you. I'd be glad to," Ted replied.

Reintroducing a herd of free-roaming bison to the surrounding ranch land had been Ryan's passion project. Ted had thought his days of animal husbandry were long gone following the sale of the cattle. At the Kincaid ranch, however, he'd learned to never say never. He would appreciate a chance to speak with the people who dealt with the animals on a daily basis. But he'd also prefer to do so with his boss and no one extra.

The San Francisco Zoo wasn't providing the animals but had cared for a herd since the nineteenth century. With generations of hands-on experience, Ted appreciated the insights from personal anecdotes the keepers would provide. The upcoming trip was scheduled for Meg and Hank to attend an auction that included an antique photograph from the Kincaid collection. Ryan was their plus-one.

"The data in the email is remarkably straight forward and optimistic." Ted interlaced his hands on the table. He liked feeling the worn top of the solid piece of furniture. With time, the rough edges had been smoothed and softened.

Joe nodded. "The more positives the better. I've been informally polling the town. I'd like to get ahead of any problems. The biggest concerns revolve around property. Most folks are worried about destruction. One lady used the word *stampede*."

Ryan snorted. "We're not suddenly descending into the chaos of the eighteen nineties. We won't be welcoming bandits next."

"Change is hard." Ted stroked his chin. While Ryan always did his best for the town, he wasn't a selfless philanthropist. He prioritized his business and—for the most part—the town benefitted.

Ted did not want any part of the bison project to be misconstrued. "We should look into the fence on the boundary closest to town. I need to be sure it's in good shape. The blockade will discourage the wanderers from heading toward town. Hard to anticipate the herd's patterns but I'd like to be prepared."

"From the old records I've seen," Ryan said, "the herd mostly kept to the original Kincaid land."

"Yep," Joe added. "In fact, part of the reason for the success of the cattle on the ranch was the presence of the bison. They established a critical ecological balance the settlers didn't appreciate."

Ted shook his head. Man forcing his will on nature was an old tale. Eradicating the bison threatened the entire prairie. Not that the proud settlers understood their folly.

"After the summer drought, anything to help the landscape will be welcome. But a boundary would serve to show our endeavor is real and valuable and not just a bandage to an old wound," Ryan said. "The expansion onto the neighboring ranches will help create a buffer zone. But I'll ask the zookeepers if there is anything we need to be aware of. If they get easily spooked by loud noises, that sort of thing."

"I'm sure the conservation group bringing the animals will have more information about the particulars of the herd," Joe added.

"Are we still on track with the feed truck?" Ryan asked. "Extra hay?"

"Yes. We can make do in the horse stable for the time being," Ted replied. "We might need another barn. Is the Hawke property available?" The last of the original ranches, the Hawkes sold their land minus a couple acres around their ranch house, to Ryan years ago.

"No. I don't want to develop that side of the ranch," Ryan said. "But the Whittier land is available. I had an idea we might repurpose an old building over there into a restaurant for Abby. Offering her a more permanent spot could benefit everyone. She could operate year-round and help with the events in the off-season."

"Are you serious?" Joe asked, aghast. "You would give her a building?"

Ryan shrugged. "It's an idea. I'm never opposed to trying new ventures."

"Yeah but...a restaurant? Food service is a notoriously hard industry. Turning a profit isn't guaranteed. The hours are long. Most new places close in the first year." Joe shook his head. "Not to mention who you'd be getting into business with. Can you trust her to do her share?"

Ryan frowned, deep furrows marring his brow.

"Let's table expansion talk," Ted interjected. He didn't want anyone to speak without more thought.

Joe's temper was short on any topic peripherally related to Abby. Ted hoped—for everyone's sake—the pair found common ground. But glaciers made faster progress. Joe and Abby weren't his top concern. "We won't want another barn for the animals too close to guests."

"Even if we do give Abby one of the old buildings out there, we still have plenty of space for bison on the Whittier land. No one will mind," Ryan said sharply.

Ted shared a look with Joe. The other man only shrugged. "I think I'll go take a look at the fence closest to town. Get a sense of what we need to do. Can Maddy stay with Hank for a little while longer?"

Ryan nodded. "He'd insist on it. Let me know what you find."

Ted slipped out of the room and hopped into his truck, steering toward the boundary with town. He was glad for an escape from founding families talk.

The Whittiers had founded the town along with the Hawkes and Kincaids. Ultimately, however, the Whittier family fell from grace and left town under a cloud of scandal. While the current Kincaids didn't often speak to the publicly held sentiment that the good for nothing Whittiers got what was coming to them, they were as susceptible to town prejudice as everyone else. Joe—an amateur historian working on his first book about the region—often fought for a more open-minded view. But even he wasn't one to speak up in their favor.

On the horizon line, the split rail fence came into view. The barrier had never been much of a deterrent for trespassers and wasn't used as such for the past hundred years. After the Hawkes and Kincaids booted the Whittiers from town, their vengeful reputations kept too many from crossing into this part of the land. *Don't cross a Kincaid man* was some of the first advice spouted to Ted, not that he'd ever seen any cause for the phrase.

Ted parked close and hopped out of the cab. The fence ran along the perimeter of the property where the ranch met asphalt roadway. From a distance, he spotted flaking white paint but nothing major to concern him. He'd replaced several sections six months ago but hadn't touched this part.

He'd come to the corner by two intersecting roadways. To get to the other side, he'd have to drive the long way around, or he could hop the fence. He chose the second option.

He tested the post's structural integrity before climbing onto the bottom rail. Swinging one leg and then the other up and over the top rail, he intended to jump to the ground. He'd done the motion countless times over the years. Muscle memory should have been enough to give him a little boost. But today, conditions conspired against him.

In the second after he'd lifted his second leg, as he supported the bulk of his weight with his two hands on the post, he heard a noise. A car. He was far enough from the roadway, the fence set onto the ranch property and not at the line, to allow for egress should a car need to pull off the two-lane roads.

But then he'd glanced up at the car. A little sedan driving along with music blaring from the stereo and out the partially rolled down windows. He knew the song because Maddy had educated him on the music of Taylor Swift thanks to Stephanie's influence.

Instead of paying attention to what he was doing, he focused on the car, hoping Stephanie might be the driver. And she was. He swung down his leg, glad for a chance to chat again and make sure she was okay.

Except, he didn't land on the ground with his usual grace. His jeans snagged on the top rail and his back foot caught. His palms scrapped against the rail. He fell in a heap on the ground, denim ripping as the weight of his leg pulled his foot free.

Tires squealed as the car stopped on the shoulder.

"Ted? Are you okay?" Stephanie shouted.

He winced and sat up, easing his legs out in front of him. Testing his muscles, he'd ache in the morning but hadn't twisted any major leg joints. He waved a hand. "Yeah, I'm fine."

"No, you're bleeding. Hold on," she called.

He sucked in a breath and flipped over his palms. She was right. He'd torn through the top layer of skin and bled in several sections. The wounds didn't look deep enough for stitches, but he'd have to keep bandages on and use his work gloves for a few days. He should have worn the gloves before he'd hopped the fence, but he'd been so sure of his abilities that his ego led to his fall.

"May I see?" Stephanie asked in a soft voice.

He met her concerned gaze and swallowed the lump in his throat. With her knees pressing into the ground, she was close. Almost as near as last night when she'd kissed him.

His cheek burned from the memory of the tender press of her lips. Kiss was a rather hopeful word to define the peck. But he couldn't stop from hoping she might kiss him palms. He didn't think that would make him all better but he wasn't about to stop her from trying.

"May I?" she asked again.

"Of course." His voice sounded scratchy, and he coughed, clearing his dry throat. "I mean. Please."

She furrowed her brow as she studied the angry dashes on his palms. Then she reached into her purse for a small red case with a cross on it. "First aid kit. Occupational hazard." She smiled.

He returned the grin, liking the conspiratorial gleam in her eyes.

When she wiped his palms clean with a wet towelette, however, his smile faltered. The shock of cold and the sting of the alcohol was fleeting. She produced antibiotic ointment next, careful to dab but not rub the cream into each wound before covering each palm with a large square bandage. "All done." She sat back on her heels, putting space between them.

"Thanks. I'm a little surprised you had normal bandages and not something covered in cartoons."

She chuckled. "Oh, I have those too." She rifled through the kit and produced a fluorescent purple bandage with unicorns. "But your injuries required something a little larger."

"I'm not sure if that's a good or a bad thing." He shook his head. "It's strange to see you dressed down."

"What do you mean?" She held out her arms and stared at her olive-green corduroy jacket and dark rinse jeans.

"I like the bright colors you wear to work. You know the smiling crayons and stuff." Was he rambling? He felt like he was.

She shrugged. "I do have a full adult wardrobe in my closet. It's not all yoga pants and over the top sweaters. But . . ." she tapped a finger to her chin. "Now that you mention it, I've never seen you in anything but flannel and old jeans."

"I can clean up when I need to," he said. "I just don't need to."

She giggled.

"I'm grateful you stopped by and helped." Although, he'd admit to himself, he might have had a chance at staying whole if she hadn't.

"I am, too. I don't know what you are doing out here. But I suppose we're even now. You saw me cry. I saw you cry."

He rolled his eyes at her smirk. "Friends don't need to keep score but sure, we're even." He made his next mistake by meeting her gaze again only to study her lips. She hadn't kissed his boo-boos. Had he imagined the charge between them at the saloon?

"What are you doing out here?"

"Inspecting the fence. Looking to see what sections need to be replaced before the bison arrive. Once winter hits, I won't be able to fix anything and the snow drifts can last long into *spring*." He made air quotes with his fingers and winced, as he reaggravated his palms. "I'll need to paint the fence again but I was starting to walk the perimeter when I . . . fell."

She pressed her lips together and her eyes sparkled.

Suppressing a giggle at his expense? He appreciated the effort.

"Bison can jump fences. They are powerful creatures," she said.

"But at least we can try to establish boundaries for them. Hopefully they'll get the idea."

She leaned back on her palms and scanned the fence behind him. "When I was a kid, I helped paint a fence. My friend had the brilliant idea to toss the paint from the can, and I would very quickly use my brush to spread it around."

"And how did that work out?" He grinned, already knowing the answer.

"We were taken off the job by my friend's dad." She smirked back. "I can help if you need an extra pair of hands."

"No, I'll be fine. It's my job, not yours." He shook his head. "What were you doing out here?"

"Helping a friend."

This time he threw back his head and laughed, a deep belly chortle that rose up from deep inside him. She joined in, her giggle light and melodious and a perfect harmony for his. Spending time with her was nice, almost intoxicating. If he wasn't careful, he'd get addicted to the joy she exuded. And then he'd want to give up all of his good intentions and get closer to her.

He slowly got to his feet. Besides a twinge on one side, he was fine enough to keep going about his work. And he needed to before he did something crazy, like kiss her on the cheek.

"Are you really okay?" she asked, getting to her feet and dusting her palms on her jeans.

"I am. Thank you for stopping. See you afterschool tomorrow?"

She nodded and flashed a thumbs up before turning her back to him and striding towards her car.

Ted wasn't sure but he thought in the moment before she nodded, she might have been about to argue. Instead, she walked away. Once he heard her car door open and shut, he did the same, heading in the opposite direction to inspect the fence. He was glad. In large part because a little distance between him and Stephanie might be the cure for his odd sense of longing. Or he'd be in even deeper.

CHAPTER 9

On Monday morning, Stephanie sat behind her desk, scanning her email, and eating a sandwich. She could go to the teacher's lounge for her break. But the forty-minutes passed so quickly, while the kids ate in the cafeteria and played on the playground for recess, she often lost track of the time. With the earliest lunch slot of the school at ten thirty, she and the other kindergarten teachers were usually still nursing a coffee and finishing breakfast.

She could have gone to Lauren's class next door, sneaking through their shared bathroom, or wandered across the hall to Kelly's. She'd had a lot of dealing with people at the event, however, and was glad for a break. She needed downtime to recharge.

Besides, her muscles still ached from manual labor at Lauren's house and her heart ached after her encounters with Ted. She couldn't accept another round of kudos for her help. Focusing on others instead of herself brought her clarity and control. She didn't seek praise and found it uncomfortable.

She chewed her last bite of sandwich and crossed the room to the sink by the door. She wouldn't have to worry too much longer about any wrong impressions. Maddy's mom was expected to return soon. This would be the last week of the atypical carpool. And then she'd have no reason to see Ted.

She'd just found her voice around him. She hadn't wanted to stop talking. And maybe, just maybe, he felt the same. Friday night, he'd followed her to the kitchen to check on her. He'd noticed she was gone. He'd noticed she was upset. What was she to make of that?

He was concerned because he's kind and a good friend. She pumped foaming soap into her hands and rubbed, covering completely every inch of skin. Scrubbing for thirty seconds was too long for her to be alone with her thoughts. The weekend was too long.

She replayed the quiet moment in the kitchen. *We're friends . . . right?* He asked so softly, and she wasn't sure how to answer. She wanted to be more, but she'd have to settle for friendship. When she spotted him on the side of the road, she'd been glad for a chance to help him. Up close and personal, holding his hands, she hadn't wanted to let go. But she had. She hadn't wanted to push her luck.

She rinsed her hands under the running water, grabbed a paper towel, and was drying her hands when she turned toward the door and jumped back.

A woman with brown, shoulder length hair neatly styled, a full face of make-up, a cream-colored shirt, and pressed jeans stood with her fist to the door. "Oh, hello." She smiled. "I'm Grayden's mom. I'm here to volunteer."

"Oh." Stephanie gasped. She took a step back, glancing at the clock over the door. She only had five minutes until the kids returned to the classroom. "I didn't get a call from the office."

Grayden's mom crossed the threshold and strode toward the cubbies, swinging her purse off her shoulder and into her son's marked spot. "I checked in and scanned my I.D. They must have thought I'd be going to my older daughter's class. Oh, well. Here I am."

She was tall and strode with purpose, like she belonged. Her confidence caught Stephanie off-guard. Tossing the balled-up paper towel in the waste basket, Stephanie shook her head. "I'm sorry for the confusion. We don't have volunteers in our class yet. Sign-ups will be posted after Back-to-School night. I'm going to need to ask you to leave."

"What?" The woman turned and frowned. "Kindergarten is always asking for help with the reading and math centers. I was in my older daughter's class at least once a week."

Until we hired more educators and aides this past summer. "Typically, sign-up sheets aren't posted until Back-to-School Night." Stephanie reiterated slowly. "But our classroom won't need too many volunteers this year. We are lucky the district hired plenty of help." Stephanie aimed to keep her tone light and the conversation vague. She hated confrontation and shied away from it at every turn. Her palms felt clammy. She shouldn't have thrown away the paper towel.

"Oh, it's no trouble." The woman smiled and waved a hand in the air. "I'm happy to help."

"I . . . ugh . . . I'm . . ." Stephanie stood in between the door leading to her shared bathroom and the door leading to the hall. She darted her gaze across, willing Kelly to save her from this situation.

No, she'd have to step up for herself. She'd let Candace Vane walk all over her on Friday night and still felt terrible. While this mom wasn't waging a war with the same venomous tone, she wasn't backing down and taking a hint either. Stephanie never let parents call the shots over the good of the kids, and she couldn't start now.

"Did you receive the newsletter on Friday?" Stephanie knew the answer before asking the question. Earlier, she'd checked the clicks on the links embedded into the email. Every parent had received and opened the message.

"Well . . . I did." She stretched the word to three syllables. "An oversight, I'm sure."

Stephanie stood her ground, pulling back her shoulders as she faced the stranger. "I'm sorry for any confusion. I need to ask you to leave. I'll be stepping out to get the kids soon, and I don't want anyone upset."

The woman flushed. "Well." She turned toward the cubbies, grabbing her purse. Swinging the bag onto her shoulder, she momentarily lifted her gaze to Stephanie. She pursed her lips, giving herself a pinched, just bit into a lemon, look. She continued past and out the door, without a backward glance.

Stephanie waited until the woman left, then she hunched forward, drooping as she let out a heavy breath. She felt horrible. Was this what she could expect her whole year? Saving the kids from having their feelings hurt by constantly battling one entitled parent after another? Why had the woman come? If she had an older child, she knew it was too early for volunteers.

"Was that Grayden Foxx's mom?" Kelly asked.

Stephanie spun around.

In the shared bathroom between her class and Lauren's next door, Lauren and Kelly stood shoulder to shoulder.

They must have been working on a project together in Lauren's class. They had been nearby the whole time. They had her back. But she wasn't at ease. She waited for another parental ambush. She'd never had such an encounter before. Until last week, she'd thought she had a very good, open, understanding style in communicating with parents.

Stephanie nodded.

"She's best friends with Candace Vane," Lauren said, gripping her belly underneath with both hands.

Stephanie glanced from one to the other. Her friends had tight expressions, mirroring each other. At her sides, Stephanie's hands shook. She took a deep breath, willing a calm. In a couple minutes, she'd have to get the kids. She couldn't be upset or they would feed off that energy and her day would be ruined. Young kids were finely attuned to emotions. She strove for peace and contentment for everyone's best interest.

Still, she was rattled. "Do you think Candace put her up to it?"

Lauren frowned. "Why would she?"

Because I didn't email her. Because she threatened me the other night. Stephanie couldn't say the words. She hated feeling like a naughty child when she hadn't been wrong. The email hadn't required a response. Just because everyone else in Candace's life kowtowed to her didn't mean she could expect that treatment across the board. "I figured I was in the clear until Back-to-School Night with the other parents. The sign-up sheets for volunteers don't go up until then anyways. I want to explain why visitors are limited in person. I've never had someone just walk in without advance notice."

The office should have called. Unless the parent gave another reason for striding into the building. Stephanie shivered. She didn't want to see a conspiracy everywhere she looked. But the oversight was chilling.

Kelly shrugged. "Maybe Candace said something. Or she could have taken the initiative on her own. You know we support you, but . . ."

"It's a big change," Lauren said. "Sure, letting parents help in the classroom comes with its own set of challenges. But you can't block every helicopter mom out there. Pick your battles."

Stephanie bit the inside of her cheek, fighting the burn in her nostrils. Her colleagues had become her dearest friends. Their advice was always for the best.

She had to do what was in the kids' best interests, even—perhaps especially—if she had to live through the discomfort of establishing something new. "I'm sure this is the right plan for these kids. Yes, a handful of them are blessed with very involved parents. But for the most part, the parents are already pulled in too many directions. I can't tug them in one more, and I won't let the kids feel left out because Mom or Dad can't miss work. I'm not blocking access. But I don't think it's helpful to the classroom to have the same parents underfoot every day of the week. I'll explain everything at Back-To-School night."

Lauren nodded. "We support you."

Should Stephanie be more forthcoming? Should she open up about her reticence and her nerves? She glanced at the strain in Kelly's smile and Lauren's white knuckles gripping her belly. Only a few more weeks until she left for maternity leave.

The bell rang.

"Let's go get those kids," Kelly said. She plastered on a bright smile and led the way out through Stephanie's door and down the hall toward the playground. Stephanie followed behind.

Should she have explained her situation with Ted and Maddy to her friends? They must know. She hadn't kept the arrangement a secret. But she also hadn't felt she owed anyone a lengthy diatribe about the scenario. She wasn't doing anything wrong.

In a small town, talk spread faster than a brush fire. But no one would talk about her and Ted. What would they say? No one would misconstrue the arrangement. Ted wasn't interested in her in a romantic way. She might be seen as desperate. And—since her sudden recklessness was the truth—she had no reason to lie.

Ted had had big plans for the rest of his weekend. He'd intended to barrel ahead with the deck project and get the joists in position. He'd need help. While Ryan frowned at working on the weekends, Ted counted on Ryan being unwilling to leave Ted to do a two-person job alone, especially once it became clear he was going to continue by himself until the task was accomplished.

With Maddy occupied at the ranch house, Ted had no excuses for distraction or delay. But he hadn't counted on torturing himself about Stephanie after two encounters that left his heart aching. She had slipped into his thoughts at the strangest moments. The breeze had carried a phantom hint of citrus like her shampoo. He almost swore he heard her laughter, and nearly hammered his thumb in the process of looking for her.

The relief of her imagined joy was particularly jarring. Friends didn't find such pleasure in each other's happiness. Neighbors definitely didn't.

The weekend work had been slow and frustrating. He couldn't go on plodding through work with only half his attention. Accidents happened with a lack of focus. He'd proved that when he fell off the fence. When he returned to the ranch after his inspection, he'd found his work gloves and his concentration.

By Monday, he was resolved. He knew the cure. Once he saw her again, he'd act totally normal and friendly. She would do the same out of politeness. Soon, they'd fall back into their usual ways of a cordial—if distant—acquaintance. No feelings necessary.

Reaching into his back pocket, he pulled out a bandana and mopped at the sweat beading on his brow. He had finished the joists earlier, thanks to Ryan for his help. Now he was double checking every screw and nail. The next stage of the build should move faster.

By himself, time passed in strange ways. Hours could go by without him noticing. Or the seconds stood still. With his hands busy, he struggled to focus and not let his mind slip to Stephanie and how much everything would change when Jen returned. He didn't want to miss Stephanie but couldn't seem to stop his thoughts from creeping back to the kitchen at The Golden Crown.

She'd been so broken, and he'd hated it. He didn't want to see her diminished in any way. He would have stormed out and yelled at the offending party if she'd given him the a-okay. He would have done so even without her permission, except then maybe he'd have to start acknowledging she could be someone special. Feelings remained dangerous.

He was off balance with his family life suddenly in upheaval. He'd mellow after his sister returned, and he got back into his normal routine. He stuffed the bandana into his back jeans pocket behind his phone. He owed his sister a call.

Dialing her number, he held the cell against his ear and fought the sigh building in his throat as the line rang. Jen worked nights. Part of the appeal of her new job nearby was the switch to days. Getting ahold of her could be a task but on the fourth ring the call connected. "Hey, Jen. It's me, your brother."

"Hi," she said, her voice slightly husky. She cleared her throat. "Sorry, just got up. How's it going? Thanks for the emails and texts. I miss Maddy. I'll be glad once I'm finally moved to Montana."

"Things are good. Maddy is settling in. She loves the ranch. You might have trouble convincing her to move into town." He chuckled. He'd have trouble watching her go.

"Good, I'm glad to hear. She's not too much trouble for you?"

"Never, and you know it. That girl is an old soul. She's fitting in well with her classmates, too."

"Oh, good." Jen sighed. "I've had a few emails from the teacher and—to be honest—I'm not quite sure what to think."

He frowned and dropped his gaze to the ground. He didn't want to care. But his heartbeat picked up its pace and his throat started to go dry. "Really? How so?"

Kicking at a rock, he dug the toe of his boot into the dry, dusty ground. Did Jen disapprove of Stephanie? He wanted them to get along. At the very least, Stephanie offered him a massive amount of help he could never repay. He didn't want to put either woman in a difficult spot of being forced to get along with someone they didn't like. Beyond that, he thought they could be friends. Unless he'd read them both wrong.

"Nothing bad. She sent the emails to the entire class. Just her expectations of the year and I guess she wants to limit parent involvement. I got one like a few minutes ago about needing to schedule ahead if you wanted an in-person meeting."

"I'm sure she had a reason. She always has others best interests at heart." *Even when they don't deserve it.* A flash of Stephanie's sad smile popped into his mind. Until he'd hugged her, he hadn't realized how he'd longed to hold and be held by another person. She stirred up all sorts of long buried emotions. *And soon it'll be over.* He had to get through the next week. Then they'd fall back into a more comfortable, easy friendship. He could avoid her and not have to worry about pesky personal problems. "She's been a big help to me with Maddy."

"I'll be glad to meet her and get a feel for her myself. Maddy loves her. I'm sure she's great."

She is. Stephanie would be someone worth risking pain and heartbreak for. Ted never intended to be alone and childless. But he couldn't have a family of his own. He had to be content to be close to his sister's. Because love was no guarantee of forever. While his wife had been tragically taken in an accident, his sister had been broken by simply pulling apart.

Jen and her ex moved further away from each other one inch at a time during a difficult pregnancy and the subsequent infant year. Cracks that had been patched and smoothed over, her husband's lack of empathy a major factor, could no longer remain hairline. The fissures stretched until the foundation rotted. And they split.

"You don't think she's great?" Jen asked.

"What?" He shook his head. "Sorry, I'm distracted. In the middle of a big project, you know how it is."

Jen snorted. "Yep. I'll be glad to finish packing and meet the movers."

"When does Dane leave?"

"In about a month. He'll come up to say goodbye and make sure she's settled in."

How nice of him to care about his child. Ted's upper lip curled but he didn't say the cheeky remark. Dane wasn't the guy his sister deserved, but he wasn't a villain. In fact, he'd been remarkably reasonable throughout their marriage and divorce. Co-parenting was complicated.

Ted could take a chance on love and start a family only for the whole scenario to blow up in his face. And what if his future ex wasn't as level-headed? Why bring a child into a doomed world AND a miserable marriage?

Life didn't hold guarantees. He might gamble the occasional hand with other players he could read like a book. But he never played for high stakes. Falling in love demanded a vulnerability that he couldn't accept again.

Not even for someone as sweet as Stephanie. He was jumping ahead, and he knew it. But he couldn't stop himself from analyzing a situation from all sides. "What is your plan? Have you found an apartment that'll work?"

"Not yet. Is it okay if we bunk with you for a little while? I'm having the movers take everything to storage close to the hospital. Then, when I'm ready, they'll haul it all to the final destination. Although, part of me wants to just sell everything and start over completely."

"Don't do that. You'll regret it."

"You did," she murmured.

And he had second thoughts for the first year. As a widower living in his hometown, he'd been given advice from everyone at all times. He'd been told not to make any big decisions by lifelong family friends, the bank teller, his dentist, and—more significantly—his lawyer. They'd all advised to stay put for a year and then make choices.

But the morning of day three hundred and sixty six, he couldn't stay put. He'd never had a wandering heart and always been content in their town. Once Liv was gone, she took the light out of the golden state. He sold the farm and almost all his belongings. He gave hers to her family. Now, years later, he wished he'd held on to some things. But he feared creating totems and holding himself back. He didn't need to worry about objects; his mind took over the task all on its own even from several states—and a whole lifestyle—away.

"ETA is Sunday?"

"I'll try for Saturday, but yes, realistically, Sunday. Tonight is my last shift. Then I'll just be packing."

"Okay, sounds good. Bye, Jen."

"Love you, Teddy."

He hung up and stuffed his phone back into his pocket. He had to get off the line before he stirred up more thoughts. He preferred action to premeditation. Especially when he couldn't take any deed.

Stephanie glanced at the bag in her hands and back up to the cabin's door. Nibbling her lip, she couldn't decide if self-confidence or self-sabotage had spurred her to drive to Ted's house after dark. Whatever motivated her, she was here, readying herself to knock with the lamest excuse possible.

She fisted her hand and raised it to the door, knocking quickly before dropping the heavy appendage to her side to grip the tote bag again. Like a flimsy canvas sack containing an assortment of Maddy's things—mostly socks and sweatshirts she'd slipped off during the school day—from her car would provide her with protection from embarrassment. She couldn't stop thinking about the stolen moments she'd spent together with Ted. Each had been spontaneous and natural. Tonight, she was forcing an encounter.

The door opened.

"Stephanie? Hi," he murmured, slipping outside. "I thought I heard a knock at the door but wasn't sure. What's up?"

She thrust the bag forward, hitting him square in the chest. "I've been collecting Maddy's lost clothing. I realized just how much I had and figured you'd probably need it. You know. To do her laundry?" Stephanie's voice was squeaky and awkward. Her skin flushed.

"Oh, right." He held the bag to his chest. "Thanks. I appreciate it."

She took a deep breath. She was glad he hadn't asked why she didn't just give the items to him tomorrow or let Maddy bring them inside. She'd wanted to see him. But now, once again, her small talk skills vanished. So much for the progress she'd imagined them making. "Well . . ."

"Maddy is asleep inside, and Hank is here, watching her for me. I wanted to stop by the barn and give Cupcake a little extra attention. She had a minor cut that I've been applying salve to every night."

"Did she jump a fence, too?"

He stared at her for a long second. Stephanie held her breath. She'd thought she was charming him. Was she wrong? Tonight was a mistake. She was only proving that she couldn't pursue anything because of her awkwardness.

And then he chuckled, the sound warm and welcoming. He rocked back on his heels, turning his face up toward the sky and the moon shining on his broad grin. "That's a good one. Do you want to join me?"

"Can I? I've never spent much time around horses. Would I be a liability?"

He shook his head. "You'll be fine. Hold on a sec." He opened the door a crack and dropped the tote bag inside. He shut the door and motioned for her to follow him down the path that led around the pond. He didn't speak again for several minutes.

She didn't mind. Sure, her inner voice might be telling her he didn't want to draw attention to their presence. He didn't want people to know she was here. But she squashed that unhelpful voice.

"I don't like to talk too much on my rounds," he murmured, leaning close as she fell into step beside him. "I hate to spoil the quiet out here. It's so peaceful."

She nodded, gratitude welling up inside her and cutting off a verbal response. He'd somehow guessed what she'd been thinking. She enjoyed the companionable silence the rest of the loop to the horse barn.

Set at a distance from the spa barn and lodging, the steel structure was the last new structure Susie Kincaid championed. Royal blue from the roof to the walls and the trim, the horse barn was a bright pop of color against the brown structures nearby. On a sunny day, the building shone as sparkling as the sky. During the snow-filled winter months, the sight was inspiring, reminding Stephanie of brighter, warmer days ahead.

Ted continued to the man door, unlocked it, and held it open for her.

She stepped inside, passing him by mere inches. She couldn't focus on that when the smell of hay, manure, feed, and wood overwhelmed her. With a hand, she covered her nose and mouth and stepped to the side.

"You get used to it," Ted said. He tipped his head to the right. "Come on, she's down here."

Stephanie followed his lead, passing the horses in their stalls. Neighs and whinnies greeted them as they passed. Ted offered the friendlier horses pats on their noses but didn't stop for long.

"Is this your favorite part of the job? Taking care of the animals?" she asked, remembering his degree.

"It's the most cut and dried part of my job," he said over his shoulder as he continued walking. "It's why I was hired."

She nodded. At the height of the ranching days over a century earlier, more than fifty horses lived and worked on the land. By the end of the cattle operation, however, the Kincaids only had thirty-five horses. Since then, the numbers had hovered around twenty.

At the last stall, Ted stopped. He pulled a pair of work gloves out of his pocket.

She noticed he hadn't changed his bandages and frowned. "You need to change the dressing and check for infection."

He slipped the gloves on. "I did. These look the same because they kind of are. I liked what you used so I bought some like them at the store. Thanks again for stopping to help."

"Any time."

He lifted the latch on the door and let himself inside, shutting himself in with Cupcake. He focused on the horse, pulling out several sugar cubes from his back pocket for her as he approached. But he kept talking to Stephanie. "And, while I appreciate the offer, after careful consideration, I won't be taking you up on your offer for painting the fence."

She grinned. "Your loss."

"Probably," he murmured.

Cupcake gummed his palm, happily munching and shaking her tail.

"May I see your leg, ma'am?" he asked the horse in the same tone of voice he'd speak to a human.

Cupcake shook her mane and neighed.

"Please?" he asked, holding firm with his tone, and only lifting an eyebrow.

Cupcake lifted her front leg onto a hay bale in her stall.

"Good girl, Cupcake," he said, pulling the salve from his other pocket and making quick work of applying the protectant to a raised bumpy section. "Don't tell the others, but this is why you're my favorite." He finished rubbing the product into the horse's skin and pet her nose.

"Wow. You're great." Stephanie flushed at her breathless exclamation. "With her."

"She's the easiest horse. She's probably a person reincarnated. She gets all the credit." He slipped out of the stall, careful to latch the door closed.

"I've never ridden a horse."

"Really? How is that possible?"

She shrugged. "I didn't grow up around here."

"Neither did I. But we still had horses." He bumped her with his shoulder. "Would you like to try?" he asked, his voice a breath above a whisper. "I can take you out."

"Can it be . . . not in front of other people? I don't want to flail for a crowd."

"But you don't mind falling in front of me?" he asked.

His question sounded almost wistful. "Of course not. Because we're friends. I trust you." Her voice almost shook on the last part. The more she got to know him, the man she'd had an unrequited crush on for years from afar, the more she liked him. She was probably a fool to keep putting herself in his path. She'd probably end up with a broken heart. But she couldn't seem to help herself.

"Thank you," he said. "Then I'll have to find time to schedule something soon. This is a good time of year to ride without too many people around. Cupcake is the horse to ride. She's a sweetheart."

"I'll hold you to it."

"You'd better." He grinned. "We'd better get back. It's a school night, after all."

She wouldn't forget it. Every moment together was printed onto her brain for posterity. Unfortunately, her heart carried the same burden.

CHAPTER
10

Stephanie spent Tuesday looking over her shoulder. She hadn't received any more emails from parents or surprise drop-ins. But she obsessively checked the inbox after she got home last night, when she first woke up, and throughout the school day. During quiet time and morning snack, at recess, after lunch, she hit refresh on her email account almost minute by minute. And she crept towards the classroom door, scanning the hallway, more often than she could count. By the end of school, she was exhausted.

She didn't need to glance in a mirror to see the dark smudges under her eyes. She felt the scratch every time her eyelids closed over her dry eyes. Her students were unnaturally quiet, too. Kids fed off energy, and when the teacher was completely wiped, they either acted up or were silent. Luckily, they chose calm. She wasn't sure she'd have the stamina to last the whole day with naughty behavior.

As it was, she didn't use different character voices during story time. She leaned heavily into independent work time today, passing out more coloring sheets than ever. She usually viewed her students' antics from a good-natured lens. Today, optimism wasn't so easy.

No one woke up and decided to be terrible and mean. Sometimes, a person acted up without any real justification. Honest mistakes could hurt feelings just as much as a premeditated moment. She encouraged grace among the kids and treated them with such herself. With not-so-subtle threats from two of their parents, however, she was on edge.

As the last bell rang, she dropped her shoulders and rolled her neck. Thank goodness. She stood at the front of the room, writing sight words on the dry erase board in giant letters. She recapped the marker and turned, plastering on a bright smile.

At the tables, the students stared at her with rapt attention. No jumping up to race out of the room. Kindergarteners still loved to learn.

She wanted to inspire them to keep the positive momentum going through all the years of their education ahead. "Who knows this word?"

Four hands shot up. The usual suspects.

She scanned the whole room, giving each child another opportunity.

At a table in the center, Maddy held her hand at her shoulder. Her fingers trembled, and she slowly lifted and lowered her arm.

"Maddy? Can you give it a try?" Stephanie asked, eager to give the little girl a chance. She was smart but uncertain when speaking in front of the entire class. In her small reading group, she shone. With practice and encouragement, she could build her self-confidence among her peers.

"Nn . . . oo . . ." She scrunched her brow.

A few murmurs filled the room.

Stephanie shot a stern look at each table.

"Now?" Maddy said.

Stephanie grinned, beaming for the first time all day. "Great job. That was a tricky one. Okay class, please line up, and we'll head to the multi-purpose room."

Chairs scrapped against the floor, and the room filled with excited chatter.

She strode toward the door. In forty minutes, she could be on her couch with a good book. If she could give herself a night off from overthinking . . . She shook her head and dropped her gaze to the class.

In the back, Grayden and Amelia stood close, whispering, and darting glances her way.

At least the little girl wasn't jockeying to be line leader. Stephanie wouldn't be intimidated by the child or her mean girl mother. "Ready?"

The children quieted.

She opened the door and led her class down the hall to the multi-purpose room. The students filed into the room one at a time. The second and first graders had already been seated. Her class took space on the floor at the front.

Maddy hung back, near the door.

Stephanie lifted her gaze to Kelly, the teacher in charge of this week's dismissal.

Kelly flashed a thumbs up and a soft smile.

With a nod, Stephanie stepped into the hall, Maddy at her side, and let the door shut behind them. Next week, Stephanie would be the adult in the multi-purpose room. She'd have to remember to pack extra ibuprofen.

The multi-purpose room sat at the end of the early elementary hall connecting to the front offices. From the corner of her gaze, she spotted movement. She turned and spied the back of a woman's head.

Slicked back hair in a smooth bun, the severe style didn't fit any of the teachers. Stephanie frowned, who could it be? Someone from the board of education? Then the woman's profile came into view.

Candace stood in the waiting area for the principal's office.

Stephanie sucked in a breath. She would know the other woman's determined chin and haughty tilt of her head anywhere. No one else dressed to kill. Being a female in a high-powered career meant she navigated a world where her femininity was used for and against her. Stephanie respected the difficult balance. But she did her best to avoid the woman's spiky, slim stilettos.

Stephanie took a step down the hall, out of the line of sight of the office. She extended her hand.

Maddy reached for her fingers and squeezed.

Stephanie smiled. For the thousandth time, she reminded herself helping a child wasn't a capital offense. The guilt didn't shift. They strolled down the hallway and back into the classroom.

Stephanie shut the door, scanning the hallway. She was acting paranoid. Candace Vane had other children at the school and plenty of reasons to be in the building. Stephanie crossed to her desk. "Maddy, let me just get some things pulled together, and then we'll go."

The little girl nodded, sat on the alphabet rug, and pulled a book out of her backpack.

A knock sounded at the door

Stephanie's breath caught in her throat and her chest squeezed tight.

The knock sounded again.

"Come in," she croaked and dried her palms on her slacks. She hadn't even pulled out her chair and already she was set for an ambush? She'd waited all day and still she wasn't prepared. Her arms hung heavy and limp.

The door opened and a head peeked around the frame.

"Joe?" Stephanie sighed.

He entered and shut the door behind him. With a smile for Maddy, he crossed the room. "Sorry if I'm a disappointment."

She waved a hand in the hair. "Not at all." *You're a relief.* She didn't want to lose her job or be put on the spot in her classroom where she'd always felt safe. "How can I help you?"

"I wanted to congratulate you on the poker tournament." He smiled and stopped in front of her desk.

He made no move to sit or get comfortable. Whatever he had to say wouldn't be a long chat. Good. She wanted to leave. "Thank you. It's become a real community effort. I'm glad to do my part."

He nodded. "We all chip in and help each other. Can I help you with anything else?" He tilted his head to the side and raised both eyebrows.

On the rug, Maddy dragged her finger through the lines of her book.

She probably wasn't reading as much as giving a good performance for the grown-ups. It tugged at Stephanie's heart a little bit. The little girl was living through a lot of emotional turmoil at the moment. Moving to a new state, her father leaving, staying with her uncle, her mother gone, and she'd started school. It would be too much for most grown-ups.

Maddy was sensitive and tough. She was a surprising combo of both and reminded Stephanie so much of Ted. The little girl had provided both a reason to interact with him and a rare chance to get to know him better. She'd always be grateful for both. And with only a few more days left in her carpool, she wouldn't squander even one opportunity to see him.

Clearing her throat, she met Joe's quizzical gaze. She understood his warning but she couldn't back down now. *In for a penny, in for a pound.* "We're great. Heading out now."

"Okay." He stepped back. "Bye, Maddy. Tell your Unc I said hi."

Maddy nodded.

Joe strolled out the room, leaving the door ajar.

Stephanie opened the bottom drawer of her desk, grabbed her purse, stuffed her laptop into the bag, and pulled out her keys. "Ready?"

Maddy scrambled to her feet. She hadn't taken off the backpack so she nearly toppled from her adjusted center of gravity. But she caught her balance and rose, clutching the book to her chest. "We're having dinner at the big house tonight. Mr. Hank said I could come over right after school and help. Miss Meg is there baking." Maddy licked her lips.

"Okay, the big house it is."

With one reply, Maddy began to chatter.

Stephanie smiled and tuned out the excited rush of words. She had too much floating through her mind to focus on Colby's new tricks. She turned off the lights, shut the door, and led Maddy down the hall and out the doors to the teacher's parking lot at the back of the school. She helped Maddy into the car seat and got behind the wheel. She turned the keys in the ignition and reversed out of her space. She started to relax, and then she turned forward, put the car in drive, and met the gaze of Candace Vane.

Crossing the lot to her own vehicle, Candace turned her head from one side to the other.

Maybe she hadn't spotted Stephanie and Maddy. More likely than not, she had.

Stephanie gulped. Paranoia and frustration could control her if she let them. She wouldn't. Because she refused to regret a single second of the past few weeks.

Ted strode along the covered porch of the ranch house. Under the guise of a break, he'd timed his arrival to coincide with Maddy's drop-off. Hopefully she had remembered to tell Stephanie to bring her to the main house.

Leaning against the post near the stairs, he stared across the dusty, dead grass toward the road. His conversation with Jen still nagged at him a day later. Through the day, as he made steady progress on the deck working from one side to the next, nailing in each board, he replayed his sister's words about her downsizing and relocating plans.

You did. She couldn't know the taunt from the obvious reply. He had sold his belongings in hopes that he wouldn't look at a random object and be thrown to the ground, overwhelmed with a wave of longing and nausea. But distancing himself from the things he'd owned during his marriage hadn't worked.

For the longest time, even the sun had mocked him and revived memories long-buried. At the time of her death, he'd spent half his life in love with Liv. Now he'd lived over a decade without her. And he had started to forget the details of day-to-day life. He wanted those random scraps to prove their time together hadn't been a dream.

Because he felt a pull towards someone new. And he knew he couldn't trust himself and she especially shouldn't. He'd let down Liv. If he hadn't asked her to go to the store, he would still have her. It was a random, tragic car accident. No one blamed him. Except his conscience.

In the distance, a red car appeared, driving toward the ranch. After Jen returned, she'd take over Maddy's schedule. If he bumped into Stephanie, then maybe he'd see these past few days in a different light. With distance in time and space, he hoped to stop thinking about the meaningless, chaste kiss and feeling the phantom press of her lips on his cheek. When they were on an even field, neither holding power over the other, then perhaps reality would strip some of the magic from his memories.

As the car neared, music blared.

He came down the steps, straining for the melody.

The car entered the half circle drive in front of the house and stopped.

"Sisters" from *White Christmas* filtered out of the car. The engine kept running, even after the vehicle stopped and parked.

With a wave, he jogged toward the driver's side, leaning against the side mirror. "I didn't know you liked musicals."

Stephanie turned and smiled. "I don't. But Maddy suggested this soundtrack for our drives, and I finally remembered to download the music to my phone."

"Yep," a little voice said in the backseat. Maddy grinned. "And now Miss Patricks knows all the words for her part. She's Betty, and I'm Judy."

Stephanie shot him a frown, the corner of her eyes pinched and her mouth downturned.

He swallowed a chuckle. She looked put on the spot, like she worried he'd test her.

"Your family has provided quite the education in movies," Stephanie said.

He studied her face. She looked unwell. Her eyes were almost sunken and her skin too pale. He should let her go. But he didn't want her to leave. "Thanks for dropping her off. Would you like to come inside? Hank cooks for a hundred."

She shook her head. "Not tonight."

Her words were soft and sad. He wanted to ask her a follow-up and wipe that downtrodden expression off her face. He'd seen her upset two times too many. He was powerless. He stepped back from the driver's side and opened the backseat door for Maddy.

The little girl hopped down and raced around the car. Her heavy steps thudded against the front stairs.

With a chuckle, he shut the back door. "Thanks again."

She nodded.

He stepped away from the car and waved an arm, watching her pull out of the spot and drive away. She wasn't her usual friendly self. Last night, she hadn't needed much encouragement to join him at the horse barn. Was she regretting their time together? That didn't seem to fit the companionable chat they'd had.

Joe might know what was troubling her if it involved the school. Stephanie worked so hard and tirelessly, it seemed doubtful anyone would have an issue with her. Except for jealousy. She came into town and started to impact the community in real, positive ways almost from the start.

He'd lived in Herd for years before she arrived and hardly knew another person in the community. She wasn't exactly walking around and introducing neighbors to one another, but she helped facilitate more events for the whole town to come together. If he called Joe, what would he say? How would he open the conversation without sounding suspicious?

Shaking his head, he crunched the gravel under his boots and strode up the front steps. Maddy had left the door ajar. He entered, toed off his boots, and shut the solid wood panel behind him.

From the front entry, Ted could turn his head to look into the front room or up to the top of the stairs and the gallery overhead leading to the second-floor bedrooms. In both directions, he spotted a wide collection of chew toys, blankets, and no less than three dog beds. A certain cowboy, who once declared pets were frivolous and that animals served only work purposes, had changed his tune. Careful not to step on one of the squeaky stuffed animals, he picked his way toward the kitchen, following his ears and nose.

Melted butter, braised beef, and a rich broth floated on the air. Water rushed out of a faucet. Low timber laughter mixed with a high-pitched giggle.

Ted strode through the open doorway and into the kitchen. In tourist season, when the ranch house doubled as the check-in, a swinging panel blocked the heart of the home from visitors. With the summer over, the door was propped open and invited everyone to come in.

The large kitchen overlooked the backyard and backside of the wraparound porch. At the sink, Meg tied an apron around Maddy's waist as Maddy washed her hands. An eight-burner stove took up the short wall to the right. Hank stood with a spoon, stirring a stew.

In the corner at a farmhouse table battered and bruised from generations, Ryan sat behind a laptop screen, his face brightened by the glow of the computer, in his seat to the right of the head of the table. Nearby, a fifty pound, black and white mutt slept on yet another dog bed. Snoring louder than Ted's college roommate, the dog's tail thumped a nearby cabinet as she beat an out of rhythm syncopation.

Although he was glad to be welcomed into the warmth, the kitchen scene was domestic chaos. Only a few months ago, the equal numbers of females to males, dog included, would have been strange. Since the passing of Hank's wife, Susie, the ranch had been a testosterone zone. Hank was a good cook, but the conversation was lacking. After a few words of gratitude and compliments on the meal, talk usually turned into a companionable run down of the day's work, and maybe conversation of whatever sport was currently televised.

Now, with the addition of Meg and Colby, he never knew what to expect. Meg ran the antique store in town and had a penchant for learning interesting facts. She loved to read, talk to newcomers, and always picked up tidbits here and there. She wasn't a gossip and never spoke ill of anyone. Rather, she discovered anecdotes and articles that made a person stop and consider a different perspective. Over the summer, she had changed the tenor of the mealtimes for the better.

While Maddy was a new arrival, she clearly fell into step with the crowd. It did him good to see his found family and his blood come together. He knocked on the doorframe.

Four heads turned in his direction.

"Thanks for having us over," Ted said.

"Of course." Hank turned back to the stove.

"Maddy and I are going to make the biscuits," Meg said.

The little girl hopped off the stool at the sink. "All yours, Unc."

He chuckled and walked to the sink. After thoroughly scrubbing his hands, he approached the table, sitting opposite his boss.

Ryan lifted his gaze off the screen. "I sent you the itinerary for our trip. It's going to be a busy few days. But you can always call if you need anything."

Ted knew, but he wasn't planning on reaching out. The trio would be busy, squeezing in several big meetings into a few days. Before Memorial Day, Hank's last-ditch attempt at setting up Meg and Ryan involved cleaning out the old shed and—by luck—the uncovering of a treasure trove of antique souvenir cards and photographs from Buffalo Bill Cody's Wild West Show. With the items now up for sale at an auction house in San Francisco, Hank and Meg had been planning to attend for months.

Ryan was an add-on to the original trip, citing the bison as his reason for joining. Ted wondered if Ryan didn't have an ulterior motive for the trip as well. The city by the bay was romantic for a proposal. While Meg and Ryan had only dated for a few months, their fate seemed written in the stars. A quick engagement and marriage wouldn't surprise anyone.

"I'm sure we'll be fine," Ted said. Over his shoulder, he glanced at the still sleeping dog. The hardest part of his weekend would be keeping Maddy from trying to play with the mutt around the clock. Colby liked rest.

"When is your sister comming?" Meg asked.

Lifting his leg, Ted sat sideways on the bench to keep an eye on everyone.

Standing at the counter with Maddy, Meg oversaw the cutting of the biscuits.

"Probably Sunday," Ted said.

"Are you okay to bunk here at the big house with Colby?" Hank asked.

"Absolutely. We'll take good care of her," Ted said.

"I've got a sleeping bag, Mr. Hank," Maddy chimed in.

"Oh, I'm not worried about you, darling." Hank winked at the little girl.

"What else is happening?" Ryan asked. "Do you need more room at the cabin? Are you cramped? You can use one of the guest cabins while your sister and Maddy get settled."

"Thanks." Ted nodded. "We're good. I like having the company."

He glanced at his niece. Her broad smile brightened him from the inside out.

What would it be like when she moved away? Would the quiet become oppressive? He couldn't think about losing her. Her arrival had been an unexpected blessing, as the good things usually were.

Life on the ranch offered more than he could ever have imagined. Change was good, bad, and inevitable. As long as he limited his variables, he'd be fine. If he expanded his social circle too quickly, he'd pop like an overinflated balloon.

CHAPTER 11

Nothing could snap Stephanie out of the doldrums faster than being helpful. When she had arrived home on Tuesday night, she answered an urgent call from Kelly. Lauren's doctor put her on bedrest effective Friday. The surprise school baby shower had to be moved up a few weeks to Thursday.

Tuesday night, she called Will at the general store and ordered the cake and balloons. The science teachers would no doubt frown at the use of helium as the world's supply of the resource dwindled but needs must. She'd pass out if she had to inflate the balloons herself. She reached out to Abby Whit, owner of the barbeque food truck, and scheduled a lunchtime treat for the staff. While not every grade took lunch at the same time, Abby would be parked outside for several hours to give everyone the chance for a complimentary meal. It was the biggest expenditure for the party but well worth it.

On Wednesday, she sent emails to the entire staff about the change. Those who were able coordinated with aides to watch their classes so, at the very least, they could be present when Lauren walked into the lounge. With a firm deadline, Stephanie focused.

The old adage *if you want something done, give it to a busy person* was almost her guiding life principle. She didn't like downtime and had never done well with time on her hands. She found her purpose and happiness in working and helping others.

As a result, her kids perked up. Wednesday was the smoothest day of school so far. No tantrums or tears. Everyone shared nicely and actively engaged in learning. She left the building feeling light as a feather with a broad smile.

Until she dropped off Maddy and saw Ted and reality slammed into her. She'd only have two more—rational, non-stalker—days to see him. Nothing had changed. Since she found her voice, she hadn't gone back to silence. But they sort of stagnated at pushing any further ahead.

She had no other conversation starters. Once again, they had nothing in common and no shared interests. How could she bring up his love of ska music or the movies of his youth without coming across as a total creep?

The age gap didn't matter to her, and she didn't think anyone in town would particularly care. But he must see it as a non-starter. Technically, they were from different generations. He grew up in the last era without social media. That was a huge blessing. Navigating puberty through the lens of influencers had been a nightmare. If anything, that pushed her to work with children too young for the various platforms. She couldn't imagine having to explain the ins and outs of the apps or warning signs to be on the lookout for when everything changed so rapidly.

She would be glad for Maddy's life to return to her new normal with her mom's move. Stephanie would be glad too that any hint of impropriety would be gone in her interactions. But she would miss Ted. Deep in her bones she knew for certain they could be happy if he let her in. She swallowed the sigh building in her throat and sat still in her chair.

Jumping out and yelling at a very pregnant woman was probably exactly the sort of thing Lauren's doctor wanted her to avoid. Stephanie scanned the room. In the teacher's lounge, with all the lights on, everyone gathered and sat, waiting for the guest of honor. It was decided slowly walking into a room full of people was enough of a surprise without causing a shock.

Kelly's voice filtered down the hall.

Stephanie sat straighter.

Lauren entered the room, stepping through the curtain of blue and pink streamers. With wide eyes, she twisted her neck from one side to the other. She covered her mouth with her hands.

Stephanie held her breath. Oh no. Had she miscalculated? Should she have let Lauren start her leave without a celebration? Stephanie pushed back her chair and reached her friend.

Kelly stood on Lauren's other side.

Lauren sniffed and met Stephanie's gaze with watery eyes. "Did you do all of this? For me?"

"Is that okay?" Stephanie asked.

Lauren nodded, tears streaming down her face. "Uh huh."

Kelly pulled out a tissue and handed it over not a moment too soon.

Lauren blew her nose, loudly. "Thank you all. So much." Her shoulders shook as a sob wracked her body. "You are too kind to me."

Stephanie wrapped an arm around her friend's shoulders and squeezed.

Lauren tilted her head, resting on Stephanie's shoulder.

Kelly stepped forward. "Okay, let's eat cake. I know a lot of you have to get back to your classes. Don't forget, Abby Whit is in the parking lot serving lunch today. It's our treat."

A cheer sounded and the room erupted into applause.

"Is this okay? Do you want to leave?" Stephanie whispered into Lauren's ear, rubbing her back.

Lauren nodded her head and stepped away.

Kelly handed her another tissue.

Dabbing at her face, Lauren balled up the tissue and lifted her red, splotchy face. "This is wonderful." She extended her hands.

Stephanie grabbed one and Kelly the other.

Lauren squeezed their hands. "Thank you both. For everything. I was really hoping to make it to Back-to-School night."

"We'll cover for you," Stephanie said.

"We always have each other's backs," Kelly added. "Come on, let's get you and the babies some cake. You need to put those feet up."

Stephanie dropped her hold and winked as Lauren rolled her eyes.

Kelly rarely played her leader card but, when she did, the other two knew better than to fight her. With a tug, she led Lauren toward the table in the center. The older grade teachers formed a line to grab a pre-plated slice of cake and then file past Lauren and offer their congratulations.

Joe approached Stephanie with a wave.

"Hi," she said. "You're getting quite cozy in the elementary wing lately."

He chuckled. "Mere coincidence, I assure you. I have to ask. When did you have time to throw this together?"

She lifted a shoulder in a shrug. "If it's important, you make time. Friends are always worth it."

He nodded. "Maybe you'd be better at party planning for Hank's big ninetieth celebration next summer."

She turned toward him, studying his face. His tone was forced. Was he pretending he'd just had this brainstorm idea? Or waiting for the perfect opportunity to unload? "Well, I probably would."

He frowned.

She stifled a laugh. *If you don't want the answer, don't ask the question.* "I'm already swamped with Frontier Days at the same time. And if I'm working on the ranch again next summer while finishing up the school year here, I'd really be too busy. But . . . to be honest?"

He faced her.

He looked hopeful. She hated to be the one to dash his plans but owed him the truth. "I already asked Mr. Kincaid if he wanted me to take over, and he refused."

Joe sighed, rolling his shoulders forward.

His animosity with Abby Whit was well-documented and unavoidable. Although it didn't make a lick of sense to her. The food truck owner was kind, friendly, and helpful. A recent transplant, she'd become a pretty indispensable vendor for both civic and private events. What could Joe possibly have against the woman? She smiled too much?

"Thanks for trying. I'd better give Lauren my regards before I head upstairs," Joe said.

She nodded and stepped back, her legs hit something. Startled, she turned and spotted the principal seated at the table she'd walked into. "Oh, sorry." She frowned.

On the tabletop, a splash of coffee formed a ring around the mug nearest her boss.

He waved off her concern, pulling a paper towel out of his pocket. "I don't go anywhere in this building without paper towels."

Smiling, she pulled out a chair and sat. "Thanks for your help with this last-minute switch."

"Of course. I'm honestly surprised she lasted this long. When my wife had our twins, she went on leave at seven months."

"Wow."

He nodded. "She was on bedrest for a month. A very, very long four weeks. Hopefully Lauren's time will be easier."

Stephanie smiled. She had nothing to add but made no move to leave. She sat, giving her principal plenty of opportunity to request a meeting or speak frankly. Following the run-in Monday and spotting Candace on Tuesday, she hadn't heard a peep from administration. Neither had she received any more emails from the parents.

"Good to see you and Kelly coming together. Kindergarten is a real team," Bill said.

Stephanie smiled. "We are. Lauren will be missed, but Kelly and I will help her sub."

"Good to hear. If you'll excuse me, I have to get back to a few meetings." He pushed back from the table.

"Of course. Don't let me keep you."

With a nod, he turned and made his way over to Lauren.

With a deep breath in, she held the air in her lungs for a count of five and slowly exhaled. She could and would continue to advocate for her students and the entire student population.

Luckily, with only herself impacted by her choices, she wasn't risking much.

Ted loaded the last of the luggage into the back of the SUV and frowned. The back of the vehicle was packed floor to ceiling with suitcases. The small SUV was the tiniest of the vehicles they could have chosen. Meg had argued against one of the trucks, pointing out the complexities of parking in a city.

Perhaps she had a false impression of how much was needed for their trip. For a long weekend away, the trio had probably overpacked. The worst offender was Hank, dropping off two large rolling upright suitcases at the last moment.

Luckily, Ted didn't mind a challenge or re-doing all his hard work. He emptied the trunk and reconfigured the bags in record time. He didn't want to be the reason the group was held up. Not that any of them would blame him.

Ryan decided to leave Thursday afternoon instead of Friday morning, squeezing in more time at their destination. For someone who planned everything, the sudden spontaneous switch was suspicious. And had more likely than not been his schedule all along. As to the reasons, he didn't share the details with his traveling companions or cowboy. Ted had his guess.

Taking a step back, Ted shut the trunk door and wiped his hands on his jeans. He strode to the driver's side. "You're all set. Have a safe drive."

With the window rolled down, Ryan leaned against the door, behind the wheel. "We will. Meg's practically opened up a coffee shop in the front seat." He pointed at four travel mugs, occupying every cupholder.

"I don't love starting a long drive late in the day. Caffeine it is." Meg leaned over Ryan. "If you have any problems with Colby, please call."

Like, trouble getting the dog to walk? Colby hadn't left the couch to bid adieu to her humans. The dog expended no extra energy. Ted had no non-cheeky response. He nodded.

The backseat window rolled down. "Hey, do me a favor," Hank called.

Ted approached the back seat. Hank sat in the center with pillows on either side of him. Either he'd be asleep in no time, or he'd comment on Ryan's driving from the safety of his comfortable perch. Maybe a little of both.

"Yes, sir. What do you need?" Ted asked.

"Keep an eye on Abby and Joe. If you can nudge those two together, I'd appreciate your assistance," Hank said.

In the driver's seat, Ryan rolled his eyes. "We're off. Bye, Ted."

Raising his hand to his shoulder, Ted stepped back and waved.

The SUV pulled through the end of the drive and turned down the road. Once the vehicle disappeared, Ted grabbed his phone out of his back pocket. School had ended, but it would be a bit before Stephanie and Maddy arrived. If he started a chore now, he'd be stuck at it too long. Night would fall, and he'd have to turn on the lights to finish. Maddy would be left alone in an unfamiliar in the dark house.

He didn't need to do more than heat the oven to make dinner. The kitchen was fully stocked for the weekend. Hank had prepared one of Maddy's favorite dinners, stuffed peppers. Ted could wander the property, alone with his thoughts for a while. But then he'd circle back to Stephanie and the dwindling time together. And then he might do something stupid like come up with an excuse to see her over the weekend. Asking her to stay tomorrow night after drop-off for a movie as a thank you hovered on his tongue.

He had only one alternative for how to occupy his time. With official confirmation of Hank's meddling from the man himself, Ted owed his friend a heads up. Dialing Joe's number, he pressed the phone against his ear. "You're right," he said without preamble as soon as the line connected.

"I usually am. What is it this time?" Joe asked.

"Hank is setting you up with Abby. Any luck getting yourself off the birthday bonanza project?"

Joe's whoosh exhale answered first. "Stephanie can't help. Bad timing."

Why? Does she have plans? Ted didn't like the boulder that had settled in his gut. Nor could he shake the surge of jealousy. He pinched the bridge of his nose. Hank's birthday wasn't until May. She could hardly plan that far ahead for a date. And if she did? He'd have to be happy for her. She deserved everything she wanted as long as he wasn't included in her plans.

"Ted? You there?"

"Sorry." Ted coughed. "Why can't she help?"

"Frontier Days and working at the ranch, if you'll have her."

Of course I will. He dropped his hand to his side and rolled his shoulders up and back. He needed to focus on the present conversation and not on himself. He'd have his hands full enough over the weekend and didn't need to add on with his own issues. "Hank probably already took that into consideration when the idea first came to him," Ted said. "If you tried, you couldn't get out of it. Why don't you just stick up for yourself with Mr. Kincaid and tell him you don't like Abby."

"As if I haven't made my distrust clear enough already?" Joe snorted. "Do you think my opinion would stop him from his goal? Have you ever tried to stand up against his matchmaking?"

No, he hadn't. After Hank settled Joe, however, would the old cowboy turn his attention in Ted's direction? Or was Ted a lost cause? Maybe Hank would help Stephanie find love. *I don't want to watch that.*

"Can I speak frankly?" Ted asked. While he prided himself on truthfulness, he also understood not everyone could handle bald facts and strong opinions at all times.

"Of course," Joe replied.

"I don't like the way you speak about Abby. Hank isn't even around half the time you speak poorly of her. You don't need to have such a personal vendetta against her."

"I'm only being honest."

"No, you're almost mean when her name comes up."

"When?" Joe's question held barbs and prickles, deflecting the accusation.

"During the conversation the other day with Ryan about helping get her a proper building for her restaurant. She's a good partner for the ranch and a kind neighbor. She needs a little help. So what? Why do you care? Leave your feelings aside and realize she's an important part of the community. Like you. Like all of us."

"Fine." Joe sighed. "You're right. But if I ease up now, I'll only convince Hank I'm softening on her. My best bet is to fall in love over the weekend. The sooner I'm taken, the better for me. If I can find someone in the next seventy-two hours, I'll propose on the spot. I'd love for him to get back and focus on Abby and some other poor schmuck."

Ted rolled his eyes. "Do you have anyone in mind?"

"Of course not. I don't spend my time thinking about her."

The reply had a sharp edge to it that was a little too venomous for the situation. Or did Joe do the opposite? How much of his day was spent circling back to his issues with Abby Whit? "Isn't she friendly with Ian?"

"The blacksmith? No. That wouldn't work. Not at all."

The delivery was crisp, clear, and concise. *And confusing*.

"Why not?" Ted asked. Before the turn in the conversation, he never really noticed or cared. But Joe sure had opinions. "Isn't he helping her with her new smoker? Shared interests is a solid start for a couple. Seems like that pairing would be a good set-up for Hank to pursue next. Take some heat off you."

"Just because I want to save myself doesn't mean I'm going to throw someone else in her path."

Ted shook his head. "What do you have against her? She seems nice enough to me. Every time we've needed help, she doesn't hesitate."

"She's hiding something, and I hate it."

Ted couldn't figure that out. As far as he was concerned Abby was an open book. What could she hide? But he wouldn't say anything to Joe. There was no point. "Okay, I relent. I didn't call to fight. You know I'm out for poker again this weekend?"

"Yep, already told the guys. After your sister gets back, you'll be expected at the saloon every week. No excuses."

After his sister came back, he'd have none. Neither would he have a reason to see Stephanie until the late spring. At least she was planning on working at the ranch next summer. Perhaps by then she would be in a relationship, and he could return his focus to his work and family. His status quo was in the midst of a shake-up. He hadn't planned on change but was finding he didn't hate it. He would hate missing her. "Sounds good. Bye."

"Catch you later."

Ted hung up the call and strolled back towards the house. With the fading daylight, the sky was awash with pinks and blues. He loved the autumn sunset, the soft colors easing the end of his day, but he hated the long nights. In summer, the days stretched into eternity, matching his working hours. Montana hadn't been meant to become his home. He settled down while he was busy ignoring the future.

Was he again at a crossroads? He'd stumbled into a good life and, despite the career changes, managed to keep his world controlled. Something different pulled at him, tugging where his heart used to be. Could he love someone else, even knowing he'd be doomed to fail her? Stephanie would be so easy to fall for and so hard to get over. She was the town's darling, and he wasn't ready to be exiled for hurting her.

He kicked at a large chunk of gravel in his way and strode toward the house. Colby would be expecting her evening meal and then her bed. For one woman, he could meet expectations without tangling his heart in the mix.

CHAPTER 12

Stephanie smoothed her hair behind her ears and dried her clammy hands on her long, flowy pants. Striding down the hall, her heeled steps echoed off the tile floor. Without the buffering of childish giggles or a teacher instructing her class, she only listened to her self-created noises.

The corridor looked like an optical illusion sketch. Could she actually reach the end or would she hit a solid wall painted as an illusion? Could she pick her preferred option?

She had never felt so alone, and her senses confirmed her solitary status. With twenty minutes until the end of the day, she'd thought she was in the clear. Yesterday, at Lauren's baby shower, she had expected a comment from the principal. When he didn't take the opportunity to ask her for a meeting, he gave her hope she had been mistaken.

Perhaps Candace's appearance in the front office earlier in the week after Mrs. Foxx's sudden visit was mere coincidence. Or—more likely—with older children also in the building, Candace simply had other targets for her attack. Last night, Stephanie had slept easier, knowing she only had to make it through one more day and then she'd have fulfilled her obligation and take the weekend to rest and recharge.

Of course, she wasn't totally free of her feelings. Her heart still twisted when she considered next week and the long months ahead until she had a reason to be at the ranch. Couldn't Ryan hurry up and propose to Meg already so the town could celebrate together?

Then, she'd have an excuse to help out around the ranch again. Only, this time, she would have no power imbalance with Ted to get in the way. Although, she didn't think that was the issue. He held himself in check. He wasn't the sort to express any big emotion, swinging from one extreme to the other. Was it because he lost his wife? Did he still grieve her? Stephanie only wished she could have an ounce of that sort of affection directed at her.

She had been happily going through her day. Until a few minutes ago when a knock had sounded on the door. She'd set down the book she'd been reading to the class and opened it to an unknown face holding a note. Could she please come down to meet with the principal as Mrs. Lamb watched her class? Stephanie had smiled to the kids, reassured them she'd be back soon, and strode out the door.

Now, she reached the glass door leading to the front offices. With a hand on the cool, metal pull, she filled her lungs to capacity, tamped down the hot emotions flooding her face. She could do this. Sure, she'd never been asked to come to the principal's office during the day nor had she ever been surprised with a substitute at the door. That didn't mean anything. First time for everything.

She opened the door wide and entered, smiling at the school secretary. "Hello, Wendy. I'm here to see B—"

"He's expecting you," the older woman interrupted.

Stephanie widened her eyes and froze at the curt greeting. Well-past retirement age, Wendy was an excessively kind, grandmotherly type woman. Dressed in matching pastel sweater sets with her silver hair permed, she greeted everyone with a smile and soft word of welcome.

Not me. Not today. With a nod, Stephanie continued past the desk to the open doorway. She stopped outside and knocked on the panel.

Behind the desk, Bill focused on a desktop angled away from the door, toward the windows overlooking the parking lot. He turned toward her, pushing back his chair. "Come in, come in." He smiled and waved to the chair in front of his desk.

She stepped over the threshold and crossed the short distance to the chair. The carpet muffled her steps, but nothing could slow the rapid beat of her heart.

He shut the door.

The click of the lock settling was like a shot. She jerked and lifted her gaze.

Unbuttoning his blazer, he settled behind his desk. He rested his forearms on the top, leaning forward. "Thanks for coming down. I'm sorry for the short notice."

She lifted a shoulder. That was the best response she could give. Inside her chest, she felt fluttery and dizzy. Like she could float off or fall down.

"I'll come straight to the point." He cleared his throat and tugged at his Windsor-knotted neck tie. "Allegations of favoritism and exclusion have arisen from your classroom."

She dropped her jaw. She'd never been accused of either. She knew Candace plotted something unseemly. These words were particularly cruel and carefully chosen, mirroring what she had endured as a child.

"I've been made aware that you have turned away help from a parent in your classroom."

She shut her dry mouth and swallowed. "Yes."

He sighed. "I was hoping that was an exaggeration."

She frowned. "Typically, we don't even put out the call for volunteers in the class until after Back-to-School night next week. The other classrooms haven't sent out any sign-up sheets. I was stunned the parent showed up."

He propped his elbows on the desk, steepling his fingers. "But the parent has older children and would have a reasonable expectation of being welcomed as a volunteer."

How did the parent get inside the building? She couldn't fling that accusation at the principal. But the lapse would need to be addressed at some point for the safety of all. "I was ambushed."

He widened his eyes.

She lifted her chin. "I believe the parent was set up to fail by someone else. I feel bad for the entire situation. I could have handled the impromptu appearance better. But I think Mrs. Foxx was used."

"That's quite a lot to claim."

"It's what happened."

He scrubbed a hand over his face. "Stephanie, you're a great teacher and an asset to this entire school."

But but but her mind rang with the word. She didn't want to supply his lines. She wanted to escape this room and this conversation.

"Are you still driving one of your students home?"

She nodded. He knew she was. Was she on a collision course with losing her job? Over one infraction? About something she'd cleared with the administration? Should she laugh or cry? She wasn't sure one wouldn't inevitably lead to the other. "Today is my last day."

"I wish you would have told me what happened with Mrs. Foxx. When it happened. I could have helped before. . ."

"I didn't want to give it more energy." Her voice cracked from the weight of her honesty. She'd had thought coming to the principal with a *she said-she said* argument was counterproductive. Clearly, someone else disagreed. With everything that had happened since the poker night, she'd pushed the incident from her mind.

"But now you have put yourself, and the school, in a difficult position. You are directly assisting one family but turning away others. I know you are trying to help, but the appearance is misleading and has created a tense situation."

Driving Maddy was a short-term situation. She had asked Mrs. Foxx to leave because, once she allowed one volunteer into the classroom, she would have a rotation of the same few helpers involved every week for the long-term. The kids with working parents would be left out. She never lost sight of her end goal. But she couldn't deny the optics were off.

"I am sorry to say that there is a hint of impropriety, too," Bill said. "Whispers have reached me about your connection with your student's temporary guardian. You have been seen spending time together beyond dropping off your student."

It's nothing. Her ears burned. Any response dried on her shriveled tongue. Ted definitely didn't have any sort of feelings for her, but she couldn't deny her regard.

"The look of the whole thing is the problem. Until I can straighten out the drama, I need to ask you to take a paid leave of absence starting after school today."

What? She gasped. Her mind whirred, and she darted her eyes from side to side, searching for any way out of this situation. "Because I'm driving a child home? I'm in trouble with disciplinary consequences for that."

"It's a little more complicated. Your choice to limit classroom access has created a tense situation for some of our more outspoken parents. Apparently, a petition has been floating around to start a disciplinary hearing into your behavior."

Her jaw dropped. She couldn't believe what she was hearing. But she did. Everyone warned her. Candace Vane was determined and difficult. On a good day. Stephanie shook her head, reaching up to press her cool fingers against her throbbing temples. "I was helping a family. I would do the same for any of my kids. You know that."

He held up a hand. "I believe you. When you first told me about the situation, you were upfront and honest. Today is the last day you'll be driving her home?"

Stephanie nodded, sniffing.

He extended a box of tissues over the top of the desk.

She grabbed one and blew her nose.

"It's a temporary review. You aren't being fired. But we have to go through the motions." He left the tissues on the desk and interlaced his hands.

"I haven't done anything wrong."

"No, you haven't. But perception is reality. Mrs. Vane is convinced there is impropriety. Until we straighten out the mess, we can't have you teach. We have to be seen as taking the correct steps. We support you. I'm doing everything I can to get you back in your classroom as soon as possible."

Perception is reality. If only that were true. Did some people in town think there was more going on with her and Ted? Or was she the desperate woman willing to do everything—including risking her reputation—for a man who wasn't interested?

Or was a cunning person crafting a narrative to manipulate the system and get her way? Stephanie had never heard anyone whisper anything about her and Ted. Would she now? Had Candace spread gossip in town?

"I am sorry to have you gone for any amount of time but especially with Lauren's maternity leave. Hang in there. We will get this figured out. Come to my office on Monday at 10:45 in the morning. We'll talk more then."

She stared at the tissue box. Tears burned her nostrils and clouded her vision. It would be all too easy to curl into a ball and sob. She could crumple.

Tucking her fingers against her palms, she dug her nails into the meaty flesh of her palms. She refused defeat. Instead, she could leave with her head held high and cling to her dignity. She hated when tears were weaponized and wouldn't be caught in that trap herself. No matter what happened next, she wouldn't be accused of manipulation.

She pushed back her chair, stood straight as an arrow, and met his gaze. "Thank you. I'll wait to hear more."

Tipping her head in a tiny nod, she swiveled on her heel and retraced her steps. She wasn't going to cry because of a mean girl's power play. Nor would she glance left or right and catch sight of a frown or commiserating head nod by a member of staff.

With her chin lifted in the air, she strode in determined steps down the hall and back into her classroom. She'd say goodbye for now to the kids but not for good. She'd drive Maddy to the ranch, and then she'd head home and plot. One setback wasn't enough to stop her. She'd found her strength, and she wasn't going to lose.

Ted had never resorted to begging a dog to move. But he'd never taken care of Colby by himself before. Standing at the ranch house's front door, he jingled the leash in the air.

From her perch on the couch in the front room, the dog lifted her head and set it back down on her front paws.

He was sure he'd heard a sigh. Could have been his. Since he returned to the ranch from the school drop-off, he'd tried to encourage the dog to leave the couch with the same poor results. What was he doing wrong?

Didn't dogs love to walk? Wasn't that their thing? A chance to sniff and go to the bathroom and chase squirrels? He frowned. Not many squirrels on the ranch but plenty of other rodents of interest to a canine.

Last night, with Maddy's help, he progressed through the dog's routine with ease. They'd fed her, walked her around the perimeter, and made sure she was comfortable in her bed next to Hank's. He'd been feeling proud of himself and brushed off the notion he'd need to call Hank or Meg. His success had all been an illusion.

As soon as Maddy left, the dog nestled on the couch. He'd come back to check on her as the hours passed, but the dog had only moved from laying on her side to her back. The black and white mutt was unimpressed by him from the start of the day. He just hadn't been smart enough to realize.

The dog gave him the cold shoulder. He wouldn't have thought a dog could snub a human. This one did.

For most of the day, however, leaving the dog in the house to sleep had been the easiest option. He'd checked on her water and petted her as he passed. But if he wasn't offering food, he was of no interest.

He glanced at his watch. Maddy and Stephanie would be home soon. He needed his niece to convince the dog to leave the couch. This was too pathetic. A grown man hired to care for animals shouldn't be overwhelmed by one spoiled, finicky pet. She was probably upset he wasn't Hank or Meg.

What if the dog was ill? Should he drive her into town to see the vet? Doc Hampton would probably make a house-call if necessary. But what if the dog was fine, and he'd charged an astronomical fee to the account for his own stupidity? He was tempted to call Meg but didn't want to worry her over nothing. He had to make another try. "Please come on? A quick walk and then we can eat?"

The dog tilted her head.

"Eat? Do you want food? After our walk?"

The dog hopped off the couch and padded over, her nails clicking with each step. Stopping a foot away, she yawned and stretched her legs one at a time. She sat very still.

"Okay, good. Let's go quick, and you can have dinner." He bent to attach the leash to the collar.

The dog's crooked tail swished over the slate.

If he hadn't spent all day internalizing, he could have made better progress. Who knew the dog understood English? He looped the leash in his right hand, opened the door, and strode outside. The more he thought about it, however, the more obvious it became.

Colby spent her days with Hank and Meg, arguably the two most talkative people in the whole state.

Ted, on the other hand, was so used to keeping his own company that he often forgot to speak. Sometimes, he felt awkward when he remembered the social niceties and found his voice following what was inevitably a too long conversational pause. *Never with Stephanie.* He liked the not needing to explain himself. No wonder he misunderstood her general friendliness as affection.

Shutting the door behind him, he jogged down the front steps and led Colby on the path around the house and toward the barn. Exercise could help clear his head where his day's labors had failed. Stephanie wasn't interested in him more than anyone else. She was outgoing. Soon, she'd find someone else.

Too bad Joe had already declared her off-limits, or he'd solve his own problems with Hank. She'd be so easy to fall in love with. Who wouldn't want to hear her light, lilting laugh? Or stare deep into her blue eyes as she considered a trademark thoughtful response?

She was perfect.

For someone else.

And Ted would have to try really hard not to hate that guy when he showed up. At least it wouldn't be Joe. He couldn't stand to be the third or fifth wheel on nights out with Meg, Ryan, Joe, and Stephanie.

Shaking his head, he dropped his gaze from the sky to the dusty ground, matching the pace of the dog at his side. For a couch potato, she was remarkably fluid and walked like she'd been trained to follow a human. Would she go to the bathroom? Or was this another moment he needed to give her permission?

Dogs and women. Why were they so confusing, discerning, and adoring? Did he need to be upfront with Stephanie? Did he owe her a full accounting of why he couldn't be the guy for her? He'd focus on one problem at a time. "Colby, please find the toilet."

The dog tilted her head in his direction and walked a little further out, pulling the leash another foot. And then she took care of business.

Was that the secret to both? Talking? Then he was doomed. While he might adapt as necessary for family, he wasn't a chatty person. A big part of the appeal of the ranch lifestyle was the solitude.

In his back pocket, his phone rang. He frowned, pulling out the screen and swiping his thumb over the image of his friend. "Two calls in two days? What's wrong?" He chuckled at his joke.

"It's Stephanie," Joe said.

"What?" Ted gasped and tightened his grip on the phone, pressing the hand against his head and readjusting his clammy hold on the leash. "What's happened? What's wrong?"

"I don't know specifics. No one is really talking here. Hopefully nothing."

"What do you know? Is she hurt?" Ted shut his eyes. If something happened to her and Maddy, how would he go on?

"Ted?" Joe asked. "Can you hear me? Are you there?"

"What was it? An accident? Where is she? The hospital?"

"Oh, no. I'm . . . I'm an idiot. Sorry. She is physically fine."

Ted let out a shuddering breath. He rocked back on his heels like he'd dropped a heavy saddle off his shoulders. "What are you talking about then?"

"School. Something has come up here," Joe said. "I should have led with that."

Ted dropped his tense shoulders. *Yeah, you think?* He pinched the bridge of his nose.

Colby yelped.

"Sorry, girl," Ted murmured. He'd forgotten they were attached. He'd lost track of everything as the adrenaline rushed his body, electrifying every cell and nerve. If she was hurt. . .

"Girl?" Joe asked, his tone dripping with disgust.

"I'm walking the dog. She responds to verbal contact."

"Oh, huh. Makes sense I guess," Joe said. "Meg acts like the dog understands English. Maybe Colby learned a few words. About the other thing. I wanted to give you a heads up. I know this is the last day she's dropping off Maddy. Stephanie might be upset. Be easy."

"How do you know she's in trouble? What sort? What happened?"

"I stopped by the office to grab a package and watched her storm out of the principal's office. I've heard rumblings about the PTO president being upset with Stephanie. My guess is she's made trouble and filed a complaint."

"What could she do? Can the PTO fire a member of staff?" Ted was incredulous. How could one self-absorbed parent impact someone doing so much good for a classroom full of little kids? Why should one too loud voice ruin others' lives?

Without Stephanie, Ted knew Maddy wouldn't have adapted half so well to her new living situation. To move away from the only home she'd known, and say goodbye to her parents, not knowing when she'd see one of them again, and stay with her uncle was traumatic for someone three times her age. But Maddy had soared, hardly noticing the little hiccups as she settled in, and he learned caretaking on the job.

He owed it all to Stephanie. Had her helping him but her in a bad spot? She swore it hadn't. But had she been trying to protect him?

"Candace Vane is a powerful enemy," Joe said. "I'm in my car, heading home. I'm guessing Stephanie will probably stop by in the next ten minutes or so. I wanted you to be aware of the situation. I'll give her a call over the weekend to see if she needs my help."

Would she need mine? Ted hated to be powerless on the sidelines, watching. "Thanks."

The crunch of tires on gravel echoed through the otherwise still air.

"They're here," Ted said. "Better go."

"Yep. Bye."

Ted hung up the call, slipping the phone into his back pocket. With long strides, he retraced his steps. Colby matched his gait perfectly. If the dog was treated less like a human, she'd probably be the ideal animal. *Except she's prized for her companionship skills.*

He shook off the thought as he rounded the edge of the house.

Maddy skipped out of the car and up the front walk, chattering a mile a minute.

Stephanie walked with her, smiling sweetly.

With each inch forward, her expression came into clearer view. She looked soft and thoughtful. How dare a brazen, brash, bossy broad ruin this woman's happiness? No one should have their joy stolen. Especially not Stephanie.

She turned her head and met his gaze.

Her face froze in a look he couldn't quite read. He cleared his throat. "Good evening. Just walking Colby. Thanks for dropping off Maddy." He'd reached the bottom of the steps and glanced up at her and his niece at the front door.

"And Shakes," Maddy said, holding the little yellow stuffed animal in a tight squeeze.

"Very nice to meet you, Shakes," he said.

"It's been no problem. My pleasure," Stephanie said with a wink at Maddy before turning back to him.

Something glistened in her eyes. Unshed tears? What happened? What was wrong? He could assure himself later he'd only said it to be a kind, caring friend. It wasn't because he didn't want her to leave. It was because he had a heart. He would have helped anyone who looked so sad and broken. Because Stephanie needed his help was beside the point.

"Come inside. We're making our own pizzas for dinner and watching a movie. Please join us," he said, resting his free hand on the railing and looking up at her.

She held his gaze and slowly nodded.

"Yes," Maddy murmured, opening the front door, and barreling inside. "Colby let's get your dinner."

The dog lunged forward, nearly taking off his arm.

At least he had back-up. He climbed the steps and stood inside the door. "Please, come in."

She passed by him, biting her lip.

He was glad. If she was truly upset, she shouldn't run off home. She shouldn't be alone. She could do or say something she'd regret.

Was he about to sow a relationship with a fateful consequence? A sigh built in his chest. He forced it down, turning to shut the front door. For a little while, he could content himself with a little taste of how easy it could be to spend time in her company. And then she'd go home, and he'd feel better. Two lonely souls making each other a little lighter for a while. He couldn't—and wouldn't—ask for more.

CHAPTER 13

Stephanie had never been more grateful for her carpool than driving home from school on Friday following her official rebuke. Which, all things considered, did a better job arguing she'd expressed favoritism than the hearsay evidence Bill presented. If she hadn't had Maddy in her car every day, Stephanie would have avoided her career doom.

But the little girl made Stephanie smile and lightened up her afternoons with conversation varying from wisdom to whimsy in seconds. Adding in the opportunity to talk to Ted each day, and she had no regrets. In truth, she hadn't known what she'd been missing.

With her friends and her projects, she was busy but not necessarily engaged. She'd participated without fully immersing her mind, her heart, and her soul. And now she would lose the companionship when she needed it the most. She probably shouldn't have accepted the invitation to stay for dinner. But she had.

As she stepped over the threshold of the old ranch house, she passed him, breathing in his mint and leather smell. Had she swayed into him, sniffing his collar? She hadn't received her official punishment yet. Was she now in a sort of double jeopardy state? If she was accused of favoritism due to a personal relationship, could she pursue said romance? Should she?

She stepped to the side, tamping down the streak of wild, recklessness surging through her veins. "Shakes shouldn't give you too much trouble. Take lots of pictures as he tags along with Maddy. She'll present a slideshow on Monday and talk about their weekend together. You can send an email with the photos on Sunday night." Stephanie sucked in a sharp, stinging breath.

No, he couldn't.

She wouldn't be there.

Swallowing, she forced her scratchy, dry throat to open and close. "Actually, I'd better give you Kelly Strong's email. She's another kindergarten teacher. She'll know what to do."

He nodded. "Follow me into the kitchen. I'll grab a piece of paper from the junk drawer, and you can jot it down?"

She lifted her gaze to his. With her admission and acceptance of her altered schedule, she lost some of the spark of indignation and daring that fueled her. She should excuse herself and send him an email from home with the pertinent details. She couldn't stand being alone right now, as fragile and transparent as a sheet of glass. He was strong and stoic. She longed to lean into his arms and break down knowing he'd hold her.

Instead of leaving or launching herself at him, however, she cleared her throat. "Kitchen?"

Nodding, he pointed toward the back and an open doorway. "We can't make our own pizzas out here."

She'd only been invited into the Kincaid house a few times and on those occasions the home had been overflowing with guests and laughter. She'd been awed by the craftsmanship and scale of the home. The building had stood strong for over a century and would keep shielding and protecting its occupants, come what may. Tonight, with only three humans and one dog, the four walls felt cozy and warm. Intimate.

Her cheeks flushed, and she strode down the hall and into a large eat-in kitchen.

At a sink overlooking the back of the wraparound porch, Maddy stood on a little stool and washed her hands. She tucked Shakes under an arm, clutching him tight around the neck, and struggled with the plastic bag holding a pre-cooked pizza crust.

Loud crunching echoed in the room. In the corner, Colby happily munched, her crooked tail swinging side to side. Ted entered behind Stephanie and crossed the room quickly, helping Maddy open her bag and the other one on the counter as well. Together, Maddy and Ted positioned the crusts on cookie sheets spread across the stove.

Stephanie should excuse herself. But her tongue stuck to the roof of her mouth, and she wasn't sure she could loosen her jaw to speak if her life depended on it.

Ted turned around and flashed her a quick smile. "Just one second." He carefully removed Shakes from Maddy's embrace and set the stuffed animal a safe distance away on the counter to observe. He strode along the counter, pulling open a drawer and approaching Stephanie with a notepad and pen.

Stephanie smiled and jotted down the details, aware he'd moved away.

"After pizza, we're watching a movie," he said, drawing her gaze again.

He grabbed an apron off the counter and slipped into it, standing near the stove.

His movements were smooth like a dance. She stared trying to figure out the steps. He grabbed another apron off the counter. Stopping a few feet away, he extended it. "You're going to need this. Trust me."

She stuck out her hand, thrusting the notepad and pen forward with too much power and hitting him in the process. Her cheeks burned.

"Specifically, we are watching *White Christmas*," he said. He swapped her pen and notepad for the apron, his touch light and fleeting.

She was grateful he hadn't commented on her jerky motions. But she refused to fall back into silence around him. Teasing suited her. "Isn't it a little early to watch Christmas movies?" She arched a brow.

The corner of his mouth lifted.

Her stomach flipped.

A loud gasp sucked all the air out of the room.

Turning toward the sound, she spotted Maddy pushing up her sleeves with a wide-eyed gaze. On a stool at her side, Shakes sat at attention, equally unimpressed by the lack of seasonal cheer.

Ted chuckled, shaking his head. "It's okay, squirrel. She doesn't know what she's missing." He stepped away from Stephanie but not before shooting her a wink.

She felt the flutter down to her toes. She slipped the apron on and tied it around her waist.

Ted helped Maddy with her and snapped a picture on his cell phone of his niece and the class pet. He opened a jar of sauce and set it on the counter with a spoon for Maddy. Then, he arranged containers of cheese and toppings nearby.

Maddy focused on creating her dinner.

He shot Stephanie a look.

She took the hint, washed her hands, and strode to the workstation. She took the space on the end with Maddy in between her and Ted. "What am I missing about watching Christmas movies in September? Don't most people stick with the holiday season?"

"It's a family tradition," Maddy said.

"When I was a kid, my mom taped all my favorite Christmas specials onto a VHS for me to watch whenever I was home sick. It always cheered me up," Ted said with a smile, staring at the pizza crust as he evenly spread sauce like a professional. "I find the movies comforting when I'm not feeling good."

Stephanie could definitely use cheering up. She'd imagined herself safe only to have that security snatched at the last second. The timing of the afternoon meeting felt particularly cruel. Bill had assured her he had her back. What happened?

"Although . . ." He lifted his chin and met her gaze. "I'm guessing that's one of those things you didn't deal with as a kid."

Sadness? She frowned.

"VHS. Video tape? I wore out the tapes. I loved everything that recorded, including the commercials. Maybe especially the commercials."

"Hmm." She tapped her chin with a finger. "I think I've heard of commercials. From the dark ages. Before fast forwarding live TV."

He rolled his eyes and chuckled.

She curled her toes. Anticipation swept through her at the low rumble of his laughter. She liked teasing him. She'd never been much for banter but with him, she had the impulse to say the coquettish retort.

I'm not that young. The words tickled the end of her tongue. She didn't say it. With his niece between them, she had to be careful not to cross over any boundary. Although, of course, she wasn't sure dividing lines existed anymore.

"Regardless, it is a family tradition to watch holiday movies whenever we feel like it. And I feel like it today. How about you, Maddy?"

The little girl nodded. "And now you can watch the dance routines and learn your part."

Stephanie nibbled the inside of her cheek. She definitely needed cheering up. Choreography might be the cure. "Will you and Unc perform along with the actors?"

Maddy grinned.

"Oh man, what has she told you?" he asked.

Maddy's giggle was the only answer anyone needed.

Stephanie met his gaze over the top of the little girl's head. For the first time all day, she felt light. As of this moment neither owed the other anything. Her staying at his invitation started something new. And she was glad for it. If she was already in trouble, her career at risk, why not actually be held responsible for following her heart?

For the first forty minutes of the movie, Ted was an active participant.

Maddy loved to sing and dance through the opening numbers with a partner. Tonight, she chose one human and one stuffed animal. By the time the cast of the movie reached the inn, however, she settled down on the couch and stayed in place. He snapped a picture of the pair, careful not to include Stephanie in the frame.

When she had explained where to send the email about the class pet, she had looked shell-shocked. Her situation had become real in that moment. Instead of crumbling, however, she had stood straight, her eyes had gleamed with valiant determination. How could anyone not admire her strength? He clung to reason, ignoring any deeper meaning.

Maddy snored. With a full belly, a warm blanket, a stuffed animal turned pillow, and a sleeping dog next to her, she curled into a little ball. Colby joined her in a symphony of nasal congestion that threatened to overshadow the movie.

Stephanie turned her head, widening her eyes.

He flashed a thumbs up. He knew what he was doing. A full belly and favorite movie were the secret ingredient to babysitting success on a weekend night.

But he didn't turn off the movie. He loved the scenes of struggle at the inn. As he got older, he respected the nuance of the film; showing how people could be forced out while still in their prime, how second chances weren't a given, but how magic could change everything.

Sitting in silence, he observed Stephanie as she stared at the screen, her eyes bright. Transfixed? He hoped so. Watching a beloved classic with an outsider was an act of vulnerablity, like showing someone his bedroom as a child. But she didn't make a sound.

Fighting the urge to sing and deliver the lines, he forced himself to watch the movie as much as he was able. Her presence proved more distracting with each second as the onscreen characters lost and found each other.

As the credits rolled, he studied her again from the corner of his eye. Curled on the couch with a blanket, she didn't show her reaction. No swooning. No laughing. No tears.

He rubbed a hand to his side, easing a sharp pain in his ribs. Did she hate the film? Did she think less of him for loving the movie?

He wanted her to connect with the story and the characters. That was probably a tall order. Life in a small Western town was not quite the same as the fictional Vermont of the fifties. Some things, however, were timeless. Reaching for a dream, continuing against the odds, and finding love remained primary motivations for so many.

"What did you think?" he asked, cutting through the silence and turning toward her. Whatever her opinion, he'd take it face to face.

"I loved it." She turned, widening her eyes. "I can't believe I've never seen it before."

"Me either."

She rolled her eyes. "Not another comment on the age gap. The real difference between our generations comes down to good luck and opportunity. You graduated college with plenty of both. When I graduated, I had neither."

A retort stilled on his tongue. He'd never thought of their differences so starkly before, but she was right. The dot com burst and 9/11 came during her formative years. Before she'd have much luck in the workplace, she'd hit the housing market crisis.

"You have a tendency to make yourself sound like Hank's peer. I'm pretty sure he wouldn't understand your references either."

Ted chuckled. "Fair point but face it. My favorite movies are your classics. Something like this, that came out when my parents were children, is practically part of the silent era to you."

She turned toward him, resting a hand on the back of the couch. "My lack of pop culture knowledge would be the same if we shared the same birthday. I didn't really watch much TV or movies growing up. I was too busy."

That he could believe. She didn't just randomly start being the overly involved town doer in her twenties. She must have been the kid with a packed schedule from birth. He could picture her in every afterschool club available. "I shouldn't have absorbed as much as I did. I spent plenty of time reading and playing outside. I've always been drawn to stories. I couldn't help but pay attention to the TV if it was on."

"Too bad you didn't read to Shakes tonight. I'm sure he would have appreciated one of your dragon books."

"There's always tomorrow." He held her gaze. His palms itched to trace the curve of her cheek. "Thanks for all of your help. I'm sorry about what happened."

"Joe called." She lifted her mouth in a sad, half-smile. "I wondered if that was why you didn't question me about the email. I'm sorry if pity was the reason you asked me to stay."

"No, I wanted you to," he murmured. He was approaching a delicate topic. Raising a fist to his mouth, he cleared his throat. "I wanted to thank you for your help. Are you okay? Do you want to talk? I'm sorry you are in a bad position because of us." He pointed at the sleeping child.

Maddy's blanket covered torso rose and fell with her deep even breaths. She was truly asleep. The little girl slept harder than anyone he'd ever known. He could speak freely without worry of upsetting his niece.

"Maddy's mom is coming up this weekend?" Stephanie asked. "For good?"

He nodded. Living with his sister again would be challenging. Jen was a messy, multitasker. She operated best at a hundred miles per hour, tackling more in sixty minutes than most did in sixty days. She exhausted him.

He liked the cozy little cabin with him and Maddy. He enjoyed the daily meet-up with Stephanie. Everything was about to change. He'd finally accepted his new normal. He felt a pang of nostalgia for the past couple weeks.

Maddy missed her mom, and he didn't begrudge the little girl for wishing the time away. The pair would stay with him for another few months before settling in a new home or an apartment. For someone who sought solace in the status quo, the constant upheaval should be upsetting. He was more worried about the shifting dynamics. He'd only found his footing. He wasn't ready to let go.

Stephanie lifted a shoulder in a shrug. "I think I know what I like most about the movie."

If she wanted to jump to another conversational topic, she'd come to the right guy. He was a master of deflection. "My singing and dancing?" he asked.

"Both are excellent." She smiled.

The expression was the same soft, sad twist of her lips she'd had when he said hello and invited her in. He would never push. He knew too well that people built up their walls to protect themselves. If he wanted his personal safety respected, he owed others the same. But still, he almost did push her. Maybe he was the only one who could.

"No what I liked most is it made showbusiness seem like such a natural job opportunity," she said, her tone wistful.

"Isn't it?"

"If only. No career is easy."

"We can get lucky. Find ourselves in the right place at the right time." He had. If he hadn't stopped in Herd, he didn't know where he would have ended. Coming to the town felt like kismet when it happened. Everything that happened in the years since only reinforced his feelings.

"I don't know how many details you've heard. But I'm on leave pending a review. I don't know what to expect."

His chest tightened. Because of Maddy and him? He reached a hand to stroke his jaw, swallowing the metallic aftertaste filling his mouth. He should ask her why she did it. Why she helped him.

She could claim it was helping a child. She'd have done the same for any of the students in her class. But she hadn't. She'd done this for him. She risked her position and reputation. Her job needed her. The town needed her.

Did he? "I'm really sorry," he said.

"Don't be sorry. I knew what I was doing." She stretched her arms over the back of the couch again. "I thought I had administration support. I didn't. But don't be sorry because I'm not. I don't live with regrets."

He wished he could say the same. He would have claimed it even a few hours ago. But that was in the time before when their interactions were an equal exchange at every turn. And now they'd reached a different moment. Words couldn't go unsaid any longer. They'd reached either the end or the beginning. He wasn't sure what he was hoping for.

"Be honest. Do you really think the age difference between is us fourteen years?" she asked. "Not what the passage of time says. But does it *feel* like we have a double-digit gap separating us?"

He opened his mouth.

"Because I don't feel it. You've had more experiences than me. Everyone has. Age and time are fluid concepts. Hank could be in his thirties for how cheeky and wry he is. Some days, I feel ancient."

"You're right," he said, quickly and reached a hand to hold hers. If he didn't stop her, he'd never get a chance to speak. "The years between us is more of an outward concern than inward."

Her hand twitched.

"I don't care what society thinks about me," he said. "I'm lucky to be here in this place. We value our neighbors."

"But?" she murmured.

"You are so sweet and so unaffected. I'm dark and moody. You need someone better. Don't get lumped in with me."

She snorted and rolled her eyes, tugging back her hand to fold her arms over her chest.

"It's true." He glanced at his sweet niece. He'd spared her the worst of his sad and angry days by moving out of their hometown long before she was born.

As long as he'd stayed on his farm, he couldn't shake the tragedy. He'd been long gone when his sister announced her pregnancy. While he'd had a momentary pang for moving away and missing out on Maddy's day to day growing up, he'd been glad that she hadn't known the version of him he'd been in California. With Maddy and Jen's move, Ted came out ahead, finding home and family in the same space again. "I told you I'm a widower."

She nodded and arched a brow.

And? Her expression spurred him on, challenging him. "I had a whole, full life with someone else in another place."

And? She didn't move.

"I was different before."

"I didn't know you then."

"I can't be that man anymore."

"I'm not trying to change you, and especially not into a stranger," she murmured.

Her words were soft and honest and heartbreakingly poignant. He'd always love his wife. But Liv was gone. And if the roles had been reversed, he would have wanted her to move on and have the family and home they'd dreamed about. Even if it was with someone else.

He drew in a breath but instead of hitching along every rib, he was lighter. He could no longer remember why he'd built a wall around his heart. Why was he acting like there was no future but also refusing to live in the present?

If they had no tomorrow, why not be honest and a little reckless tonight? If it's all going to end, why not take the risk? He leaned forward. With his fingertips, he reached out and grazed her cheek and chin.

She licked her bottom lip. Her tongue darted quickly across her mouth.

The air changed. The space between them suddenly charged. He leaned forward. He couldn't go back once he did this. He wouldn't. No matter what came next.

She sighed, and her eyelids fluttered close. She tilted her face towards him.

From the corner of his eye, he saw a spark. He dropped his hand and turned. Maybe he'd imagined the streak of lightning. Then came the ground rattling boom. He'd be glad for a thunderstorm if it meant rain.

She sucked in a breath.

He faced her, tipping his head to the side and considering her pale face.

Lifting an arm, she pointed out the window. Her hand shook. "Fire," she murmured.

CHAPTER 14

Stephanie had imagined herself in a dream. All too soon, she found herself in a nightmare. Swiveling off the couch in one smooth movement, Ted could have been a dancer. As her mind formed the thought, she knew how unhelpful her brain was. But she couldn't focus on what or where she was needed. She stood on wobbly limbs, locking her knees to stay upright. She was moving through gelatin or quick sand or anything else better suited to a sitcom than a life or death problem. A real emergency unfolded, and she couldn't quite send the signals from her brain to her body and back again.

Thankfully, he didn't have the same problem. He raced out of the room and flung open the front door. It crashed against the wall and snapped her back to the present.

She padded toward the entryway. The tiles were icy under her sock covered feet. A horrible, acrid smell filtered into the room. Why did the outside smell like plastic? She'd always been comforted by the smell of woodsmoke. But this overwhelming stench was different.

Wrapping her arms around her torso, she crept onto the covered porch. In the dark, she squinted. Beside the orange light of the flame, she couldn't see anything. It was a cloudy, moonless night.

She pulled the front door closed and walked down the front steps. With each step, she adjusted to the dark. When she spotted him, she sighed.

Holding a hose, he followed a thin line of fire, soaking the ground. He was fighting with success. And he moved fast. The grass fire was nearly put out. Thank goodness. The ground was so dry, they could be encapsulated in a ring of flames within seconds.

How had it started? She hadn't heard thunder. Was she too distracted to notice? She cupped her hands around her mouth. "Hey."

He lifted his head, briefly acknowledging her presence. Then lowered his chin again.

The ground shook. A streak of lightning brightened the sky with a terrible glow.

He dropped the hose on the ground, turned toward the house, and took off at a jog disappearing from view.

Where was he going? Had he heard her? He'd sort of acknowledged her but not in any significant way. He hadn't asked for help or offered instruction. She hated not knowing what to do.

Facing the house, she saw the next bolt of lightning and felt the heave of the earth with the boom of thunder. If the streak wasn't so close to those she loved, she would have marveled at the ferocity. Instead, she ran.

She chased after him, rounding the side of the house. She raced ahead and collided with his back.

He was frozen in place. Why? Then she saw it, the most awesome and frightening sight she'd ever beheld. Flames licked the left side of the barn. An old structure that had seemed immortal now succumbed to Mother Nature.

"Oh no," she murmured. Her heavy limbs trembled. What could they do?

Crackling echoed in the otherwise silent night. It was horrible. Shouldn't something so devastating and destructive sound an alarm? Wasn't the outbuilding retrofitted with sprinklers?

He grabbed her shoulders. "Call Joe and James and Ian. Call the brigade. Call anyone."

She nodded, wide-eyed and took a step forward. She'd help. She could throw a bucket of water onto the flames.

"No, don't. Go back inside. Take care of Maddy and Colby. Get the fire extinguisher by the front door."

She opened her mouth to object.

"Please." He squeezed her shoulder and dropped his hold.

The single word was a shaky plea. With a nod, she spun and raced back around the house to the front. She let herself inside and shut the heavy door. If only she could shut out the bad things happening on the other side as easily.

She was helpless.

A whimper came from her left.

"Maddy? Colby?" she murmured, tiptoeing away from the door toward the front room. She retraced her steps. She should turn on a light. She didn't know this house well enough to navigate in the dark. Why didn't she have any issues finding the door when she'd left?

The TV had been on.

She bumped into a table, the sharp edge hitting her thighs. She sucked in a sharp breath, wincing at the pain. She'd found her way out thanks to the ambient light of the television, and the front door left ajar by Ted. Now the space was plunged into darkness. The power was out.

A transformer had blown somewhere. She went to the wall, flipping the switch in an act of futility. But she had to try. *Fire extinguisher by the door.* She felt her way there, finding the cold hard cylinder on the ground and then slowly made her way back to the couch.

"Shh, shh, shh," she murmured. To herself or the dog or the child? Didn't matter. All three needed comforting.

With her hands outstretched, she hit the back of the couch.

Colby woofed under her breath.

"It's okay, it's me," she said, cooing to herself, the dog, and any ghosts that might haunt the old home. "Maddy? Are you here?"

"Uh, huh," came the shaky, voice cracking reply.

Feeling her way along the back of the couch, Stephanie returned to her spot on the right side. Close to the girl and the dog just in case. Colby was fond of humans but in a tense situation, anything could go wrong. "Sweetie, it's okay." Stephanie sank onto the cushion and reached for the little girl, smoothing her hair.

Maddy remained curled into a tight ball with Colby resting her furry muzzle on the little girl's legs. Her body wracked with shudders, shaking the furniture with the same force as the thunder. "I've got sh . . . sh . . . Shakes." Her teeth chattered. "He was scared."

Stephanie drew in a deep breath. Outside she had been out of her depth. Whatever may or may not be happening with Ted threw her for a loop. But she could be strong for a child.

Grabbing a throw blanket off the back of the couch, she wrapped the thick knit around the little girl's shoulders. "The power is out, but we are okay," she said softly, stroking the child's hair. "I need your help. Do you know where the house phone is?" *Or my purse?* She could barely see a few inches in front of her face.

"In the kitchen." Maddy sniffed. "Colby knows the way."

The mutt hopped onto the ground, her nails clicking against the slate floor.

Carefully, Stephanie stood.

Maddy got to her feet. "Do you think I can leave Shakes here? I don't want him to be scared."

Her kindness in the face of her own vulnerability touched Stephanie's heart. "He'll be okay. He knows you need him to be brave."

"Okay." Maddy draped the blanket around the stuffed dog. Bending, she held onto Colby's back. "Follow us."

Stephanie rested a hand lightly on the little girl's back. The unlikely conga line made their way through the front room and hall and into the kitchen.

Red-tinted light poured in through the windows. The awful fire lit brightness reflected the painted barn as it became engulfed in lashing, licking flames. But she could see. In a few steps, she crossed to the wall and grabbed the cordless phone off its cradle, dialing the emergency number.

"Oh, no. Unc!" Maddy stopped near the sink.

"Shh, Shh." Stephanie pressed the phone to her ear. "It's okay, sweetie. He's fine. Let's call for help. Everything will be fine. We need to do our part. Unc has everything under control."

She hoped. Because she'd never been less certain of a situation in her whole life. And this wasn't the moment for anything less than her best.

Ted hadn't believed in signs. He had never put much stock in fate or karma either. Losing Liv couldn't have been destiny. No higher power could be so cruel and expect worship. But maybe he should reconsider. He stared at the flames on the side of the barn, frozen in place for several seconds as his brain processed what was happening.

He had to stop it, as much as he was able, before the fire spread. The hose attached to the back side of the house wouldn't stretch far enough to save the barn. He hoped the hose still running on the front continued to pour water onto the cracked ground. He'd build a moat around the house to protect Maddy and Stephanie if he could.

Instead of water, he'd run inside the barn to grab the extinguisher. With his elbow, he slammed the glass case near the entrance, shattering the door and pulling out the fire extinguisher. The old beams and boards released a pleasant smell of woodsmoke. After the grass fire, the scent was a relief. His eyes watered from the plastic, chemical like emission.

He pulled the pin and scanned his surroundings, shocked by the turn of events. The barn had stood for generations. *If it burns, we can rebuild*. Hank had expressed the sentiment with a shrug of indifference, frustrated by the efforts to retrofit the building instead of new construction due to sentimentality.

Ted would never have guessed he'd be alone, fighting to save it. If he had, he would have pushed to add a sprinkler system when he'd learned of the updated codes while overseeing construction of the spa barn. Grandfathered in with building codes, Hank and Ryan had waved off the safety concerns over a decade ago.

Ted heard a crackle and then a creak. He glanced up in time to see one of the beams overhead catch fire. He raced out of the door. He wasn't a hero and wasn't sticking around to die like one. He had to make sure Maddy and Stephanie were safe.

By the time, he felt cool night air on his cheeks a wave of heat pushed him forward. He turned, fire extinguisher at the ready.

The roof collapsed inward. The crash of heavy beams and splintering wood echoed.

For a second, he didn't move. The horror of watching something that had stood sentry for generations rattled him. A family's history gone in an instant. It was horrible to witness.

He couldn't save the building, but he could make sure the flames didn't spread. He started to run. Lapping the barn, he sprayed the perimeter with retardant until he reached the deck. Then he had to lengthen his strides, jogging past his hard work. The fire had already begun to catch on the lumber he'd toiled over.

By the time he returned to his starting point, the smoke thickened. Panting from exertion, he breathed in the billowing air and coughed. His throat and lungs burned. He stopped, bending over to drag in deep shaky breaths.

The fire extinguisher ran out of the contents. He threw it to the ground, his mind racing as he triaged the situation. He couldn't do more for the barn. As much as he hated to walk away from the deck after months of work, he had to focus on containment.

He raced to the side of the ranch house, turning on the spigot and grabbing the garden hose. Stretching the hose as far towards the barn as possible, he sprayed the ground. The water rolled off the cracked earth and brown grass. It might take as long as half an hour for the drought-stricken land to absorb the moisture. He wouldn't worry about time. He'd stay and do his best.

This was why he'd been right to be alone. No matter how much Maddy's childish jokes brightened his whole day. No matter Stephanie's shy smile made him feel like he was living a good life. Caring about people meant he was vulnerable. He couldn't handle losing someone he loved again. He was a coward, but he wasn't a fool.

Please let the rain come. He snorted and shook his head. If willing was manifesting, he would never have arrived on the ranch. He'd be at home in California with a couple of kids by now.

Flashing lights and a siren drew his attention to the side of the house.

He exhaled, nearly collapsing forward, and dropped the garden hose. Help had finally arrived. He strode around the covered porch.

Joe and the rest of the volunteer firefighters reached the ranch.

Ted cupped his hands around his mouth. "It's the barn." His hoarse voice croaked, and he started coughing.

The fire engine drove around the house without slowing or stopping.

The flames must be visible from the road. He'd strained his voice for no reason. *Powerless.* He hated the feeling. He raced back around the house.

The fire engine parked. The crew descended and got to work on the barn. Two of the team worked in tandem to unfurl the hose and douse the flames. Another produced an ax and walked around the back.

With their training on full display, Ted realized he was out of his element. The adrenaline drained out of him, leaving him numb. How much time had passed since he sent Stephanie inside? The minutes stretched to an eternity as history turned to ash. But where was Maddy? Stephanie? Why weren't the lights on?

He backtracked to the side of the house, turning off the water and letting himself in through the back door. "Maddy? Stephanie? Colby?" He coughed again, shutting the door, and slipping out of his boots. He couldn't see. Crossing to the wall, he flipped the switch but nothing happened. The brief electrical storm had cut the power.

"Unc?" A little voice asked.

His heart cracked as a small body collided with his legs. Bending, he squinted and reached for Maddy. Embracing her, holding her tight against his chest. A rough tongue licked his cheek. "Oh, hi Colby," he croaked and coughed.

Maddy giggled.

The dog continued lapping his face with her sandpaper tongue.

"Okay, okay, enough." He petted the dog and stood, holding onto Maddy's hand. He couldn't lose track of her again. When his sister came back, he'd be able to resume his rightful place in the sidelines of his niece's world. His ultimate fear almost came true again. He can't protect those he loves. He desperately wanted the love of his family, but he couldn't be in the midst of it. He'd endanger those he held most dear. Because when the worst happened, he was useless.

"The fire is almost out," Stephanie said.

Silhouetted by the kitchen window, he couldn't see her face. Her hunched posture looked defeated and fragile. Holding tight to his niece's hand, he stood. "Thank you for taking care of them," he murmured, forcing the words out of his scratchy throat. "Squirrel, let's go in the family room. I can't find the way upstairs without the lights."

"Okay," Maddy whispered.

Holding his niece's clammy hand, he led the way back down the hall, humming one of the songs from the movie musical. He felt Maddy relax, her tense grip lightening. He settled her on the couch, tucking the blanket around her.

Colby jumped up and laid down next to the little girl, resting her head on the girl's legs.

"Good dog," he murmured. "I have to go outside for the firefighters. Stay here with Miss Patricks. Please?"

Instead of a reply, a snore escaped the little girl.

Stephanie sat on the other end of the couch. "Go. I'll take care of her."

Ted wanted a few more moments with Stephanie. But in the dark, after the fire, he didn't know what to say. Maybe another person would be compelled to seize the day after surviving a life or death scenario, but not him. He couldn't take a chance on love again. He couldn't be the man she needed or deserved, so he left.

CHAPTER 15

Stephanie stretched her arms over head, her fingers hitting something soft and solid. Her bed had no headboard. This morning, she touched fabric and not drywall. She opened her eyes and stared up at a ceiling. She pressed her hands to her sides and raised herself against a smooth, cool cushion. Where was she? She surveyed the room including the massive stone fireplace and hardwood floors.

Realization slammed into her. She was angled on the leather couch in the front room of the Kincaid ranch. Next to her, Maddy and Colby slept, curled up in twin tight balls. On the ground, Shakes, the stuffed retriever, laid on his side. His glass bead eyes somehow bore into Stephanie, peering deep into her soul. Ted was gone.

Slowly rolling off the couch, she stood. She stretched her neck from one side to the next and twisted her torso. After the fire, she hadn't left. She told herself, the power was out, and she wasn't sure she couldn't leave if Ted needed help again.

In the morning light, she saw how slim her excuses were. She remained because she wanted to be here. She was touched by his tenderness. He knew exactly what to do in every situation from fighting the fire to calming his niece. She'd been awed. She felt safe and secure with his steady, stoic presence. After her rollercoaster day, she really needed him, and he came through.

She had been relieved when he hadn't asked her to leave. Exhaustion slammed into her within seconds. Curled up on the couch, she had fallen asleep, unconcerned with what anyone might think or the crick she'd get in her neck from the awkward positioning on the cushion.

Last night was long gone. Thin streaks of sun poured through the front window. She grabbed the stuffed toy off the floor, tucking him next to Maddy. She crossed the room and gazed at the front yard and circular drive. A patch of burnt grass was visible from the front window. The sky remained full of clouds but these didn't seem heavy with rain any more than the ones from last night. How bad was the barn? She shuddered. She was grateful the fire had been contained.

On her drive over after school, she had mentally talked herself into acting like the consequences wouldn't matter. She thought she could live like there was no tomorrow. She hadn't been prepared for the terror of thinking her days might end. On tiptoes, she turned and crept toward the kitchen. Last night's fire had proven her new mindset was the right one.

As she entered the kitchen, a blinking light caught in the corner of her eye. She turned her head. The microwave and oven flashed twelve o'clock. The power was restored.

Turning toward the table, she spotted her purse on the bench. Inside, her phone was on silent. More likely than not, she would have missed a couple calls and texts from Kelly. She hoped not from Lauren. If Stephanie stressed her friend and risked Lauren's well-being, Stephanie would never forgive herself. But neither of her friends would expect an immediate reply. She wasn't quite sure how early it was and didn't have to race out of here.

Doing so would be irresponsible. She couldn't leave while Maddy was inside unaccompanied. At the very least, she'd have to find Ted and say goodbye. She might as well make coffee before doing so.

A yawn hit her hard. She spotted the coffee maker next to the sink. She filled the reservoir, located filters and grounds in containers next to the machine, and hit brew. As the percolating started, she stared out across the backyard toward the remains of the barn.

A pile of red and black wood occupied the space.

She recoiled. She hadn't grown up in Herd. Like many, she was a transplant. The small-town was either the starting point or the final destination, but not many people stayed their whole lives. The Kincaids were the exception. Ryan and his grandfather Hank were both born and raised. Seeing their historic barn reduced to ashes shocked her down to her core. What stood for generations was gone in one night. Everything could be erased in an instant.

The night taught her one important lesson. Stop wasting time by not being honest. She owed herself that much.

The coffee maker beeped.

She jumped.

"Miss Patricks?" A little voice asked. Stephanie turned and spotted Maddy and Colby standing inside the doorway.

Maddy flicked on the light switch.

Stephanie blinked. Now she was definitely awake. She plastered on a smile for the child. "Good morning, Maddy."

"Do you know where my unc is?"

Good question. "I'm not sure. I just woke up, too."

A stomach growled. Colby woofed.

"Me and Colby are starving," Maddy said. "Shakes, too."

"Sure." Stephanie wiped her clammy palms on her pants and crossed to the fridge. She rooted around someone the fridge like she belonged there. Already pushed out of her polite comfort zone. After she fed Maddy, she would march out of the house, find Ted, and kiss him. She vowed to stop wasting time waiting for permission.

She scanned the fridge's well-stocked contents. Every ingredient needed more preparation to craft a meal then she felt comfortable tackling. She didn't want to turn on the stove and make eggs or whip up French toast in the oven. "Toast with cinnamon and sugar?"

Maddy licked her lips. "Yes, please." She strolled to the dog's bowls set in the corner.

Stephanie made her way to the corner of the counter, housing the toaster, bread basket, butter, and spices. She made quick work of the easy breakfast, as the sounds of kibble hitting the metal bottom of the dish and running water at the sink for the water bowl filled the room.

Stephanie opened the upper cabinets, finding the glasses, mugs, and plates. She pulled down a few of everything and opened various drawers, utensils clattering with the tug of each handle. The morning soundtrack was reassuring.

She buttered the toast, sprinkled the cinnamon and sugar over it, and carried the plate over to the table. Shakes was propped on the top, waiting for his temporary owner. Maddy approached with a carton of milk, Stephanie poured the glass and returned the half gallon to the fridge. Movement outside the window caught her attention.

Ted walked toward the destroyed barn, his chin down and shoulders slumped.

Now or never. "Maddy, I'm going to go talk to Unc. Can you and Colby stay inside?"

Maddy shook her head.

"You can't?" Stephanie's stomach dropped. She'd just talked herself into what she had to do and hadn't factored in resistance.

"I need to take Colby out. I'll put her on the leash."

"Can you stick very close to the house? I don't think it's good for either of you to get too close to the burned sections."

"Okay," Maddy said through a mouthful of toast.

Stephanie chuckled and strode toward the mugs she'd set next to the coffee maker. Filling both to the brim, she held both mug handles in one hand, opened the back door a crack and slid outside, shutting the door behind her.

A chilly breeze snaked past her, blowing the smell of smoke. She shivered and curled her bare toes against the ground. She should go back inside and get shoes. Hadn't she warned about the dangers out here? If she turned back now, however, she'd lose her courage.

Under her feet, the ground was cold and hard, rising in misshapen lumps with footprints scattered across. She'd heard water running but hadn't realized he'd turned on the back hose. Heat from the mugs warmed her chilly hands. She put one foot in front of the other, heading toward the barn. With each step, the smell became stronger, and acrid. Stopping as close as she dared without shoes, she breathed in charred wood mixed with melted metal and plastic. The flames had been indiscriminate, burning the whole structure.

"Stephanie?"

She turned her head, gaping. He stood near what had been the deck. From her position, she shouldn't have been able to see him. A building should have blocked her view.

Her heart sank. All his hard work reduced to nothing. His time wasted. But not hers. If he hadn't worked on the project, he wouldn't have needed help with pick up. She wouldn't have chatted with him so much. She held up a mug. "I brought coffee."

Walking in a loop around the ash, he accepted the coffee. "Thanks." He took a long sip and glanced down. Meeting her gaze, he frowned. "Where are your shoes?"

"I didn't . . . I wasn't . . ." She cleared her throat. "I hadn't planned on coming outside until I spotted you." *And I couldn't waste a second once I did.* She sipped her coffee. She preferred creamer to cut through the bitter taste but was glad for the extra jolt of caffeine. "How can I help?"

"Is Maddy awake?"

"Yep, and Colby. I fed her, and she took care of the dog. She might walk Colby on a leash close to the house." Stephanie drank again. With the mug raised, she glanced at him over the brim. He was quiet.

She was used to his stoic, reserved personality. But this morning was different. He stood in front of her but was hiding somehow. His jaw was set, and his eyes clouded. Only a few feet away, he was distant. The friendly man of last night had vanished.

Not surprising. He was probably trying to figure out how and what he'd tell his bosses. The fire was hardly his fault, but it was a major catastrophe and would impact the business. Not just in the immediate clearing of debris and rebuilding but long term.

Their community had never been so dry as this year but that was only after last year's record-setting drought. Wildfires burned faster and longer. If every year became the worst in a century, the community couldn't count on problems only every couple generations.

"What can I do?" She pulled back her shoulders.

He looked at the ground again.

She rested one foot on top of the other. "After I get shoes on, of course. I can help. What do you need?"

He shook his head and took a long drink of coffee.

"Come on, it was a good thing I was here last night. Let me keep helping." She hadn't intended turning the conversation in this direction. But now that she was here, it felt right. She had to be helpful. If she wasn't, if she didn't advocate, who else would? She wasn't backing off the conversation about where they headed next. Instead, she was providing a more natural opportunity for the talk to spark organically. "I can help."

"You can't. One person can't change a thing," he snapped. His words were sharp in a foreign tone. He turned away.

She wouldn't be put off so easily.

He faced her. "You don't have to always be the one leading the fight. Sometimes you just need to sit and listen. There are other people who can step up. Doesn't always have to be you."

She wasn't sure she understood. "Maybe you're right." She said the words softly. She didn't believe them. If he did, however, he wouldn't respond well to badgering. "I can't stop everything bad from happening."

He snorted, his shoulders shrugging.

She inched forward. "But what if one person could make real change? They just had to be brave?" She reached a hand toward his shoulder.

He stepped away. "Then I'd wonder if it was courage or foolishness. We have differences too big to overcome."

She drew back her hand and clutched the mug. His words had been a verbal slap. He'd shifted from a broad discussion to a narrow argument so quickly that he'd almost pushed her away. She wouldn't be so easily put off.

She drank the last of her coffee. Was he going to break up with her before anything had started? All she was going to get was one almost kiss? She refused to accept that. The bitter coffee couldn't compete with the foul taste filling her mouth. She could pretend she didn't understand him. But she did, all too well. She was tired of games. "Are you talking about our age gap? If I was older?"

"No, that's not it."

"If I had some big tragedy?"

He sucked in a breath.

She'd put her foot in her mouth in spectacular fashion. Good thing she forgot her shoes, or she'd start choking. She was a jerk for even thinking it.

"I would never want that for you," he said. His words were almost a growl. Was the huskiness from smoke inhalation or emotion? "You deserve happiness. Always."

Just not with you? "Tell me why?" she asked, her voice cracking.

"Because I lo—" He shook his head and faced the ashes. "Just go, please."

For a painfully long second, she couldn't function. Her brain couldn't process how to make her limbs bend and move. She couldn't save herself from this pain. A laugh built low in her belly. The shudders wracked her torso and restarted her locomotion. She had just enough dignity not to linger.

She stalked back to the house, grabbed her purse, kissed Maddy goodbye, and was out the door and in her car. At least she wouldn't have to face anybody. Since she was on leave. What a joke. She was being blamed for favoritism and following her heart. In truth, she'd skidded in a brick wall and been too oblivious to avoid the head-on collision.

Ted drummed his fingers against his thighs and stared—unblinking and unseeing—at the horizon. He didn't look down at the mess on the ground. Since waking a few hours ago, he'd toured every inch of what had been the barn and deck. With only the foundation intact, the whole thing needed to be rebuilt.

Now he focused on keeping still. On not turning around and apologizing and agreeing he wanted to give them a chance. He needed to let Stephanie walk away. It was the kindest thing he could do. For either of them.

He curled his hands into fists, counting to a hundred. When he left her sleeping on the couch, curled up next to Maddy and the dog, he almost reconsidered. She looked so peaceful despite the awkward twist of her body to fit onto the sofa. He knew she wouldn't complain. She was so accommodating and yet firm, a perfect mix of strength and spontaneity.

But he couldn't. Overextending himself emotionally, he'd stood on the brink of ruin last night as the terror of the fire highlighted everything he stood to lose. He couldn't endure another tragedy.

Stephanie wouldn't give him a chance at peace or rest. Her angelic, sleeping face hid the truth of her constant need for advocacy. She wasn't a person who spent much time relaxing. His quiet evenings spent reading alone would be gone. He appreciated her fierce spirit. But he couldn't imagine joining her in every battle she waged. If his ultimate goal was calm, he wouldn't find it in a relationship with her. He was right to push her away. He forced a momentary hurt for her good, not that she could see it yet. She'd probably leave if her job was gone. Why stay?

His jaw tightened. He opened his mouth and shut it, forcing the muscles to clench and unclench. Taking in a deep breath, he filled his lungs with the still smoky air. A relationship with Stephanie was doomed to fail.

"Unc, what are you doing?"

He turned and squinted, rubbing the crust from his eyes to clear his vision.

Colby tugged the leash, panting as she led Maddy down the yard toward him.

"Stop there, squirrel." He jogged the few yards toward her. "I'm not sure how safe it is. There are sharp things like nails mixed with ashes in the ground. I don't want you getting hurt."

"You're dirty."

He scrubbed his face with the hem of his shirt. Soot and sweat collected on the cotton. "I need a bath."

"Miss Patricks left."

He swallowed the sigh building in his chest. He knew.

"But Mr. Joe is here." She pointed toward the house. Joe raised a hand and waved from the porch.

Thank goodness. This time he didn't hold in his heavy exhale. He needed another able body. Stephanie could have been the help, but he couldn't separate out his feelings from his needs.

"Squirrel, can you go inside? Are you hungry? Do you need food?"

"Miss Patricks made me cinnamon toast." Maddy licked her lips and widened her eyes. "We need to show Shakes the ranch, remember?"

He chuckled. He'd probably regret the little girl eating sugar first thing in the morning, but he wouldn't second-guess what had already happened. If he started down that path, he'd wallow in self-recrimination for the rest of the day. Stephanie did the best she could in the circumstances. He had to do the same. "Okay. I'll be in soon. I need to talk to Mr. Joe."

She shrugged and tugged the leash. "Come on, Colby." The dog happily sniffed the ground, wagging her tail and leading the way.

Probably eager to lay on a bed. He waved a hand to Joe. who crossed the yard, greeting the ladies as he passed. He wore heavy work boots.

Ted wasn't sure what compelled Stephanie to traipse outside in her bare feet. Had it been him? Hoping for a resolution to the almost kiss? He shook his head and stared at the ground, kicking a rock with his boot.

"Hey, good morning," Joe said.

"Hey." Ted lifted his chin and nodded.

Joe whistled and approached the remnants of the barn.

Ted followed and stopped at his friend's side. "Yep."

"I was afraid of how bad it would look in the morning. Somehow this is worse than what I imagined."

Ted had no response. He agreed. He could only be grateful the fire had been successfully contained and put out by the crew. The rain never came. The ground remained dry as kindling.

"Any luck reaching the Kincaids?" Joe asked.

"Nope." Ted dragged the toe of his boot into the thin layer of ash. With a rake, he might be able to scrape off the soot. He wasn't sure any efforts would ease the shock of the changed landscape. His feeble words wouldn't offer much consolation either. He raised his gaze to his friend and shrugged. "I left messages for Hank and Ryan this morning. I'm not likely to get a call back. I think it might be a big day."

Joe widened his gaze. "Are you talking about a proposal?"

Ted nodded. While Hank was known for losing his cell phone, Ryan was fused to the device. Last night, Ted had decided against waking the men. By the time the fire was out, the hour had grown too late.

This morning, Ted tried again. Ryan's must be powered off. Every call immediately received the voicemail message. Only a big reason, like a proposal, would justify Ryan turning off his phone. Ted was happy for his boss and friend but his ribs tightened and his eyes burned. He'd admitted to himself—and almost to her—that he loved her. He couldn't offer her the happiness she deserved. He wouldn't begrudge anyone their joy. "I haven't seen a ring but I have my suspicions. I wasn't a kid detective though."

Joe chuckled at the jibe. "Hank will be truly incorrigible if Meg says yes. He'll take all the credit."

Ted shot his friend a pointed look. Meg and Ryan were destined for each other. Everyone knew it.

"Alright." Joe pulled a pair of work gloves from his back pocket and slipped them over his hands. "Where can we start? And don't push me away. You can't do this alone."

It's not hard when there is nothing to salvage. Ted nodded and strode to the gravel parking lot on the side of the building. Earlier, he had driven to the spa barn and collected every trash can he could find and parked close to the ruins.

In silence, Joe followed.

Together, they grabbed the empty cans from the bed of the truck and filled each one with sharp items they found amid the debris. After they had the loaded each garbage to the top and neatly arranged all in the bed like a puzzle game, they closed the hatch.

With a sigh, Ted turned to survey. Their hard work had barely made a dent in the clean-up. Now he'd have to drive the load to the dump and see about arranging several dumpsters for the rest. All of that would wait. He didn't want to permanently remove any piece of history from the ranch without Hank's say so.

"Thanks for stopping by. And for last night."

Joe shrugged. "I'm sorry for all your hard work on the deck."

"It's not worth anything anyway."

Joe drew back his chin and stared.

Flinching, Ted turned away. He couldn't help his cold attitude. Despite an hour's work, he remained cold from the inside out. "I'm glad you came quick last night. I'm grateful to you and the crew."

"I got the call from Stephanie." Joe crossed his arms over his chest and leaned forward. "Was she here last night?"

"Yes, but it wasn't like that." Ted hated the suggestion of any untoward behavior. Stephanie didn't deserve to be the subject of gossip.

"How was it?"

Joe asked with such tenderness and care that he threatened Ted's hard exterior. "She dropped off Maddy. You told me she was upset. I didn't want her to think no one cared or appreciated her. She stayed for dinner." He scrubbed his face with both hands. He wasn't going to rationalize or justify yesterday's actions. "Doesn't matter because it's over."

"Is it?"

Whirling around, Ted crossed his arms over his chest. "Zip it, Joe. Why did you come here?"

"To help." Joe held up his hands. "But you want to be alone."

No, not now and not ever. That's the problem. He sagged his shoulders. "I'm sorry, and thank you. I think there's nothing left to do here at the moment. Hopefully Ryan checks his messages so he won't be shocked when he gets home."

"I don't think that's possible."

Ted agreed. From a long-standing structure to charred remains, the landscape's sudden change was shocking. The point of a surprise was being totally unprepared for it. It's why he'd always hated the unexpected. He had no time to steel his response and lessen the impact. Love the first time had been a long slow build giving him ample opportunity to jump ship before reaching the next level of seriousness.

In life, he could only control his actions and responses. Never another person. Growing up with Liv had meant knowing her well enough to anticipate her needs and yet still enjoy the thrill of her questions and answers. She'd surprised him in the best ways with her contagious joy.

Stephanie was both a stranger and a friend. But he had the same awareness of her, understanding her wants, during a much shorter amount of time. He shouldn't know her as well as he had known his wife.

This time, he'd been smacked on the side of the head with love. And he'd never be the same. Because he couldn't give her what she needed. She deserved much better.

CHAPTER 16

Angry pop anthems and rage cleaning could only do so much for Stephanie. *We could be happy if you let us.* The words thrummed through her veins, pulsing in time with her heart. As she stripped her sheets, washed every linen, beat her rugs, and scrubbed her grout, she couldn't shake the mantra. She should have said it to his face.

He was frustrating. He was such a puzzle at a time when she didn't have time to fit pieces together. He opened up and invited her in only to push her out and slam the door.

He provided a good distraction from her work frustrations, but she wasn't content to categorize their exchange so superficially. He couldn't get hurt if he wasn't actively engaged so he hovered on the fringe of life. And once he finally started to interact with her, he couldn't let it continue.

She understood him better than he wanted. She was terrified of tragedy. But instead of hiding, she took action. She guided her path. After the fire, she wasn't going to sit around. He might have been short with her, but it wasn't anything new. She'd heard the whispers for years. *What's the deal with your savior complex? Do you live for the praise?*

She'd argue she needed no accolades and hadn't received any. If she didn't make something happen, it didn't happen. She preferred action. Clarity slammed into her.

He wanted to wait around. He wasn't ever going to let himself love or live. Stephanie left, and he didn't stop her. They had been getting close. She felt it in her heart and soul, but she couldn't make him love her back.

She redirected her feelings into cleaning, losing herself, until a text message interrupted her playlist. Lauren was admitted to the hospital for observation. Stephanie pushed aside every concern, racing to her friend's beside.

As she signed in at the front desk, applied her name tag, and waited for the door to open, she focused on her breathing to still her dread. She would not get emotional. She would not upset her friend. And—under no circumstances—could she discuss her leave of absence.

Her steps echoed in the hall as she plodded toward the room.

The door was ajar, propped with a doorstop. Kelly and Lauren's muted voices filtered out. Raising her fist, she knocked.

"Come in," Lauren called.

Stephanie pulled the small gift bag out of her giant tote and entered.

Lauren pushed herself up from a pile of pillows on the bed. Kelly stood next to her.

"I brought you contraband." Stephanie wiggled her eyebrows and set the bag on the tray table next to the bed, and squirted some of the giant bottle of hand sanitizer into her palm.

Lauren reached for the bag, looked inside, crinkling the tissue, and grinned. "I'm hiding this from the nurses and Steve." She tucked the bag under her blanket.

Stephanie laughed. "I'm sure you're allowed a little treat." Gummy bears and corn chips weren't a combination Stephanie cared for, but Lauren had a weakness for both. Stephanie had purchased the junk food to bring to the hospital after Lauren's delivery. But with doctor mandated bedrest, she needed the distraction now.

"Not according to anyone here." Lauren exhaled a heavy sigh. "I'm being monitored and evaluated. Everything is being recorded including my food. It's so boring. I thought it was bad at home. It's so much worse here. I have none of my stuff. I can't do any work. The TV has limited channels."

"Really?" Stephanie looked to Kelly for guidance. "Having someone else cook and clean sounds pretty good right now."

"I agree." Kelly nodded. "And she should enjoy the chance to rest before the babies get here."

"What do the doctors think? How much longer?" Stephanie asked.

"Maybe by the end of the week. They've given me some steroids to help with the babies' lung development. Which sounds really scary, but Bill told me his wife had the same. Their twins didn't have to stay in the hospital too long after they were born," Lauren said.

Stephanie offered a tight smile. "Oh, well. He would know."

Lauren folded her arms over her belly, interlacing her fingers. "Yep, he knows quite a bit."

Stephanie glanced from Kelly's frown to Lauren's pursed lips.

"You've heard what happened." Stephanie felt spotlighted by the overhead fluorescent bulbs. Her nostrils stung with the alcohol stench of the sanitizer and cleaners. She wasn't escaping this conversation. She nibbled her lip, her teeth sinking into the flesh. She didn't want to aggravate her friend. The dark smudges under her eyes and heavy breaths told Stephanie how worn-out Lauren was.

"You aren't going to stress me out by talking about your leave of absence. Kelly told me everything. What can we do? How can we help?" Lauren asked.

Stephanie lifted her chin and met the determined set of Lauren's chin and the soft smile in Kelly's gaze. Her friends always had her back. They had warned her. But she hadn't listened. Instead of telling her *I told you so* or shaking their heads in contempt, they consoled her. The unease of the last twenty-four hours drained the last of her anger, leaving only exhaustion and sadness. The tickle in her throat became a gasp as her eyes overflowed with tears and her nose started to run.

Kelly handed over a tissue box. Lauren squeezed her arm.

It was going to be okay. With the support of people Stephanie cared about, she would manage her way through. The truth stung. She couldn't hide from it and expect to feel resolution enough to move on. She grabbed the tissue and blew her nose. With another, she dabbed at her cheeks. "I was taken aback by how far the situation escalated. I didn't tell either of you, but Mrs. Vane confronted me at poker night. She threatened the future of the fundraising event."

"Why didn't you tell us?" Kelly asked.

"At first, I was shocked. I couldn't believe she was willing to be so flippant about a program that has become so vital to the community." Stephanie shrugged. "I didn't want to believe it was true. But I should have understood the warning. She was determined to bring me down. Guess she has."

"But you told Bill you were driving Maddy. It was only for a short time. He knew." Lauren wrinkled her brow.

Stephanie nodded. "He knew. I couldn't really fight back though against the claims of favoritism. If I'm honest, I'd admit helping Maddy wasn't an entirely selfless act." She paused.

They didn't exchange knowing looks. They just listened without judgement or condemnation. How had she gotten so lucky to find these friends? And why had she almost ruined her relationship with them after their warning? "I would help any child in my class. By assisting this student in particular, I had the chance to spend time with Ted."

"And how has that been?" Lauren asked.

Stephanie snorted and grabbed another tissue, blowing her nose again for good measure. "Foolish. He's not interested in me."

"Someone else?" Kelly asked.

Luckily, no. Stephanie wasn't sure she could stand by and watch that. Was that what happened next? Was she just the wrong person? Would he find love with someone else? Her heart ached. She shook her head. "Kelly, he'll email you the pictures from the class pet's adventure-filled stay at the ranch. I don't know who my sub will be. Maddy was so excited about taking the stuffed animal for the weekend. I didn't have the heart to cancel."

Kelly nodded. "I'll take care of that. Don't worry."

"What comes next?" Lauren asked.

"Bill asked me to come to a meeting with him Monday morning, before the closed-door board meeting," Stephanie said.

"What are you going to do?" Lauren asked.

Stephanie frowned. "About Ted or my job?"

"Both," Lauren replied.

"I don't know," Stephanie murmured.

Kelly reached for Lauren and Stephanie's hands.

Lauren extended her other hand.

Stephanie accepted both and squeezed.

"I hope you fight to stay," Kelly said. "You're a wonderful teacher. We'd miss you. So would the kids."

Stephanie smiled but didn't reply. She wasn't sure. After facing down a fire and a formal reprimand, she wasn't sure who she was or what she'd be.

But she couldn't pick up from where she had been before. She had a day to process before her meeting with Bill. She wasn't sure what the future held for her career. She proudly stood by her moral code and wouldn't back down on taking action. Not to placate the people who couldn't support her. She wanted someone to be at her side and not hiding in the wings. If that wasn't Ted, then good riddance. If only her heart could catch up to her brain.

Ted had spent the rest of his Saturday taking care of the horses and his niece. Cupcake the mare was particularly upset. While the stables were moved far enough from the barn not to be under threat from the fire, the smoky haze carried on the wind, irritating the sweet old girl. He'd given her extra oats and a thorough brushing. The horse had responded well to both.

With Shakes tucked under her arm, Maddy had offered her words of encouragement.

So did Colby. Or, rather, low barks of commiseration.

He'd finally heard from Ryan around eight pm. Ted's suspicions proved correct. Ryan proposed to Meg and spent the day with his phone off to enjoy the celebration. He didn't want bad news to ruin his plans. He'd been smart.

Ted hadn't slept easy. With their arrival scheduled for Sunday afternoon sometime around when he expected his sister, he had plenty of chores before the Kincaids returned. But that wasn't the reason.

Long after Maddy fell asleep, Colby curled up on her legs, on one of the two twin mattresses in the guest bedroom, Ted had headed downstairs with his book. Reading always transported him far away from his cares. It was hard to remain rooted in the real world when on the back of a dragon, soaring over a fantastic kingdom and engaging in the various plots and intrigues of a royal court.

But he couldn't stop thinking about Stephanie. His beloved mythical beasts were tinged with the memory of her astonishment the first time she dropped off Maddy and scanned the spines on his bookshelves. He smiled, thinking back on her cute, surprised face. He liked catching her off-guard. He enjoyed letting another person see the playful side of him he didn't freely share. With her, he embraced it.

And now that he pushed her away, he had to return to the man he'd been. The steadfast and safe person who others could depend on. He wanted to cry. Despite the words blurring in his vision, he must have fallen asleep. Because he started Sunday on the couch, aching and cold.

After waking, he fed Colby and Maddy, cleaned the kitchen, and led the pair on a long walk around the property. Exercise had always been his balm and antidote. Angry? Sad? Confused? Working his muscles and body gave his brain the freedom to either solve the problem or give up and move on. Topping out at forty minutes, however, he wasn't any lighter mentally, but his companions were exhausted.

He glanced down at the panting dog and his winded niece, their shallow breaths evenly matched. He fought the chuckle building in his throat. The pair were adorable. Always. He might not be ready to take on more dependents, but he was glad for them. "We're almost back. I promise we walked in a loop."

"Unc, are you sure? I don't recognize any of this." She frowned, twisting her neck from one side to the other.

The landscape was very monotone in the autumn. Dormant, golden grass stretched into the horizon. In a few weeks, snow would blanket the ground. On cloudy days, the line between heaven and earth would be indistinguishable. In the bright sunshine, the glare from the frost-covered landscape would be blinding. He didn't love all seasons but respected the process. The weather's constant change was a reminder to him that nothing was permanent.

"If you squint, you can see the bar—where the barn used to be." He reached up and rubbed his tight chest. Would he always ache at the events of Friday night? If he hadn't had the ultimate sign from the universe, he would have kissed Stephanie.

Tires crunched over gravel, the sound broadcast in stereo on the other wise silent air.

"Mommy!" Maddy shouted and dropped the leash, racing ahead.

He stepped forward too late.

Colby ran off after the little girl, happily barking and shaking her tail. Like she was always ready to run and not the dog who loved to snooze.

He shook his head and jogged behind them. The pair certainly found their second wind when properly motivated. He continued forward, rounding the ranching house, reaching them on the drive and catching the leash. Jen held Maddy in a tight squeeze, lifting the little girl in her arms until Maddy's feet dangled.

He chuckled. His sister wasn't a very big person, and Maddy wasn't a baby anymore. For motherhood, however, she tapped into a strength she otherwise hid.

Colby woofed under her breath, wagging her tail.

"Hey, sit," he commanded. With one more low bark, the dog complied, her tail dusting the ground.

"Thanks for taking care of her, Ted." Jen set her daughter on the ground, keeping her arms wrapped around the little girl's shoulders.

"Of course. Squirrel is easy," he said.

"The fire was hard," Maddy added.

Jen widened her gaze. "Fire?"

He nodded. "The old barn burned down. Luckily it was contained. No one was hurt."

"Yikes. Are you okay?" Jen asked, narrowing her gaze. "How long were you exposed to the smoke? I have to head over to the hospital soon to pick up my badge. I was going to take Maddy. Should you come and get checked out?"

"I'm a little bruised, but I'll live." At least he'd stopped coughing or his sister wouldn't give him a choice. He didn't want to elaborate about the location and severity of his injuries. Breaking his own heart wasn't something a nurse could fix. "I was outside for much of it, and the wind blew in the opposite direction. Glad you're here. Our cabin is fine. Are you still planning on staying with me for a bit?"

"As long as you'll have us. My start date was pushed back a week. I thought I might tour a few places, just so I know what is out there when the time comes to move. I'm guessing I won't be able to sign a lease until January," Jen said. "I'm sure you want your space and some quiet."

"No rush." He meant it. He wasn't sure how he felt about being alone or left in silence for too long. "The new year is fine."

"Mommy, this is Shakes. He's pleased to meet you." Maddy held out the stuffed animal like a talisman. "He's our class pet, and Miss Patricks let me take care of him this weekend."

Jen shook the stuffed dog's front paw. "Shakes, it's a pleasure. Sounds like you have had an exciting visit."

"And we took pictures," Maddy chirped. "Unc can show you. I get to talk all about his visit at school tomorrow. Can he take a picture with you?"

"Sure, honey. Even better. Maybe he can get an I.D. at the hospital, too." Jen smiled.

A car horn honked.

"Come on, let's stand on the porch," he said, grabbing the leash and leading the dog out of the way.

The white SUV appeared, driving fast, and stopping with no care for the shocks. The vehicle doors opened and slammed shut in a syncopated rhythm.

Colby howled and lunged forward.

"Alright, go and say hi." He dropped the leash.

The dog leaped from the porch to the ground, clearing the stairs, and launched herself at Hank Kincaid, knocking him backwards into the SUV's door.

"Oh, I missed you, too," the old cowboy cooed, stroking the dog as he was lavished with kisses.

Meg and Ryan strolled forward, passing the pair.

"She used to be my dog," Meg said.

"What's yours is mine and vice versa, right?" Ryan asked, lifting their intertwined hands, and kissing her knuckles.

A flash of light from Meg's left hand caught Ted's attention. Being right usually felt more triumphant. After the tumultuous weekend, however, he could only manage a pleased smile.

"When is the wedding?" Ted asked, glad to jump on this topic.

"I was thinking we could combine it with Hank's birthday extravaganza," Meg said.

Hank grinned from ear to ear. "I can't wait to update Joe and Abby." He rubbed his hands.

"I'm thinking all the events might be on hold," Ryan said. "Ted, you burned down my barn?" He arched a brow in an exaggerated, joking manner.

Meg glared at her fiancé.

Ted shook his head. He wasn't sure he was ready to find humor in the terrifying situation.

"How bad is it?" Hank asked, holding Colby's leash, and striding forward with a slight hitch.

"Come see for yourselves," Ted said. He led the group around the side of the house. Once they reached the yard, their murmurs stopped.

Joe had helped clear away what he could. Ted needed machine power, a dumpster, and a crew for the rest. Piles of charred wood and asphalt shingles were neatly contained within the general outline of the foundation. No part of the structure remained intact or in position.

"You didn't say it was as bad as that!" Jen hit him in the ribs. "Teddy!"

Ted rubbed his side, taking in a sharp breath and glaring at his sister's pointy elbows.

"It's okay, Mommy. Unc had it under control, and the fire men came. The scary part was being inside without power. But Miss Patricks kept me company."

"Miss Patricks?" Meg, Ryan, Jen, and Hank said the words in unison.

Could he quadruple jinx them and keep them from talking or asking questions for the rest of the day? As he scanned each face, ranging from inquisitive to skeptical, he was sorely tempted.

"Sure. Miss Patricks drove me home and stayed. We made pizzas and watched a movie. It was really fun." Maddy shrugged. "I thought she liked Unc, and Unc liked her. But she left yesterday morning, and I haven't seen her."

"Miss Patricks spent the night?" Hank asked.

Maddy nodded.

"Hey, squirrel." Ted bent to address his niece. "We had a really long walk. Why don't you and Colby go inside and get some water, okay? I need to talk to the grown-ups for a little bit."

"Okay. Come on, Colby." Maddy turned and waved to the dog. The duo went inside through the back door.

Meg shook her head. "I don't think Colby even noticed I was here."

Ryan wrapped an arm around her shoulder and squeezed. "I did."

"Do you want to survey the damage to the barn?" Ted asked.

Hank rolled his eyes. "No, I want to get back to you having a lady over and her spending the night under my roof."

Heat crept up Ted's cheeks. Blushing? In his forties? He hadn't done anything wrong, but the events sounded scandalous when laid out by his niece in her matter-o-fact way. "Not like that. We were watching a movie, it ended, she was going to leave and then lightning struck."

Hank stroked his chin. "According to Maddy, in more ways than one."

Ryan rolled his eyes. "The fire was an act of God? I worried bad wiring started the blaze."

Ted shook his head. The entire evening had seemed to be the work of the almighty. He'd made his displeasure at Ted's romantic feelings known.

"You must have been terrified," Meg said. "Especially with Maddy. I'm sorry you had to live through that, Ted. I'm glad you had another adult to help."

Ted was grateful too. But not just any grown-up could have stepped in quite the way Stephanie had. "I owe her a great deal. She kept Maddy and Colby safe and called the firefighters while I did what I could. The power cut, and she stayed. She could have left, but she didn't."

"Are you interested in her?" Hank asked.

Ted scrubbed his hands over his face. He didn't want to lie to himself or his friends.

"Are we open to outside opinions now?" Meg asked. "Can we finally be honest and tell you you're making a mistake and throwing away happiness by not pursuing her?"

"You knew?" Hank spun and stared at her, incredulous.

"I know Stephanie's interested." Meg shrugged and turned to Hank. "But you said you weren't going to put pressure on Ted so I thought it was okay to let the pair figure out their own path. I didn't realize they needed a helping hand."

"Of course they need help." Hank shook his head. "You two would never have taken the initiative if I hadn't pushed."

"Wait, I'm confused," Jen said. "Maddy's teacher that she loves and raves about? She's interested in you. You seem to like her. What's the problem? Why aren't you together?"

"You know," Ted murmured.

"Because you're a widower? I loved Liv, but she's been gone for a long time. She would not have expected you to remain alone for the rest of your days," Jen said. "You aren't honoring her memory by living like a monk."

He did not want to have this conversation ever and especially not in front of his employers. He glared at his sister. "No."

"What's wrong?" Jen asked. "If someone makes you smile, you need to run after that person and hold them tight for as long as you can. Life is too short and unpredictable to waste any time."

"Here, here," Hank said. "I blame myself. I've missed out on matchmaking this whole summer. I've been too distracted by other pairings. I'll fix that."

"Please, don't." Ted drew in a deep breath. "I'm not ready. It's not just about loving and honoring Liv. I miss her every day. It's . . . more complicated."

"How?" Ryan asked.

Had all his friends deserted him? "I'm not judging anyone."

"But . . ." Jen fixed him with a stern look.

"What if I end up married and divorced? You said yourself, life has no guarantees. I got lucky once. Why would I take the chance again when I can get hurt?" Ted asked.

Jen sighed. "Why are you affected by my failure?"

"Don't say that. You got Maddy. You won."

"You're right. But . . ." Jen shook her pointer finger, emphasizing the word. "We are talking about you and how you internalize others actions instead of taking action yourself. Divorce wasn't easy, but once I determined to do the best for daughter it wasn't the hardest choice to make. Navigating each other's adult feelings is hard. Leaving emotions out is difficult but not impossible. Why do you think you'll end up divorced? Don't use me as an excuse to stop from living your life." Jen folded her arms over her chest.

Ted glanced at the ground. She'd nailed a direct hit. No one could call him out like his sister. Except maybe Hank. With the people closest to him holding him accountable, he couldn't hide anymore.

But he could run. "I'm glad you're all back. I need a night off." He turned and strode away, seeking refuge away from those closest to him, and hoping for a break from himself.

CHAPTER 17

After a final round of hugs in Lauren's room and promises from Kelly to keep an eye out for Maddy's email, Stephanie lingered in the antiseptic scented hallway. Slowly ambling toward the exit, she tried to process the whirlwind weekend. She'd endured more highs and lows than a night at the carnival. Now she wanted off the ride so she could regain her balance somewhere sturdy. She wished Ted could have been what she needed. Her eyes watered, and tears sting her nostrils.

She hadn't expected to feel so emotional and raw after visiting Lauren in the hospital. While she was worried for her friend, her deep vulnerability exposed Stephanie's own insecurities.

She was so used to putting on a brave face, to tamping down her own feelings, to reframing her struggles as lesser than in the grand scheme of the whole world. And while she still believed all of those to be necessary functions as an adult, had she grown so used to discounting her own sense of self that she had no identity any more besides her work?

Fighting for her feelings hadn't done her any good. She had wanted Ted to see who she was and to be brave enough to take a chance. But maybe she had to do the same. She couldn't be afraid to be herself.

"Miss Patricks," a tiny voice called.

Lifting her chin, Stephanie plastered on a smile and spotted Maddy. With Shakes firmly clutched under her arm, the little girl beamed and held hands with her mom. Tall and lanky, Ted's sister shared his smile.

Happiness exuded off the pair as expansive and unending as the Montana sky. Despite her pain, Stephanie was glad. She didn't have to worry about her new pupil. She felt a little lighter and hopeful at witnessing the family reunion.

Stephanie stopped a few feet away. "Hi, Maddy. It's nice to see you and Shakes. This must be your mother?"

"Hello, yes, I'm Jen Cade." Jen extended a hand. "It's a pleasure to meet you."

"The pleasure is all mine," Stephanie said. "You have a wonderful daughter. She is a joy in class. Maddy, what is Shakes doing here? I hope he isn't having health issues."

"Oh no. Don't worry I'd take him to a vet if he was sick," Maddy said solemnly.

Jen chuckled. "I'll be joining the nursing staff here. We wanted to take a quick tour."

"Shakes is going to get a badge like mommy," Maddy added.

Stephanie was bursting with curiosity about Maddy's mom. Only the thought the other woman was probably brimming with wonder about the woman who had grown close to her child and brother reminded Stephanie to keep her tongue in check.

"I hope you are alright?" Jen asked. She scanned Stephanie like she had x ray vision. "Are you here for an appointment?"

Hopefully a broken heart wouldn't show up under such scrutiny. *The fire.* Stephanie shook her head. "I'm perfectly fine, thank you. One of my colleagues is pregnant with twins, and she's been put on bed rest and observation. I was visiting."

"Not Mrs. Strong?" Jen asked.

Stephanie frowned. No one would make that mistake. And then realization hit. Jen must be taking over all duties including Shakes' photo project and had the email address for Kelly. As Jen should. She was the mom. Still, it felt like giving up one last link to the unexpected connection with Ted. Stephanie shook her head. "No, not Mrs. Strong. I'd better get going before one of your new colleagues has to escort me out."

"Thank you for all of your help," Jen said. "Truly. I appreciate it more than I can say."

At least someone did. Stephanie forced a smile. "No thanks needed."

"We'll see you soon?" Jen asked

Stephanie pressed her tongue to the roof of her mouth. She never lied in front of a child. Starting now wouldn't do her any good. "Have a good afternoon." With a nod and wave to the mother-daughter pair, Stephanie continued down the hall toward the exit. She couldn't mourn what she'd never had. The best she could do was to keep moving forward.

She didn't stop until she reached the parking lot. Then she took in deep gulps of the air, breathing in the faint hint of smoke. Or so she imagined.

For the rest of her life, she would never forget the terror of the fire. As the flames licked the side of the red barn, she had been frantic looking for him. And then she saw him. And she knew. He was her home.

But he didn't feel the same way. And he rejected her enough times that she really needed to start listening to the message he'd so clearly delivered. She had to be enough on her own. She couldn't keep doing for others and ignore herself deep down. Inside her pocket, she grabbed her phone and tapped the speed dial.

"Hello?" A deep voice answered on the first ring.

"Hey, Ty, it's me."

"Steffy. Hey, Melissa has been asking about you. Are you coming to visit soon?"

Her little brother's low baritone was like a soothing balm. He should have gone into radio or voiceover work. But he found his passion in engineering, and she'd been proud of how he managed a demanding career with starting a family. His question should have been obvious before she made the call. She had the time. She should put it to good use. "Maybe."

"What's wrong?" Her brother asked.

Emotions bubbled up in her chest, and she felt like she was drowning and couldn't get air into her lungs. "I'm on leave. From my job."

"Oh no, what happened? Are you okay?"

She pinched the bridge of her nose stemming the tide of tears that threatened. "I don't know. I'll be ok about my job. Something will work out."

"Why do you sound so demoralized? Is there a guy?"

"Yes." Her voice cracked, and she blubbered. "I'm sorry. I didn't mean to call and get all emotional."

"It's okay. I wish I was there. What happened? Do you need me to beat somebody up?

She snorted. "Do you want to take on a big lug of cowboy probably 200 pounds?"

"Hey, I'm not your kid brother anymore. I'm two twenty on a good day."

"Do you mean when Melissa is making healthy meals?"

He chuckled. "Something like that. If you need to get away, you should come visit us. You know we'd love to have you. And you don't have to worry about a thing anymore. I'm a grown-up now. I'm fine. It's ok to take care of yourself a little bit."

She knew he was right. And she knew she had people who would show up for her. She wasn't scared little girl anymore, worrying about being left at dance rehearsals long after pick up or not having mom or dad show up for parent day at school. But she didn't know how to let go of it all. "Do you ever get mad?"

"That's a very vague statement. Of course I do. Want to provide a little context?"

"Didn't you want Mom and Dad around more?" Her tummy tightened, her insides twisting like the binding on a battered spiral notebook. She breathed through the sharp pain. "Don't you ever wish things were different when we were growing up?"

"Not anymore."

"Really?" She spent too much time thinking up what if scenarios. Had he been so unaffected?

"I don't want to throw the whole it's different when you're the parent thing at you because that's not fair. Plus, I've been a dad for about two minutes. Everyone is entitled to their feelings about their experiences and to frame their life however they need," he murmured. "Please don't think I'm discounting you. All parents are learning on the job. We assume a huge responsibility with no training. Our parents were busy and dealt with any issue they were aware of. You had trouble advocating for yourself."

She still did. He had a point. But it was frustrating that her little brother could be so rational and insightful. Although, as an engineer, he dealt in logic.

"I know how much you did for me," he said. "You saw what I needed and took care of me. I couldn't do the same. I was too young to understand you had needs too."

She wasn't sure how much she really did in the grand scheme of things. Her brother was a good kid. Silly at times but determined to always do the right thing. And precocious. He'd skipped two grades and graduated college a semester before she did. On a fast path to success, he seemed to soar without any hurdles.

"I want to encourage you now. Don't be held back by fear. Learn from your insecurity about attention and make it your strength."

How? With Ted, she had taken charge and asked for what she needed. And she was still turned down flat. Maybe her problem was tying up her sense of security in one person. She had to be enough for herself. She had to speak up. She sighed. "When did you get so smart?"

"I made one good choice. Falling in love with Melissa. She taught me everything including the gift of forgiveness. That's why I want you to find someone who cherishes you. So, if you need me to come up and beat up this cowboy I will. Or maybe you can move by us."

If she didn't love the community as much as she did, relocating would be tempting. She knew better than to think she could simply run away from her problems. And she definitely couldn't leave behind her heart. She might be able to keep breathing, but she wouldn't keep really truly be living if she left. "I love you, Tyler. I think I just needed to talk it all out."

"If I can help, I will. Will you keep me posted on a visit? I know we owe you one but with the baby."

"Absolutely I will."

"Great I love you, sis. Bye."

"Bye." She ended the call on her cell phone and slipped the device back into her pocket. This time when she filled her lungs, she didn't breathe the smoke it truly had been in her imagination after all. Maybe Tyler was right, and she wouldn't understand the sacrifices her parents had made until she became a parent herself. Maybe she hung onto childish feelings as a way to deflect growing up.

But she was an adult. And she couldn't run away from her problems. She'd stride into the principal's office tomorrow morning, accept her punishment, and figure out the next phase in her life. Because she was going nowhere.

Ted swiped the broom against the hardwood floor, scraping the bristles along and against the grain. If he kept at it with such vigor, he'd probably scratch the boards. At present, he hadn't done much good. For his efforts, he was rewarded with a plume of dust, as he worked his way through the bunk room.

With summer in the rearview, maintaining the residential space for the seasonal employees was a monthly job. And a quiet one. And the most annoying. Which almost guaranteed he wouldn't be followed by any of those overly involved friends that had become family. Or—potentially worse—his actual family.

He hated the way everyone had invested so much of themselves in him. Because he was bound to disappoint. He'd done Stephanie the kindness he couldn't bring himself to do for anyone else that he loved. Leave them alone.

Loved? He grabbed a bandana out of his back pocket and blew his scratchy nose. He'd kicked up too much in his fevered attempts at cleaning. He wasn't scared of the word or the emotion.

He didn't think letting someone else into his heart was a betrayal of what he had felt for Liv. Not anymore. On the contrary, the last few weeks of getting to know Stephanie, reminded him of the capacity for living he only experienced when he was completely open and vulnerable with another person. He only reached that point of enlightenment once before when he'd fallen head first for his wife.

He'd nearly succumbed again. But then nature intervened. The fire had burned through him as fast as it did the old barn. Maybe quicker. He was drier than the timbers of the historic building, ready fuel for the blaze.

And the absolute rush of adrenaline, he had clarity of his purpose. He couldn't lose someone else. Even if that meant forcing himself back into a black and white world after living in Technicolor for the past several weeks, he'd do it.

"Whoa, whoa," a deep voice called followed by a sharp whistle.

Ted met Hank's gaze as the older man stood in the doorway leading from the TV room.

"You weren't kidding," Hank said, his breathing shallow. "Reckon, you really wanted to be alone to come all the way out here and do chores." He coughed, leaning against the door frame for support.

"Hank, you shouldn't have followed me." Ted crossed the room to the older man. Without asking, he draped Hank's arm over his shoulder and steered Hank back into the main communal gathering space, lowering him onto the couch.

Ted crossed the room to the sink, filling a glass of water and returning to his boss.

Hank stopped coughing and accepted the cup, drinking deep, and nodding. "Ahh. Thanks. Needed that. Tickle in my throat."

Ted wasn't so easily convinced.

At eighty-nine, Hank was definitely not spry and nimble. He tired easily and was now on even more prescription medication following a hospital stay earlier in the summer. He was so mentally fit and focused, it was easy to pretend he was a young man who would live forever. No one could.

"Take a seat and stop hovering," Hank said, curling his upper lip. "Makes me feel old when you're staring like that."

Ted understood. He didn't like fussing either. He sat on the sofa's armrest, propping one leg on the furniture and keeping the other foot flat on the floor. In case he needed to run again.

"I am here. To apologize to you," Hank said, cradling the empty cup in both hands. "I overlooked you, and I underestimated you. I'm sorry."

"I'm the one who was here when your barn burned down. I should be the person apologizing."

Hank stared at him. Hard. "We both know I'm not talking about the barn. But I am sorry to see it go. Losing a piece of your history, especially something you've taken for granted your whole life?" Hank shook his head. "I was cavalier about the old timbers. I floated the idea of tearing it down. I was wrong to be flippant. Probably caused the fire with my careless words."

"No one would ever accuse you of taking your legacy lightly," Ted said.

"Maybe. But I did. Those old boards have always been there. Like a beacon. To lose it?" Hank pressed a hand to his heart. "It's like getting knocked off your favorite horse. Hard not to reevaluate everything. In your case, though, I think it brought up some old trauma."

Ted couldn't disagree. He still didn't quite understand what Hank was sorry for. In his experience, however, Ted would only get the answer if he let Hank speak.

"A lot of change happening around here lately. Now even more with the wedding." Hank smiled.

Ted grinned, too. He couldn't help it. Hank's excitement was contagious for good reason. When two people found each other, and in this case after years of mutual uncertainty, it was hopeful for the rest.

"I'm sorry, because I skipped you. After my success with Meg and Ryan, I jumped straight ahead to Joe. I was focused on him and Abby and couldn't see what was happening on the ranch between you and Stephanie this summer."

Ted's throat constricted. He coughed. "Nothing happened this summer, sir."

"Maybe nothing big, but changes were underway. A friendship was developing and swiftly becoming something sweeter." Hank stroked his chin. "I couldn't find a better pairing for you if I'd been looking. I'm glad. I am sorry. I was treating you with extra care and space, and I forgot something important."

"I'm a lost cause?"

"You?" Hank widened his eyes and waggled a finger. "Oh no, you're no victim. I know your pain." He pressed the hand to the center of his chest. "I don't push you, because I don't want anyone to shove me."

Ted understood. In many ways, Hank had been an example and a mentor. At Ted's lowest, most fragile, Hank had been the one to offer a job and a purpose. They'd been united in their grief and status as widowers. "You were right. I'm not ready."

Hank snorted. "I was coming around to you as soon as I had everything else settled."

"Joe and Abby are not a match, sir."

Hank rolled his eyes. "Leave them to me. Right now, we're talking about you. You never mention your wife. My Suzie practically haunts this place, as much as I talk about her."

"Liv was. . . everything. My past, my present. And I thought my future."

"I wish you'd have had it all. Growing old with someone is a gift. Are you honoring her memory? Is that what you've been doing on your own? I can't understand why you are a hermit."

"I'm not anymore. I have you and my sister and niece now. Ryan will have kids. I'm not alone."

"But you aren't together. Not really. I've seen the way you always keep yourself apart and away from us. I'd guess you're trying to protect yourself from getting hurt?"

"I can't. . ." A sob rose in Ted's throat, choking him. "I can't lose Stephanie."

"And the fire put that fear through you again?"

Ted pinched the bridge of his nose, shutting his eyes tight and squeezing hard.

"You are already loving her from a distance. You don't get to enjoy what you could have. You are only suffering pain. Why are you pushing her away? Do you need permission to love again? Because that's what I'll do. I'll give you the freedom to follow your heart. Your wife would not have wanted you to be scared. What would have happened if you'd been the one that died? What would you have wanted?"

Ted dragged in a shaky breath and dropped his hand to his leg, numb on the armrest. "For her to have a family."

"And you don't think she'd want the same for you?" Hank murmured.

You're going to be the best Dad. Liv's voice filtered through his mind. He wasn't sure he agreed. And kids were a long way off. But he had a chance at a real, lasting love. If Stephanie wasn't too mad to look at him. . . He had to take his shot.

"Okay. You're right." Ted lifted his chin.

"I usually am. What are you going to do?" Hank asked.

Ted wasn't sure. Grovel? Apologize? She was woman who kept to the sidelines and gave others a moment to shine. "I'll come up with an idea."

At the determined glint in Hank's eyes and the cheek-to-cheek grin, Ted was glad he didn't ask for assistance. He didn't want help. He was ready for his life to begin on his terms. He'd managed to escape Hank's notice for his courtship, and he'd continue under the radar for as long as possible. "Actually, I have another question. How did you know I was here?"

"I didn't." Hank pressed his hands on his thighs and pushed up to standing, his bones creaking and cracking. "I went everywhere else first. When someone is important to you, that's what you do. You don't give up. You keep fighting."

Ted got to his feet. "Did you ever think maybe you had permission to enjoy your time here without Suzie? You should take your advice. If you met someone, you wouldn't betray your wife but might enhance your life. Never say never, right?"

Hank scoffed. "I'm the oldest person in town. I'm not finding love. Thanks for thinking of me. And I promise, if someone comes along interested in my stories, I'll give her an earful over a nice dinner. Let's go. You've got work to do. Good thing my old pictures sold well at the auction. If I know my grandson, I can expect a big bill from the new construction. More than just the insurance will cover."

Ted chuckled, the laughter lifting him up and making him feel lighter than air. Hank was right, per usual. Ted had work to do, and he'd get straight to it. He'd pull out all the stops to win back Stephanie.

CHAPTER 18

Stephanie stood outside the school's main entrance at ten thirty-eight, smoothing the jacket of her charcoal gray suit over her pants. She only owned the one suit and felt like she was on her way to a funeral every time she wore it. Or to trial. Which was worse?

The door buzzed, and the lock clicked.

She grabbed the handle and strode inside, making sure the entrance relocked behind her. She hoped she wasn't on her way to being sentenced. She missed her bright, colorful outfits with cartoonish details. Dressing in shades of black and white wasn't for her.

The glass paneled foyer gave visitors a peek into the school en route to the front office.

Movement caught in the corner of her eye, and she spotted the last few kids from Lauren's class in a single file line, heading to art. Stephanie was tempted to smile and wave. But she hadn't been recognized in her austere, professional garb, almost a disguise. The long-term sub would have her hands full on the first full week on the job. She wouldn't appreciate a disruption to whatever order she'd created.

At the door to the office, she reached for the intercom button.

The door buzzed.

She grabbed the handle and looked up.

Wendy smiled. "Good morning, Miss Patricks."

Stephanie stepped inside and shut the door behind her.

Wendy gave away nothing with her even tone. She offered a warm welcome to everyone who entered the school, but she knew all. She held out a hand.

Stephanie stared at her blankly.

"I.D.?"

Right. Stephanie reached inside her purse for her government identification, ignoring the flash of hurt, and handed it to Wendy. It was standard security practice, and she went through the motions like anyone else. Had Wendy always addressed her with her last name? Stephanie wasn't sure. She was desperate for clues to make sense of the situation and the state of her career, but now she saw conspiracy. She breathed in through her nose and slowly exhaled.

Wendy handed her the sticker visitor's pass and driver's license, motioning to a chair. "He'll be right with you."

Stephanie nodded her thanks and took the seat, perching on the edge and crossing her ankles. She slipped her license into the slot into her wallet.

Her phone rang.

Kelly's face flashed on the screen. It was the kindergarten planning period. Kelly had enough on her plate today with two substitute teachers filling in for the rest of her team. Kindergarten thrived on consistency and many of the kids would cling to Kelly with the new faces. But she took the time to reach out.

Stephanie breathed a little easier and silenced the call. She switched her phone to vibrate as a series of incoming texts from Kelly and Lauren began in earnest. Her phone remained loud with the wave of encouragement.

"Stephanie?" Bill asked.

She glanced up and almost sighed. At least she remained on first name basis with her boss. "Good morning." She turned off her phone, slipped it into her purse, and stood.

"Please, follow me." He smiled.

She did her best to focus forward, not daring to dart a glance anywhere else. A worried look or polite nod from her colleagues would pierce through the faux confidence she wore like armor. With her heartbeat thundering in her ears, she followed Bill into his office and sat at one of the two visitors' chairs in front of his desk.

Since opening up about her failures to her friends, her end of the road conversation with Ted, and being placed on leave on Friday, she wasn't sure she had any emotions left. She'd been squeezed and tossed like an old sponge.

Bill shut the door and took his chair.

She watched his mouth move but didn't register the words, instead listening to a low buzz. Her boss was speaking. She needed to listen.

Anxiety crushed her. If she lost her job as well as her chance for love, what did she have? Until it had been snatched, she hadn't realized how desperately she'd been searching for her place in the world. She wanted to matter to her workplace, to her community, to Ted, and to herself.

"What do you think?" Bill asked.

She shook her head. "I'm sorry. Can you repeat that last bit?"

"I'm sorry, if you felt blindsided. You were upfront with me the entire time about the situation. I needed to straighten out the information being flung at me. I've spoken to the board. Off the record, several members feel that the PTO president is unfairly exerting pressure and power of her position. They have worried about other situations she's been involved with. Her treatment of you has only solidified their concerns. A meeting will be called, and she will be removed. A special election will be held to fill her vacancy. The vice-president is taking over until then."

It was everything she could have asked for and then some. The words held no meaning.

She loved working with the kids and being part of her community. She didn't like not having her boss and colleagues on her side. She could pursue any number of jobs to provide a paycheck, starting with the much-needed role of wedding coordinator at the Kincaid ranch. If she returned, she needed more.

The silence stretched.

She studied her boss.

He held himself perfectly still.

"Does that mean I can come back to work?" She could have cheered for how even she kept her tone despite the chill running through her body.

"Yes, please." He sighed. "I shouldn't be saying this, I'm sure a lawyer would advise me to hold my tongue, but I have to tell you the truth. You are sorely missed today. We need good teachers. And I hope you look into becoming an administrator. We need fighters."

She lifted her chin and stared at her boss. Today was the first day in a long time, she felt seen and supported in her job. Could she believe it? Or was his comment a throwaway attempt at placating her? "Are you serious? Do you think I should move into the front office? Would you want me to join you in administration? I'm sort of a lightning rod now."

"I am, and I do. You have a deep compassion for the students. It's not a universal quality. Admin would be a good move." He steepled his fingers, pressing his hands to his mouth.

Being a principal hadn't been a goal, but maybe it should be. Why not expand her work and help more kids? "I'd have to take night classes. Maybe some summer classes, too." She wouldn't be able to teach at the ranch. *Probably make my life easier if I didn't.*

"The courses can take time, but you'd have our full support."

She took in a deep breath, letting the air expand her lungs and letting go of the pent-up frustration. "You say you want fighters, but I can't always fight. If I've learned one thing, it's the value of listening."

He grinned from ear to ear and stood, extending his hand. "Then I think you'll be very successful in the role."

She pushed back her chair and rose, shaking his hand. When she thought she'd lost her career, she wasn't sure what came next. But now—with a little humility—she understood she'd always rise to the challenge and find a new way. Even when it hurt. Maybe especially then. "Thank you, sir."

"We'll see you tomorrow?" He dropped her hand.

"Tomorrow? Really?"

"Yes, please."

She nodded, grabbed her purse, and exited the room. She might have to reevaluate, but she wasn't running away. She loved her town. For better or worse. And she'd take advantage of a rare free day to do something for herself.

Ted held the cell phone against his ear. No sooner than the line connected and it went to a pre-recorded message almost instantly. Straight to voicemail. Was that on purpose? Was she avoiding him? Did she bristle and send him on his way every time his name flashed on the screen?

He couldn't blame her if she was avoiding him. He told her to go away. At a vulnerable moment in her life, he pushed her out of his. Maybe it was all too presumptuous on his part, that feeling he couldn't shake that she could change his life if he let her. Why give so much power to another person? Why let an outsider control his destiny? For all he knew, she wasn't looking for forever. One date would give him an idea of what lay ahead. That's all he wanted.

"Stop pacing." His sister shouted.

Startled, he turned around and spotted Jen walking into the living room with a laundry basket on her hip.

"If you're going to walk in place, take off the boots for goodness sakes. It's like being at an out of sync tap dance recital."

"You know you are staying in my space."

"And I'm grateful." Jen set the basket on the floor and sat in an armchair. She pulled out a purple, child-sized shirt and folded. "But having roommates means making allowances even in the short term. Shouldn't you be doing something somewhere anyways? It's Monday at ten minutes to eleven in the morning. Why are you here?"

"I can't really do much today. Ryan is meeting with the insurance company. I'm not supposed to touch anything near the site."

"A day off?"

"Not really." He sighed. "I have to get things straightened with Stephanie. I can't get ahold of her, and I'm not sure what I do next."

Jen folded pants and socks.

"You don't approve?"

She shrugged, grabbing a sweatshirt, and shaking it out before folding it in half. "Do you want an opinion? You seemed to shut down the other day."

"I was." He sat in the opposite armchair. Without activity, he felt gangly and awkward. He was a man of the never-ending chore list. Quiet time was best avoided.

"Miss Patricks is lovely, kind, and sweet from Maddy's point of view." His sister leaned back and met his gaze. "I never thought I'd see you get back into the dating pool again."

"I had thought it was all behind me. But then a series of events made me realize maybe I shouldn't be alone."

"Like me barging in on your personal space?"

"That and becoming part of a community again. I didn't try to, but I found family here."

"For what it's worth, Liv would like her."

He didn't need anyone's blessing or approval. He didn't live his life by committee. Warmth spread through him regardless.

"They wouldn't be friends." Jen chuckled. "They'd have nothing in common. They wouldn't get coffee together."

He nodded. Liv was sarcastic and sophisticated. Stubborn and savvy. She had been a take charge personality that guided him for years, leaving him bereft on his own. He'd been happy in her wake. "How do you know?"

"I met Stephanie at the hospital when I got my badge. I'm known as a pretty shrewd judge of character."

He rolled his eyes.

"For other people," Jen said. "Liv wouldn't have stayed single forever. No one would have wanted her to be alone. Same goes for you."

"I'm rusty at flirting and all that stuff."

Jen snorted. "Aren't we all? At least you were friends first. It's a solid start. And you don't have to get on the apps." She pointed at the phone. "Are you trying to call her right now?"

"It seems like the sensible idea," he said, fighting the eyeroll. Little sisters might grow up, but they never stopped being annoying.

"Well, it's a Monday, and she's a teacher. She's probably at school. She's not exactly the type to stare at her phone all day."

Or she was at her review meeting with the principal. His stomach sank to his boots. Maybe her phone was turned off. Was she getting bad news? Had she been fired? Was she already packing up her apartment preparing to leave? Was she about to say goodbye before he had a chance to tell her he felt like she brought him back into the living world? That she could be someone very special? "I'm heading into town. Do you want anything?"

"Like what? Where are you going?"

"I'm not sure. I'll find out when I get there."

Jen grinned and slowly nodded. "I understand. You're about to make a big gesture. Convince her to give you a real chance?"

"Not that I deserve one."

"No, you don't." Jen shrugged.

He rolled his eyes.

"You know I won't flatter your ego. I'm not Mom. But I am glad. What's your plan?"

"I don't know what I'll do. Talk?"

Jen shook her head. "Too late. You need more." She snapped her fingers. "I have an idea. But we need to go up to the ranch house, and we need reinforcements."

"What are you thinking?"

"We have to go classic romantic comedy."

In his mind, only one movie had captured the ideal grand gesture moment. And it didn't involve a stereo or signs. It required a marching band and an outdoor stadium. He remembered the adorable wrinkle of Stephanie's brow when she completely misunderstood a pop culture reference between him and Joe. He'd be tempted to find a brass line if he didn't worry she'd think he was poking fun at her.

"She doesn't really watch movies," he said. "She won't get it."

"Maybe that's even better, she'll think you're being original."

He wasn't so sure. Wouldn't she appreciate something more from the heart? From him? His sister was determined to use every cliché she knew. If he asked for her help, he'd have to take what she gave. How would Stephanie react to knowing his sister was involved?

In a small town, dating relationships were hard to hide from public scrutiny. Everyone would have an opinion. They probably already did. Would she be embarrassed? Would it be too much too soon?

No, he should get others involved. Showing her that she mattered to him, in a public way, in front of those nearest him nearest and dearest to him, would matter more than anything. Because she mattered to him. And if he got a chance, he would show her. "She won't be at the school today." *Or for much longer.* "But I think I know where she will be." He glanced at the time on his cell phone screen. "I don't have a lot of time."

"Let's go to the ranch house. I'm sure they'll have what we need."

He wasn't sure he liked the flash of mischief in his sister's eyes. But he was glad she was here. He'd take a little inconvenience and over-involvement if it meant having everyone that mattered close. He had one piece of the puzzle left to finish the whole picture.

CHAPTER 19

Stephanie drove to town, only passing a handful of cars on her way. Her apartment was outside city limits, on the way to a bigger town and more job opportunities. Downtown Herd was tourist central. The Old West false fronts catered to those in search of a sanitized version of the cowboy past.

With the ranch closed for the summer season, most of the businesses shuttered until the late spring. She expected a tumbleweed to blow down the street. She was heartened to see a few locals out and about, walking into the post office, stopping at the general store, and frequenting the local businesses. The off-season focused on community spirit, a very worthy endeavor.

At the end of Main Street, she steered towards the church and cemetery. She turned into the gravel lot, crunching the stones under her tires like a heraldic welcome announcing her visit.

She hopped out of her vehicle and grabbed her purse, stalking towards the food truck.

"Stephanie?" Her friend, food truck owner and go to cowboy dinner caterer Abby Whit, exclaimed. "Wowza, you clean up nice."

Stephanie unbuttoned her blazer and tugged the hem. "Thank you. I feel a little too strict in the suit. It's like a strait jacket."

"You could be a lawyer. Who knew you were a shark hiding underneath all of those oversized dresses."

"I suppose we all have a few secrets."

Abby nodded, stiffly. "Did you have to defend yourself today?"

Stephanie wasn't surprised word had gotten around town about her situation. Neither could she stop her embarrassed reaction. As she tucked a strand of hair behind her ear, her fingertips brushed her burning cheeks. "I think I'll be okay." She darted her gaze side to side. No one was around. "Between you and me, I'm returning to school tomorrow. I'll be glad to shove this suit into the very back of my closet."

"That's great news are you here to celebrate? I can offer you a wide selection of anything on the menu." Abby chuckled.

Stephanie sniffed. Instead of melting butter, smoking meat, or baking bread, however, she breathed in industrial cleaner. "Are you sure you don't mind?"

"Of course, not." Abby tossed a dish towel over her shoulder, twisted a knob on the griddle, and squirted oil liberally over the heating surface. "Deep cleaning can wait. Trust me."

"Thanks. I'm glad you're still open. Not a lot of traffic in town today."

Abby nodded.

"When will you close up for the season?"

"Soon. Business always dwindles after the poker night. But this year it seems to be an even steeper drop. And the wind is cold when I don't have the griddle on."

Stephanie nodded her head in commiseration. Her apartment complex had seen a lot of recent development nearby. She knew of at least two new restaurants going up. While not many could compare with Abby's culinary skills, location was a big factor. As well as indoor seating. Too bad Abby couldn't set up shop in a building. She'd lure customers to downtown year-round, a boon for every business. "Could you make me a wrap?"

"Absolutely. I have some barbecue chicken in the fridge that I think will be perfect. I made a batch while testing a new rub in the oven earlier. And I'll whip up a smoky chipotle ranch dressing."

Stephanie licked her lips. "That's great."

Inside the food truck, a cell phone rang. "I better get that you can go sit down if you'd like."

"Actually, I think I need to grab something out of my car." Stephanie walked back towards her unlocked vehicle. She reached inside and grabbed her lip gloss from her purse.

She wouldn't admit it to Abby, but Stephanie didn't really want to be alone right now. She'd come out victorious. And the only person she wanted to celebrate with, Ted, had shoved her aside. She wasn't quite sure what to do or where to go. But sitting on a picnic bench overlooking a cemetery wouldn't make her feel any better. Angling her body, Stephanie observed her friend from the corner of her gaze. As soon as Abby hung up the call, Stephanie made her way back over to the food truck.

"Hey, do you mind testing out a few new recipes for me?" Abby asked.

"Sure. What did you have in mind?"

"I want to try a new hushpuppy batter. And I have a new macaroni salad I'd like to try. It may take a little bit of time. Are you in a rush today?"

"I've got nowhere to be. For maybe the first time ever."

Abby chuckled and glanced away. Her movements were sharp and rigid. Determined. Practiced.

Stephanie nibbled the inside of her cheek. Asking who had called was rude. But whatever was said during the short phone conversation must have set Abby on edge. She acted sort of bristly. Stephanie wasn't sure how to proceed without making things strained. She'd try anyways. "It sure is quiet here without the tourists around."

Abby nodded and started pulling ingredients out of the fridge, whipping hushpuppy batter, her utensils clanging against the metal bowls.

"Does it ever unnerve you?"

"The tourists?" Abby focused on her work, not glancing up. "That's the whole job."

"No. Working in a haunted parking lot." Stephanie kept her voice low so as not to disturb the ghosts. She wasn't superstitious, per se. But she didn't court trouble. Avoiding cats, cracks, and ladders, she also tossed salt over her shoulder and followed every other old wives cure to ward off evil.

"It's not haunted," Abby said, deadpan.

On the otherwise bright day, a cloud passed over the sun. A cool breeze kicked up, whistling through the cemetery. Stephanie shuddered.

"Isn't it?" she asked, pushing ahead with her theory. "Unclaimed land belonging to the most hated family in town next to the cemetery?" Stephanie shuddered. "At least you won't have to worry about someone swooping in and stealing your spot soon. The land reverts to the town within the next year. I'm sure you'll manage a hundred-year lease for like a dollar a year or something."

Abby nodded but didn't lift her head.

Did Stephanie imagine her friends' tight posture? "Gives me an idea about Christmas."

Abby raised her gaze. "Ghosts?"

"Of course. What is more festive than reflecting on the past? But you are already closed for the winter by then. Too bad. It could be almost like a historical reenactment of the shunning of the Whittiers. People in Herd still hold a grudge. The crowd would be huge. I bet you'd sell out of everything."

"Before you run away on a wild tangent with your ideas, you need to know. I can honestly say I have never been approached by a phantom, a poltergeist, or spirit of any kind."

"I suppose Joe would tell everyone if it was haunted."

"And I'm surprised you are put off by quiet. Considering who you like."

Stephanie cheeks flamed again. "Don't tease me about that. It's too raw. There's nothing there. Not like you and Joe."

Abby rolled her eyes. "Now you need to stop teasing. He knows a lot about history, and I'm interested in learning. That's it."

Stephanie knew the pair were like oil and water. They separated and couldn't be forced together unless vigorously shaken. Maybe that's what the town needed next. To really enter the next phase of their community's progress, to accept moving forward, they'd all have to get a little uncomfortable for positive change.

"Okay, it's going to be a little bit. I've got to get the water boiling for the macaroni. You don't mind waiting?"

Stephanie's stomach growled loudly.

Abby laughed. "Fair enough. Let me make your wrap really quick, but you cannot leave. At all."

If you see something say something flashed in Stephanie's mind. Abby wasn't the type to make demands. But she was acting a little peculiar.

"I have my guinea pig, and I'm not letting her go." Abby chuckled again, the sound a little forced.

"I'm not going anywhere."

Stephanie meant every word.

Holding a stack of posters in one arm and a boombox in the other, Ted waited in position at the end of the street. If he was right, and he really was hoping he was in at least this one instance, he'd be hard for Stephanie to miss as she left the food truck and drove back to her apartment.

He angled the posters against his chest, trying to avoid a finger cut as he readjusted. He wasn't sure how long lunch would take. He'd called Abby to stall, and she promised to do her best. He'd been standing in place for ten minutes already. Did he have another thirty to wait?

Under his boots, he had no give on the solid asphalt. His knees ached. He wasn't much for being in one place for too long, his body wasn't used to the way his legs locked. This must be as bad as sitting for the way gravity could stress a skeleton. In another ten, he might reconsider holding the props.

No, it's a big moment, I have to. Stephanie deserved to know and see and feel how wrong he'd been about her. About them. Since opening up to the extended ranch family, he'd felt both lighter and weaker. He was a worn piece of leather, dangerously thin but buttery soft. With any luck, he'd have enough of a head start on opening up about his feelings before he had too much of a crowd. Although, he wouldn't shy away from that either. Being vulnerable and honest was a lot less to carry around than hiding.

Tires squealed as a car pulled out of the gravel lot a few hundred yards away.

Ted widened his stance. He was an immovable object. As long as he didn't get hit.

The little red coupe appeared and stopped, suddenly.

Through the windshield, Stephanie's eyes went wide, and her mouth dropped open. She looked like a ghostly fish behind the wheel of her car.

Ted felt calm and clammy. He hadn't anticipated the rush of actually spotting her.

She left her car engine running and got out of the vehicle. "Ted? What are you doing? You're going to get hit by a car. Why are you in the middle of the street?"

Dressed in a dark suit, she looked serious and addressed him in her firmest tone. What was he doing? For a moment, he stood perfectly still, too entranced to do anything.

"Get out of the road," she said.

Her worried tone snapped him out of his reverie. "No. I'm trying to get your attention."

"Mission accomplished. Wait…" She crossed her arms over her chest. "Is this from a movie? Does a man get hit by a car on a busy street? Is that it? Is this some sort of symbolism?"

The only film that fit that setup involved an amphibian puppet trying to sell a musical about his life story to Broadway producers. "No, of course not. And I'm fine. I've been here for a few minutes, and I haven't seen another vehicle go by. Read the poster."

"How did you know where I was?"

"I listened. You said you love eating at the food truck and would miss it. I figured you'd take this opportunity before Abby closed up shop for the year." He shook the posters in his arms. He'd poured his heart out into a confession of everything that held him back. "Can you read the poster from there?"

"And Abby was helping you? Did you call her?"

He nodded.

"Oh, thank goodness." Stephanie dropped her arms to her sides. "I was getting really worried about her."

"When I called you, and it went to voicemail, I remembered what you said about the food truck."

"My special treat. Abby didn't disappoint. Her new hush-puppies are amazing."

He didn't want to rush her, but he was worried they'd gotten off track. He glanced down, trying to reach the play button without dropping the cards. He should have practiced this part. He didn't think it would be hard. It was so easy in the movie. "One sec. I'm sorry." He lifted his gaze.

"You look nice. Did you dress up for me?"

He had. His dark slacks hung in the very back of his closet. The white shirt still had its price tag in it when he grabbed it off the hanger. "Will you read the poster?"

"I think I have to come closer. Your handwriting is hard to read." She wrinkled her brow, folding her arms over her chest and strolling forward. "I'm sorry. I still can't tell what it says. Am I supposed to understand the reference?"

The classic pop song filled downtown. Finding the old school stereo had been the real hitch in his sister's plan. Meg scoured her inventory at the antique store but had nothing. Joe came through via text on his lesson planning break. His love of history wasn't strictly professional. In his spare time, he fiddled with video game systems and, in a cardboard box full of parts he was working on with his class, he had a plastic, two-cassette boombox. Ted swung by the school to grab it.

Educating Stephanie on movies and TV shows promised a lifetime's worth of fun date nights. *I need to ask first.*

"Yes, it is a reference but never mind." He stopped the music, hating to end the song at the first build up to the chorus, and set the boombox and cards on the ground.

He dusted his hands on his pants. Why not segue to a reference she would understand? "How about I ask you what kind of sandwich and drink pairing you'd like for your dreams tonight? Perhaps Pastrami and Buttermilk?"

"Like the movie?" She widened her gaze. "That one I get. But seems a little personal."

Her mouth twitched like she suppressed a smile. He was glad to have a shared joke. "Good. I'm glad you understand."

She kept her mouth in a solid, straight line. She was emotionless.

He'd done that. He'd ruined the sunshine that bubbled up from inside her. With his rainy personality, he blocked her light behind his clouds. "Nothing makes sense without you. The whole town needs you." *So do I.*

She wrinkled her forehead. "Anyone can run an event or teach a class. What I do isn't special."

"You know that's not true. No one can advocate for the kids or the town like you. No one cares as much as you. And that's why I can't let you leave."

"I'm not. If your whole speech is about convincing me to stay. It's fine. Don't worry about it. I'll keep going." She smiled. "Same as I always do."

The happy expression didn't reach her eyes. Up close, she looked almost sad. Was she so practiced in smiling for her students she could wear the expression without meaning it?

"I told you I couldn't be the man I was."

"You said he was a stranger," she said.

"Yes. The man I was is so far in the past. I couldn't pretend to be him if I tried. With you, I'm someone different. You're transforming me. I've been shut down for so long. I don't know how to act or what to do."

"I'm sorry," she muttered.

He stepped forward. "But I want to try. Because I need to break down the barriers between us." He stretched a hand out, stroking her shoulder and dropping his arm away. "I'm ready to give us a chance."

"I need more than words," she murmured.

"I know." *I was counting on it.* He didn't smile. He wouldn't. Because then he'd give away just how much he already knew her. How deeply he already loved her. And he wanted to say the words to her so she could see and hear and believe him. He put two fingers in his mouth and whistled, loudly. "I'm not hiding."

She widened her gaze, her cheeks turning bright pink.

He stepped to her side and waved toward the Golden Crown.

Meg, Ryan, Hank, and Jen stood a few yards away. They waved as they emerged from the restaurant to gawk from the hitching post out front. He'd invited them. They helped him search for the items of his plan and encouraged him to follow his heart. Had he overstepped? Was this too much?

He swiveled, spinning on his heel, and several locals exiting the general store on the other side of the street. He bit the end of his tongue. He couldn't go back now. Boxed in by the community on all sides. "I wanted you to see I have no fears about everyone knowing how I feel about you. But. . . I didn't want you to feel put on the spot. In my head, this felt much more like a grand gesture and not much like peer pressure."

She met his gaze and smiled. "I can appreciate the spirit behind the grand gesture. For future reference, I'm more of a private, no public displays sort of person."

"Future reference?" He held the words to his giddy heart.

She tipped her head back and raised both eyebrows. "I like hand holding in front of everyone. But maybe not what Hank's sign is suggesting?"

"Hank made a sign?" His voice cracked. His stomach filled with lead and dropped to his ankles. Dread covered him like a sticky syrup and he slowly turned his head.

Hank's poster board was no-nonsense and direct, like the man himself The white sheet read *KISS,* the black lettering clear with its thick outlines.

Ted provided Joe a day off from Hank's meddling. Now Ted was glad he hadn't been more of a distraction. *Good luck, Joe.* "I thought I grabbed all the posterboards. I'm sorry."

"Welp. Guess I'd better respect my elders."

Ted shook his head. He saw the playful gleam in her sparkling eyes and her half-smile. But he never wanted her to ever feel coerced. "Listen, Stephanie. I'm sorry it took me so long to realize what was only feet away from me this whole time. But I'm awake now. I've snapped out of my coma, and I'm ready to live. And I want to, with you. You were right when you said I used excuses to push you away. I did. And I'll probably screw up again. I never stopped caring about you or wanting the best for you. I just didn't think I could possibly fit that bill."

"But?" She teased the word and nibbled her bottom lip.

"I love you. If you'll take a chance on an old fool like me, you won't regret it."

"You won't turn out to be one of those millennials with no savings because you're addicted to avocado toast?" She teased.

He chuckled. "It's fine. Give me your best generational slaps. I've heard them all. It's the curse of my age."

She stepped forward, draping her arms around his neck. "I love you, too."

He lowered his mouth to hers. He put every ounce of hope and every single promise he had into the kiss, tightening his grip on her waist to let her know he'd never let go. The chorus of "oohs" that could have been a canned audience response from a sitcom were enough to assure him this town would never let him forget what he'd done here today.

And wasn't he lucky.

EPILOGUE

Stephanie loved being with Ted. She didn't need much. She didn't need fancy dinners, romantic movies, or sparkly jewelry. Time together in any capacity, from working side by side to reading their books, was her love language. Every second was special.

"You're really sure you don't mind?" Ted asked.

In the shotgun seat, Stephanie squeezed his hand. "Of course not. Have I ever minded when dinner and a movie becomes a ranch event?"

He shook his head. "No, you haven't. You've been a really good sport."

She liked the way the smile reached the corners of his eyes. She liked so many things about him, more than she had ever guessed at during her years of unrequited pining. From deep conversations to silly moments and every comfortable silence in between, she connected with him more every day.

He parked in the semi-circle drive. With five vehicles already in position, he angled at the very back of the line. "One day we'll do something fun." He released her hand and turned off the engine. "I promise."

"You make our time together fun. Even when we have a bunch of spectators for our date."

"Well, not so many anymore." The words were almost under his breath as he opened his door and exited the vehicle.

In the month since they had started dating, after the failed romantic moment in the middle of the street—that ended up being witnessed by no less than fifteen people. Who knew so many people were free in the middle of the day? Bystanders and interruptions had become part of being together.

For the first few weeks, date nights at the cabin became family affairs with the tight quarters. Stephanie hadn't minded too much although it was awkward to have one of her students witnessing her casual moments. Long walks around the property had become their go-to for time together.

Instead of waiting for the new year, Maddy and Jen had moved out of the cabin at the beginning of October. An apartment building in a great location had a sudden vacancy. Jen jumped on the chance. While Stephanie knew Ted was glad to have his space to himself again, she could also see the sadness in the last week since he'd been on his own again.

Before she finished grabbing her purse and unbuckling, he had her door open.

"Thanks."

"Are you really sure you don't mind?" he asked. "We don't have to stay for supper. We could make it a quick visit."

Stephanie shook her head. "I have to see Maddie and Colby's Halloween costume. I've heard all about how hard your sister has been working on it at school."

"It's something." He chuckled. "I haven't seen the whole look pulled together. I've only been called in to help wrangle Colby for measurements. Have you ever held a dog still so it could be measured for a hat?"

She widened her eyes.

"And the weird thing is, the dog didn't really mind. I've never known a dog that likes costumes," he said. "Colby might be more person than dog though."

"Or she just likes attention. She gets a lot of it," Stephanie said. "Before we go in there, how are Ryan and Meg's wedding plans going? I don't want to say anything and step on anyone's toes."

They had reached the front of the ranch house.

Instead of continuing up the front steps, he pulled her to the back, taking the long way around the covered porch from the backyard and making their way to the door. They weren't visible from the front window yet.

He darted his gaze around the porch. "Would you believe me if I told you I think Ryan might be a groomzilla?"

Stephanie chuckled. "If he needs any help. . ."

"You're sweet to offer. Take my advice. Stay out of this one. You'll have your hands full with Frontier Days and starting your master's degree. You don't want to get involved."

She wanted to argue. Herd wasn't known for its options. She assumed she'd plan the event easily because each item only had one choice. Cake? General Store. Catering? Abby Whit's food truck. Photography? The Old West studio. "I'm sure I could handle it."

He shook his head. "You can handle logistics no problem. But dealing with a finicky groom? The situation is already tense."

"Oh really?" She wrinkled her brow. "Tensions between the couple? That's a shame."

"More like a groom and his grandfather. And the grandfather's insistence about the wedding planner."

The front door opened with a crash.

Startled, Stephanie leaned around Ted and spotted Hank.

"Come on inside. It's not getting any warmer out here, and the food is getting colder by the second inside," Hank said. His voice was deep and scratchy, almost a snarl.

Hank's words were harsher than normal. While he embraced the appearance of a gruff cowboy, he had never behaved as such. The old man was a sweetheart.

She held tight to Ted's hand as he steered her towards the door and inside. Once she crossed the threshold, she stepped back.

Hank shut the front door.

She stilled Ted with their interlaced hands and shot him a look before turning to their host. "Mr. Kincaid? Are you feeling alright? We don't have to stay long if you'd rather have the house to yourself."

"Oh, I'm sorry." Hank scrubbed a hand over his face. "Just trying to talk sense into my grandson again."

She nodded.

The pair disagreed often about big decisions. Between a wedding and a full-scale construction project, they had plenty of opportunity for strife. The town had rallied to help the Kincaids clear the debris and start the new build. In record time, plans had been drawn, submitted, and approved. With the foundation poured, the crew worked on putting up the walls and roof in a race against the weather.

"If I can be of any assistance, I'm glad to help. I could get Joe started on the timetable for planning a wedding."

"Don't you worry about it, darling." Hank forced a smile. "Joe and Abby will figure it out. Ryan is the one leading the charge and driving everyone to distraction." He patted her hand. "I'm glad you could come. Supper is on the table. You know the way."

Together, they continued down the slate tile hall to the large kitchen at the back of the home. A swinging door that had been installed to provide privacy during tourist season was propped wide open, letting light and sound spill out. The room was warm inviting and smelled of chicken pot pie. Her stomach growled. Ted led her to the table, and they sat on the bench opposite Joe, Meg, and Ryan.

"How is your book coming, Joe?" Stephanie asked as she unfolded a paper napkin over her lap.

Joe blew out a sigh. "Slow. I had hoped to make more progress by now." He shrugged. "I'll get it done. Maybe not in time for the centennial, but I'd rather do my best work than rush."

Hank took his seat at the head of the table.

"Don't eat yet," Ryan announced. "We have our special guests coming down the stairs."

Meg turned toward the door. "I am so excited to see what they are wearing. Do you have any ideas, Ted?"

"None," Ted smiled. "My sister and Maddie have been determined to keep this a secret. I was only called in for back-up but not given enough clearance for the classified intel."

Jen appeared in the room from the open doorway. "Is everyone ready?"

Nods and murmurs of agreement erupted around the large plank table.

"Okay." Jen pulled out her phone and it tapped the screen.

Familiar music filtered into the room. But Stephanie wasn't sure where she had heard it before. She couldn't quite place the melody.

At her side, Ted folded his arms and shielded his mouth with a hand. He shook slightly.

Then the opening line was sung as Maddy and Colby entered the room.

"Sisters, sisters. . ." The music played, and Ted and Jen sang.

A dog and a girl dressed in matching powder blue tuille dresses and sequined headdresses entered and spun in a circle. Maddy held an ostrich feather fan. Colby sat and wagged her tail.

"Oh, she looks like an angel," Meg exclaimed.

Stephanie glanced away from the charming tableau.

Ryan rested a hand on Meg's shoulder, his eyes crinkling and softening as he gazed at his fiancée.

Stephanie bit her lip to still her tongue from a cheeky response or a chuckle. Maddy was precious, but Meg meant the dog.

"See how well she can do? She has to be the maid of honor and ring bearer," Meg stage whispered.

"Ring bearer, maybe. You cannot have a dog as a maid of honor," Ryan replied.

The dog and girl danced and wagged to the end of the song. The audience dutifully applauded their efforts.

"You look marvelous," Stephanie said. "Do you need help getting changed for dinner?"

"Thank you." Maddy beamed. "Mommy has to help me, Miss Patricks."

"I'll help, too," Meg said and scurried away from the table. Walking away, Meg and Jen leaned close together, leading the dog and girl away.

Stephanie smiled. All three women had become friends. A few years ago, Stephanie had only considered Kelly and Lauren part of her inner circle. Over the past six months, however, she'd expanded her friend group by two and was glad. Jen had quickly become part of the community.

Stephanie turned toward Hank at the head of the table. "Mr. Kincaid? Have you ever thought about you know who and," she lowered her voice and leaned close, "Jen?"

Hank stroked his chin. "I had. She is a nice woman. But. . . no. I'm only more convinced than ever. There is somebody for everybody, and Joe would get bored with anyone else. He needs conflict." Hank patted her hand on the table. "You leave them to me. I know what I'm doing. I have someone else in mind for Jen."

Hank had brought enough strife to Joe with the event planning. Would the phrase if you want something done give it to a busy person prove true? Stephanie wasn't so sure. She couldn't argue with the mischievous twinkle in his eye. She was only grateful she'd escaped his notice but found love anyway.

Ted reached for her hand under the table and squeezed.

This was the good life. She'd savor every moment.

Check out these other great romances from Rowan Prose Publishing!

Rachelle Paige Campbell writes contemporary romance novels filled with heart and hope. She believes love and laughter can change lives, and every story needs a happily-ever-after. Check out her blog for updates on current projects, and sign-up for her newsletter to learn about upcoming releases and announcements: rachellepaigecampbell.com